ONE SUMMER IN ITALY

VICTORIA SPRINGFIELD

B
Boldwood

First published in Great Britain in 2025 by Boldwood Books Ltd.

Copyright © Victoria Springfield, 2025

Cover Design by JD Smith Design Ltd

Cover Images: Shutterstock

The moral right of Victoria Springfield to be identified as the author of this work has been asserted in accordance with the Copyright, Designs and Patents Act 1988.

All rights reserved. No part of this book may be reproduced in any form or by any electronic or mechanical means, including information storage and retrieval systems, without written permission from the author, except for the use of brief quotations in a book review. This book is a work of fiction and, except in the case of historical fact, any resemblance to actual persons, living or dead, is purely coincidental.

Every effort has been made to obtain the necessary permissions with reference to copyright material, both illustrative and quoted. We apologise for any omissions in this respect and will be pleased to make the appropriate acknowledgements in any future edition.

A CIP catalogue record for this book is available from the British Library.

Paperback ISBN 978-1-83633-642-6

Large Print ISBN 978-1-83633-643-3

Hardback ISBN 978-1-83633-641-9

Ebook ISBN 978-1-83633-644-0

Kindle ISBN 978-1-83633-645-7

Audio CD ISBN 978-1-83633-636-5

MP3 CD ISBN 978-1-83633-637-2

Digital audio download ISBN 978-1-83633-638-9

This book is printed on certified sustainable paper. Boldwood Books is dedicated to putting sustainability at the heart of our business. For more information please visit https://www.boldwoodbooks.com/about-us/sustainability/

Boldwood Books Ltd, 23 Bowerdean Street, London, SW6 3TN

www.boldwoodbooks.com

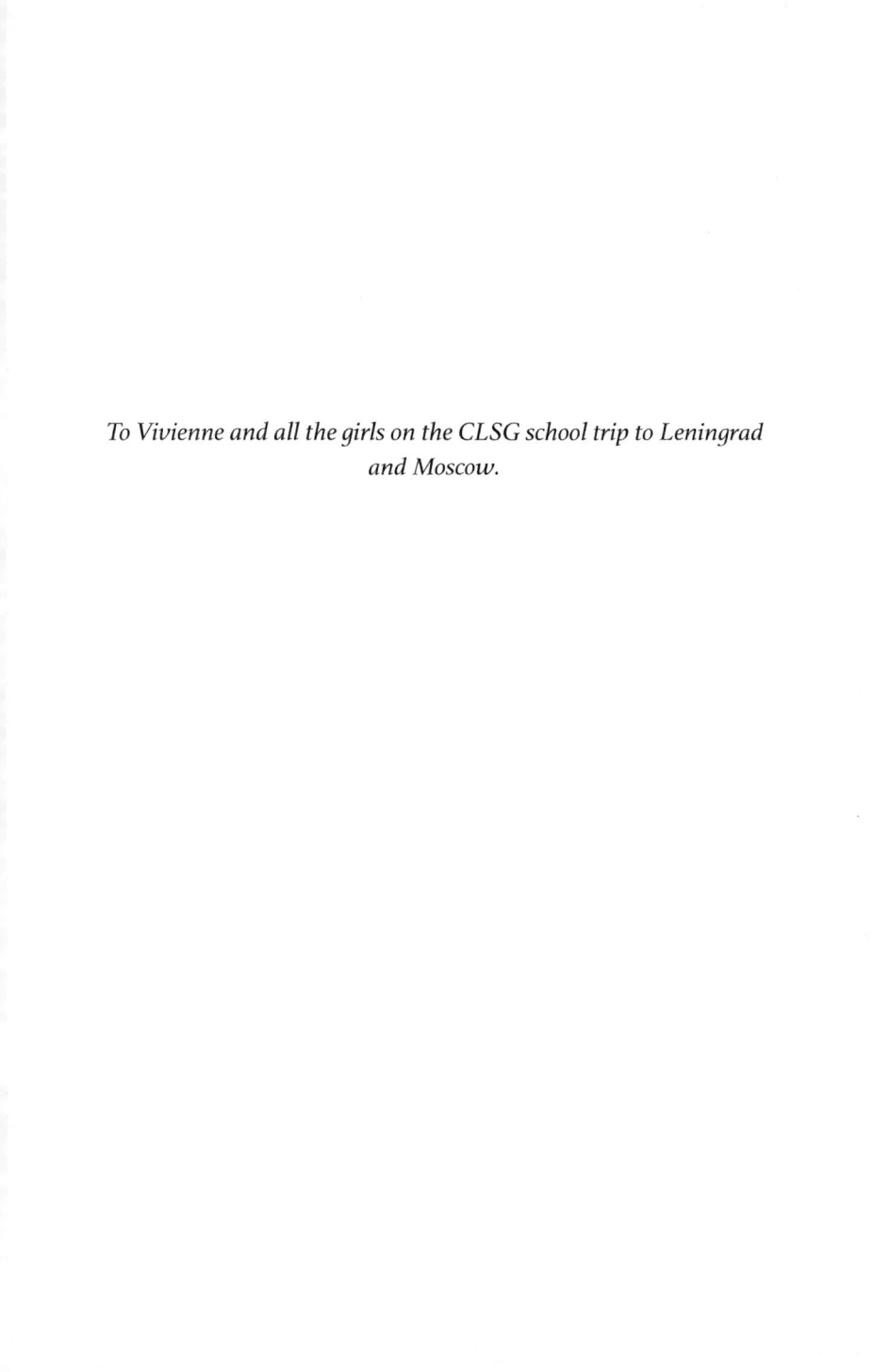

To Vivienne and all the girls on the CLSG school trip to Leningrad and Moscow.

1

Natalie studied the photograph: the prow of a gondola just passing under the Rialto Bridge, golden light bathing the Grand Canal. She could almost feel the gentle warmth of a Venetian evening, hear the voices of the jostling crowd. Her trip to Italy had been magical. Until...

A blur of bright colour moved across the glass partition. Floella elbowed open the office door, two takeaway cups balanced in one hand. She dropped a pink and white cardboard box on the desk, bracelets jangling.

'Admiring my mood board?'

'Yes, it's beautiful.'

Floella set down the cups. 'I've brought coffee and doughnuts.'

'Thanks, Flo. And I'm glad I've caught you. I don't suppose I'll see you for a while after today, at least not until the new series of *Together* gets the green light... unless something comes up in the meantime.' Natalie hoped she sounded casual, not desperate. She loved her job in TV production but being freelance made it hard to plan, let alone pay the bills.

'Something will turn up for you. Go on, have one of these.'

Natalie opened the cardboard box, releasing a sweet, doughy aroma. Globules of pink frosting clung to the lid's cellophane panel. She took a doughnut, the sugary coating sticky on her fingers.

'So, how's *Luxe Life Swap* going?' she said tentatively. The show was Flo-Go Production's flagship programme. Thousands of loyal fans were looking forward to the series returning but in the fickle world of television, that wasn't enough to guarantee the additional funding that was critical to the survival of Flo's small company.

'Marrakech and Paris are looking good but it's hard to keep the new locations all hush-hush when some eagle-eyed viewer manages to snap a picture of Mandy Miller halfway up the Eiffel Tower. But now we've got a much bigger problem. Mandy's not going to make it out to Italy.'

'Oh no! Why? What's happened?'

Floella stirred her coffee. 'If it was anyone else, I wouldn't say, it is rather personal, but you know Mandy, she's all for talking openly about women's problems.'

'She's ill?'

Floella reached for a doughnut. 'She's been suffering with severe endometriosis; poor woman's been in agony. Her PA met her off the plane from Paris, took one look at her and took her straight to A&E. Next thing she knew, they were wheeling her into theatre for an emergency hysterectomy.'

'How awful! Mandy's such a trooper, she probably didn't even tell anyone she was suffering. Is she going to be okay?'

'Looks like she'll be fine; her husband's keeping me in the loop. He says she's been charming all the staff; some of the nurses are quite starstruck. Apparently, she's been demanding her make-up bag, and wants to film a message for her fans so they hear the news from her first. The doctors have told her to rest but...' Floella tutted.

'She's probably giving an interview on hospital radio as we speak and boning up about Venice.'

Floella waved a hand in the direction of her mood board.

'We need to talk about that.' She ran her tongue over her purple lip gloss, catching a couple of errant sugar sprinkles.

'If there's anything I can do...' Natalie reached for her phone and clicked on the Notes app. She felt Floella's eyes on her. 'Why are you smiling at me like that?'

Floella began singing a theme tune Natalie hadn't heard in years. '*Panda's Place – it's yours and my happy place. White tummy, black paws, Panda's Place!* Remember that show?'

'How could I forget it? That awful tune! Those dreadful striped dungarees they made me wear! Don't tell me you've been watching it.'

'Someone's uploaded the old episodes to YouTube.'

Natalie cringed. Her one and only stint as a television presenter hadn't worked out quite as she'd hoped.

'Don't make that face. The programme was terrible but you were great.'

'I was okay, I suppose, considering the material.'

'You were more than okay. That's why I want you to be the stand-in presenter for *Luxe Life Swap*'s Italian leg.' Floella smirked.

Natalie gasped. *Luxe Life Swap* was prime-time television, a once-in-a-lifetime chance most people would kill for. And if Floella needed her, she had to help. She'd go anywhere. Anywhere but Venice.

'No! Come on, Flo, you're kidding! Surely you want Suzie Silver or Fiona McPhee? I've not done any presenting for years.'

'Suzie and Fiona are great but they're both tied up. I need someone now. Someone who's free to jump on a plane tomorrow.'

'Yeah, I guess that's tricky.'

'You don't sound very enthusiastic, Nat. I thought you'd be leaping up and down. I know you love your job but wasn't this your dream? I always assumed you'd fallen into production because the right presenting role didn't come up. And anyway, I've already cleared it with my contact at Channel Four.'

'I love what I'm doing now but you're right, this was my dream, a long time ago. And it's a fantastic opportunity – of course it is.' A brilliant solution popped into her head. 'Wouldn't it make more sense for me to do the filming with the Italian couple whilst they're over in London? Daryl could be the presenter out in Italy. It must be frustrating for him when Mandy gets all the foreign gigs.'

'Natalie.' Floella shook her head. 'Daryl won't get on a plane. It's been hard enough to get him to step outside the M25 since he and Craig adopted the twins.'

'But...' Natalie began even though she had no idea what she was going to say.

Floella raised her hand. 'Now stop being so modest.'

'But Venice...'

'Yes, Venice – such a wonderful city! Have you ever been?'

'No... I mean, yes, a long time ago... a school trip.'

'Then you'll remember! No one forgets Venice!' Floella flung her arm towards her mood board. 'Those magnificent horses on the front of St Mark's Basilica, dinner-jacketed musicians playing in the piazza, gondolas on the Grand Canal. Imagine! This is your chance to shine! Bettany will get the tickets rebooked in your name, she'll send through all the information. You know how important this show is. I need you

Nat; I know you won't let me down. And of course there's a nice fat fee, much better than your hourly rate.'

Natalie forced a smile. 'I'll finish up here then get home and dig out my passport.'

'That's more like it! Ah, one last thing. Now I'm in your good books, I've got a little favour to ask.' Floella licked some sugar off her fingers. She bent down and rooted in her capacious, leopard-print shopper. 'I need you to hand-deliver something for me when you get to Venice. It's for Eraldo, a very good friend of mine.'

Natalie took the small, padded envelope Floella held out. 'Couldn't you just post it? I'll deliver it if you want me to but...'

'I can't trust this to the post; it's far too precious to lose. Eraldo is a watch restorer. These are spare parts for antique watches; they're incredibly rare. You don't mind, do you?'

'Of course not, but I shouldn't really take something through customs for somebody else.'

'I'm not asking you to smuggle a packet of heroin!' Floella laughed.

'Sorry, silly of me. I'm a bit on edge. This presenting job: there's so much at stake.'

A burst of jazz came from Floella's bag.

'I'll have to take this; it's that woman from Netflix. She talks so much, I'll be on this call half the morning. Good luck in Venice, Nat. Don't worry about anything! You'll be a star!'

'Thanks, Flo. I won't let you down.'

'Yes, Kathleen... of course, yep, yep.' Floella headed for the meeting room, phone clasped to her ear.

Natalie gave Eraldo's envelope a squeeze and slipped it into her bag. She'd go straight home and pack. She'd concentrate on the practicalities, stop her mind creeping back to the past. She would help keep Flo-Go Productions afloat whilst showing the doubters she hadn't moved into production because she couldn't hack it in front of the camera. She would get to live her old dream for a week or two before going back to the production role she loved. Floella was right, this was her chance to shine. She had to take it.

2

The aroma of barbequed sausages drifted across the elegant dressing room. Cate hastily closed the sash window. Down on the patio, Phil was supervising next-door's teenage daughters who, bribed by the promise of mini hotdogs and a boost to their pocket money, were acting as waitresses that evening. From two floors up, she could see the tiny bald patch in his reddish-brown hair had now spread to the size of a fifty pence piece.

She opened the doors of her treble wardrobe. The neat rows of jackets and dresses lined up on padded hangers never failed to please her. She bit her lip, considering. Something with sleeves, the evening was too warm to cover her upper arms with one of the rainbow of cashmere pieces stacked up in the cedar-lined cubby holes. She practised Pilates regularly, but even so...

Quickly, she selected a deceptively simple shirt dress and retrieved a pair of duck-egg blue sandals from the rotating shoe cupboard. Phil's inlaid, hand-turned barrel design had been an instant hit, it had even featured on the front page of *World of Interiors*.

She ran a brush over her white-blonde hair. There had been no time to squeeze in another salon visit; they were leaving tomorrow and she hadn't begun packing. She'd told Phil she was too busy with the preparations for their annual summer party. But come the morning, she'd have no such excuse. She'd have to psyche herself up for the trip. *Luxe Life Swap* would be the perfect showcase for Phil's business. She couldn't let him down.

She breathed deeply the way she'd learnt on her spa retreat, inhaling the scent of freesias on the dressing table. She *would* cope with this trip to Italy. She was no longer the insecure teenager who'd gone on that school trip, hiding a smattering of normal teen acne – that felt like the end of the world – under a too-long fringe.

She fastened her emerald bracelet, a Christmas present from Phil. How lucky she was. She mustn't forget that. Why was she harking back to a school trip most of her classmates would barely remember? Cate wasn't proud of the way she'd behaved in Venice but that trip had changed everything. It had made her determined to leave her old life behind as soon as she could. She glanced in the mirror at her expensively made-up face. Cathy Laidlaw was gone. Cate Beresford had taken her place. Those girls from St Margaret's wouldn't recognise her now. Except for Natalie Spencer. Nat had known her better than anyone.

* * *

Tyres crunched on the gravel. A slam of a car door. Phil's best friend Evan and his wife Lucy had arrived.

'Hello, Cate, you look beautiful. And Phil, good to see you, old man!' Evan pumped Phil's hand up and down with unnecessary vigour. He held out a bottle. 'This do?'

'Puligny-Montrachet, very nice,' Phil said. It would have cost more than his old dad had earnt in a week.

'Phil!' Lucy planted a kiss on both his cheeks. She stepped back, a smile playing on her lips as though she was inspecting him. 'Looking good!'

'You, too.' He flicked his eyes away from the pale cleavage splendidly displayed by the low neckline of her emerald-green, floral dress; the floaty sleeves so long, they grazed her knuckles. Over his shoulder, Cate was disappearing through the glass doors clutching a fashionably unstructured wildflower bouquet.

'I would have sent the flowers ahead if I wasn't so disorganised.' Lucy gave a tinkling laugh.

'Good drive down, Evan?'

Evan ran his hand through his floppy, blond hair. 'Yah. Prunella didn't conk out.' He named all his cars after ex-girlfriends.

'Drink?' Phil asked. One of next-door's girls – he never could remember which was which – was approaching with a tray of champagne flutes.

'Thought you'd never ask... Bollinger, I presume! Bolly-jolly good.'

Phil felt a hand on his arm. Cate had reappeared minus the flowers, the scent of her freshly washed hair inches from his nose blending with the Chanel perfume she loved to wear. She gave him a smile. It was all he needed. What was wrong with him this evening? Evan was his friend. The person to whom he owed everything: his multimillion-pound, handmade furniture company, this dreamy old vicarage outside Sevenoaks, the

Bentley in his double garage. Even Cate, he sometimes thought. Cate loved him, she'd grown up with nothing like he had but when he saw the smile on her face as she toyed with her emerald bracelet, he couldn't help asking himself if she'd find him equally attractive if she was crunching over discarded drug paraphernalia in the stairwell of the council estate he'd once called home.

He took a perfectly chargrilled pepper, halloumi and red onion skewer from one of the girls.

'Excuse me,' he said. A couple from his golf club had arrived. He busied himself with introductions and drinks. The conversation would turn soon enough to the topic he dreaded.

'So, you're off to Venice with *Luxe Life Swap*! You must be so excited,' one of the wives gushed. 'We're going to be glued to the show.'

Phil cast his eye around for Cate, but she was pointing out their new summer house to two women from her book group.

'Yes,' Phil said. 'It's a business thing really, good for brand awareness. Far more subtle than social media. You know I've always avoided getting into that.'

'But staying in an Italian count's palazzo is a teeny, tiny bit of a holiday,' Lucy butted in. 'Of course, Phil's been to Venice before, haven't you? Phil and my husband Evan went there on a school trip. They've been inseparable ever since. Isn't that right, darling?'

Only Phil caught Evan's momentary hesitation before he replied, 'Yes, inseparable. Now, how's the handicap, old boy? I hear you've been playing off eight.'

* * *

Cate plunged two glasses into the sink. The aroma of pine-scented bubbles mingled with charcoal smoke wafting in through the bi-fold doors. The girls next door had been primed to keep on top of the dirty glasses but Cate just wanted a moment alone to wipe off the fixed smile on her face when anyone mentioned Venice.

Lucy's heels clicked across the poured concrete floor. Trust her to interrupt.

'Cate! You shouldn't be washing up!'

'I know.' Cate shrugged.

'Put that down. You should be out circulating, enjoying yourself. You're the hostess.'

'And you're a guest.'

Lucy nudged Cate aside and plunged her hands into the sink. Despite pushing up her sleeves, her ludicrously long cuffs still trailed in the suds.

'Are you worried about Phil? He's not himself, is he?' Lucy kept her face turned towards the Moroccan-tiled splashback.

'Phil?' He had been quieter these last few weeks, distracted, accusing Cate of imagining things when she asked what the matter was. But she wasn't going to share that with Evan's wife. 'He's fine, probably just worried he's got to go a whole fortnight without popping into his workshop or the new showroom. You know how hands-on he is.'

'One has to let go, like sending the children off to school.' Lucy swished the glasses under a running tap and upended them on the draining board.

Cate remembered how it felt driving first Oli, then Max, to Phil and Evan's old school. They still seemed like babies, but she was amazed how they'd thrived at Hillingdon, returning each holiday with a confident swagger Phil had never possessed.

She handed Lucy a linen towel to dry her hands. 'It's strange to think the count and his wife are going to be living in our house whilst we're in theirs. A fifteenth-century palazzo – it seems so unreal. I wish the TV people had sent through some pictures.'

'They'll want to capture your faces when you see the place for the first time. But it's not the house that's bothering you, is it?'

'I'm fine.' Cate smoothed her hair behind her ears. 'Let's go back outside. I might need to rescue Phil from that new golf-club buddy; he can be a bit of a bore.'

'Wait.' Lucy laid her hand on Cate's, her damp sleeve brushing against Cate's arm. 'I don't want to pry but...' She turned her head pointedly in the direction of the expanse of lawn, mowed into neat stripes.

Cate followed her gaze. Phil stood by the tennis court talking to their new next-door neighbour, leaning in close, his mouth almost touching her ear. He threw back his head and laughed; she tossed her wavy, black hair.

Lucy dropped her voice. 'If you need to talk, we could go out for a coffee. I've been through it myself... more than once. Evan's always been a hard dog to keep on the porch, as they say in the States.'

Cate stared at her. 'What are you saying? You think Phil and that woman...? No, that can't be right! Kiran's just a friendly neighbour. We've had her and her husband round for dinner a couple of times; they seem very happy together.'

'But where's the husband now?'

'Away, working. His water-filter company has contracts all over the world.'

'Well, when the cat's away...' Lucy let the rest of her sentence hang. 'Come on, let's get another glass of fizz.'

Cate followed her out onto the terrace, feeling, she imagined, like someone being led through the wreckage of a gas explosion.

'Pineapple, strawberry and mango kebab?' One of next-door's girls was holding out a tray.

'Uh, yes... thanks.' Cate stood holding the stick of char-grilled fruit. Phil wasn't having an affair. She'd know; she was sure she would. But something *was* off. Six weeks ago, he'd been thrilled they'd been selected for *Luxe Life Swap*. They'd had great fun with Lucy and Evan trying to guess where the show would send them – for some reason, they'd all thought of Lisbon. But since the information on their trip to Venice had arrived, her husband had become uncharacteristically snappy. This evening, amongst their closest friends, she could tell by the set of his shoulders, his forced bonhomie, that something wasn't quite right. But an affair? What nonsense. Phil wasn't the type.

Cate usually loved their summer parties, the perfect opportunity for their adult friends to get together during those few weeks of peace before the chaos of the school holidays began but thanks to Lucy's insinuations, she couldn't relax.

Finally, the last drink was downed, the last four-by-four reversed off the drive.

She climbed the stairs to the bedroom. Ted was lying on the rug. She'd long given up on confining him to his dog bed in the kitchen. He cocked a quizzical ear.

'I'll miss you, lovely boy,' Cate said. 'But you'll be fine whilst we're away; the Venetians are animal lovers. They've promised to walk you twice a day; I made sure of that. You'll be on TV. How do you fancy that?'

'I don't suppose he's too bothered.' Phil's voice came from

the doorway. 'But he'll be a star, our Ted. Who could resist that soppy old face?' He crouched down to pat him.

'I wish I'd got my packing done.' Cate glanced towards her empty suitcase.

'We're not leaving until lunchtime. We'll set the alarm for seven. You'll have plenty of time to pack and then I'll run you down to The Evergreens.'

'I've still got to—' Cate began.

'He's your dad, Cate. I wish I'd spent more time with mine.'

'I know you do.' Cate slipped her arms around her husband's waist, tilted her head against his shoulder, felt his head rest against hers. She breathed in the familiar scent of his newly washed shirt, the Aqua di Parma cologne he'd worn on their wedding day that she'd bought him every Christmas since.

'I love you,' Phil murmured. He said it so rarely, it meant the world to her when he did.

'I love you too.' Cate turned her neck, looking into his sincere, grey-blue eyes. Lucy was so, so wrong. Whatever had been distracting Phil these last few weeks, it definitely wasn't a secret lover.

'I can come to The Evergreens, if you like. I could have a cup of tea with the carers; you know I can't resist their ginger biscuits.'

'It's okay, there's no need. I know you want to drop into the new showroom. Just pick me up after an hour. I can manage that.'

'Okay, darling. You get off to bed now. I've just got to catch up on a bit of work in the study.'

Cate hovered in the bedroom door, watching him walk downstairs. The Evergreens wasn't a bad place. Everything about it, from the perfectly pruned roses at the entrance to the old, music-hall tunes piped through the corridors, was chosen with care. And the scent of lilies in the entrance hall – despite their unfortunate funeral-parlour connotations – was far superior to the aroma of oxtail soup and disinfectant that hung around some of the places Cate had considered for her dad and swiftly dismissed.

Dad's illness had come as such a shock. He'd progressing rapidly from seemingly unremarkable forgetfulness and harmless eccentricities to wandering out of the house in the small hours and shouting at his reflection in the window of the launderette. Cate hadn't realised it was possible to develop dementia in your late fifties. She didn't know if she'd ever get used to visiting a father who sometimes struggled to recognise her, his eyes flickering through a card deck full of fuzzy memories, trying to place the woman sitting by his side. Cate visited him twice a week, made sure he had the best quality of life she could afford. She felt compassion for him; no one deserved to end up like Dad. But she could never forgive him for what he'd done.

3

Natalie leant on the deep stone balustrade of the Rialto Bridge. She was back, in the heart of Venice. It was early in the morning but the Grand Canal was very much alive. A barge delivering fruit and vegetables was heading towards her, three mahogany-brown Venetians, sleeves rolled up, standing amongst the crates and pallets. A private taxi sped under the bridge, a woman in a greige, linen suit sitting amongst her piles of luggage, hair blowing in the breeze.

Last night, Natalie had arrived by waterbus, gliding slowly through the dark lagoon. She hadn't come that way on their school trip, had vague memoires of being herded onto a two-storey coach, PVC seats and a strong aroma of cheese and onion crisps. She would have been too excited and giggly to remember much of the journey anyway, singing along to Britney Spears' 'Baby One More Time', one earphone bud of her Sony Walkman clamped in her ear, one in Cathy's. But she did remember that first glimpse of the Grand Canal all those years ago.

Today, it had barely changed. Grand palazzi stood on either

side, the soft pink, yellow and white buildings making a pretty contrast to the pale-green water. Natalie tried to pick out the different styles she'd swotted up on: the elegant Istrian stone arches and pointed windows of the Gothic period, the later baroque buildings festooned with swags and cherubs, as elaborate as a wedding cake envisaged by the most demanding bridezilla. Not that she knew anything about wedding cakes. She was never going to get married. How could anyone promise life-long commitment? People changed.

The next day, she was meeting Lucia, the Italian fixer, before the rest of the film crew arrived. The team wasn't just going to film around St Mark's Square, The Bridge of Sighs and all the well-known sights. Viewers of *Luxe Life Swap* would want to experience another side of the city: the secret places and hidden gems born and bred Venetians like the count and his wife would know about. The places where they shopped, ate, worked and played. Grand and intimate, fancy and simple, light and dark: the programme would showcase every facet of the unique floating city. It was going to be a heck of a challenge getting the camera equipment around Venice; she was glad the organisation fell to someone else.

But now Natalie had a whole day to wander the city they called *La Serenissima* – the serene one – and get a feel of the place, thanks to Mandy's insistence that settling-in time was always built into her presenting schedule. Reluctantly, she tore herself away from the ever-changing scene. There was a lot of Venice to see; she couldn't lean on the bridge all morning.

She took a side street by the vaporetto station past stands of souvenirs to a *campo* overlooked by two large churches. Strains of opera – singers rehearsing, perhaps – came from one; a poster outside advertised a forthcoming concert. Checking her map, she followed the route to the foot of a low bridge, stepping to one side to let a man clatter his trolley down the steps. A gondola drifted silently by, the gondolier ducking low under the bridge and replacing his be-ribboned boater as he emerged on the other side.

A yellow sign high on the wall pointed the way to the Palazzo Contarini del Bovolo. It led her to a narrow alleyway between two high brick walls. A prickly sensation crept down her spine. It felt as though the breath had been sucked from her chest. *Don't be ridiculous, Nat.* It was broad daylight. She had to get a grip; she would never survive the filming if she let the fears of the past rush in.

She hurried down the *calle* into the courtyard where the palazzo stood. The distinctive red brick and white stone building with its external spiral staircase was perfect: just the unexpected, quirky place the viewers would love. She'd get Phil and Cate to climb the eighty-odd stairs to the top; they'd get great shots of them oohing and aahing at the views across the terracotta rooftops as Natalie asked a few questions on camera. She made a mental note to wear her peacock-blue dress that morning, leaving her chestnut hair loose to flow in whatever breeze there might be at the top.

Natalie would need to consult with Cate – when they finally met – to go through the outfits they'd be wearing each day to make sure they worked well against the various backdrops. *Luxe Life Swap* peddled a fantasy; beautiful clothes were an integral part of the whole viewer experience. She pulled out her phone and sent Bettany a reminder to send over the contestants' photographs and CVs; it was the one file Flo's PA had omitted in the rush to bring Natalie up to date.

Leaving the spiral staircase behind, she negotiated a maze of streets until she reached the entrance to La Fenice, the grand opera house where the contestants would get to enjoy a performance of *La Traviata*. Natalie caught her breath. The sweeping steps, soaring pillars and blue silk curtains were going to look fabulous on camera. She thought of introducing herself to the man on the desk and taking a look inside, but exactly where Cate and Phil would sit and how the camera angles would work didn't fall within her remit. Besides, she wanted to head to St Mark's Square to refresh her memory of the grand basilica and the Doge's Palace. But first, she had a parcel to deliver.

She undid the catch on her tan shoulder bag, one of the three she'd packed in order to ring the changes on screen, her fingers searching for the small, padded envelope Floella had entrusted to her. Of course, it was still there. There was no rational reason for it not to be but she was so nervous of losing the precious watch parts, she'd checked she was carrying the package umpteen times. She'd be glad to drop it off at Eraldo's premises and be shot of it.

She consulted the email Floella had sent her: Eraldo's workshop could be found on the upper floor of a souvenir shop opposite an artisan perfumery in the Dorsoduro, a quiet area of the city on the other side of the Grand Canal. She'd assumed she'd need to cross a bridge but Flo's directions led her to a wooden platform where people were boarding a large gondola. It was lacquered plain black without the leather seats and fancy trims of the smaller, more elegant versions she'd spotted from the Rialto Bridge.

Natalie rummaged for some change; a roughened hand helped her aboard. The sway beneath her feet almost pitched her into an elderly woman's lap, erasing any thought she had of copying the smartly dressed Venetians who stood up for the crossing. She perched on the wooden ledge; the craft tilted as others stepped aboard. Two oarsmen conveyed them across the canal with the minimum of fuss. She stepped off on the far bank, the paving beneath her feet strangely wobbly. It took her a few moments to feel normal again.

She followed a shop-lined *calle*, walked over a bridge and crossed through a courtyard arriving on a quiet *fondamenta*. The sweet aroma of vanilla and orange wafting from the perfumery confirmed she was in the right place. On the other side of a small humpback bridge, a round metal sign, shaped like a clock face high up on the wall advertised watch repairs. But below Eraldo's premises, the windows at street level weren't full of the Murano glass and marbled paper Natalie was expecting. Row upon row of Venetian masks stared out at her.

For a moment, she was propelled back in time: sixteen teenage girls creating mayhem in an explosion of papier mâché, feathers, sequins and glue, the teachers wishing they'd had the sense to choose a pasta-making workshop or a sketching class for the hands-on creative component some bright spark in the staffroom had decided to weave into their school trip.

She rested a hand on the bridge's balustrade to steady herself, forced herself to cross to the other side.

'May I help?' The voice came from the mask maker's doorway. A man standing in the entrance peered at her over half-moon glasses; his white hair and brown apron reminded her of a story-book drawing of Pinocchio's wood-carver father. He gestured to a diamond-pattern mask in royal blue and white. 'In the window, you can see mainly the carnival masks, such as the harlequin, but we have many more masks inside. Or perhaps you are here for a watch repair? It is through the shop up the stairs.'

She stood, feet rooted to the pavement. Maybe if she flattered this man a little, he would fetch Eraldo down from his workshop to meet her in the street so that she did not have to step inside.

She nodded towards the window. 'The masks are beautiful. Do you make them yourself?'

'Of course.' He spread his paint-stained hands. 'All my life... well, as long as I can remember. Come in, come in.'

She took a step back. 'I am looking for Eraldo, the watch restorer. I have a parcel for him, from London.'

'You are Floella? You are not how I imagined you.'

'No, I'm Natalie her, umm, friend.' She undid the catch on her bag.

'I am Pietro, *piacere*, pleased to meet you! Come in.'

Natalie hesitated. Pietro's eyes were kind, his welcome genuine; how could she tell him the very thought of walking into his shop was making her sweat?

Keeping her eyes focused straight ahead, she allowed him to lead her past a workbench piled with half-made masks, jars of brushes and pots of glitter and paint to the foot of a spiral staircase.

'Eraldo! A visitor! A friend of Floella's.'

A voice came from the floor above. '*Avanti!* Come up!'

Her eyes fell on a set of white *bauta* masks fixed high on the wall, eyes empty hollows. She hurried up the stairs.

Eraldo was bending over a wooden bench; a tangle of dark, curly hair concealed his face. He looked up at her approach, laid down his microscope and put on a pair of glasses with tortoiseshell frames. Treacle-dark eyes met hers, flooding her body with a warm feeling that had nothing to do with her hasty ascent of the spiral stairs.

'You must be Natalie.' His rich accent turned her everyday name into something sensuous.

'Yes, I am Natalie.'

He stood looking at her expectantly. 'You have something for me? From Floella?'

'Oh, of course!' She'd almost forgotten why she'd come. What an idiot she must look, standing there gawping at him.

'Please do sit down, it is not so comfortable but...' He gestured to a simple ladder-back chair on the other side of his workbench.

She sat down, taking in the cluttered workbench, the half-open wooden drawers, the overflowing cardboard boxes. 'What are you repairing?'

He turned a bracelet over in his hand. 'A secret watch. The face of the watch is concealed until the lady – for these are usually designed for ladies – chooses to reveal it. This type of watch has fascinated me since I was a young boy. They originated when it was considered rude for a woman to consult the time in public, revealing she might be bored. I love the idea of this little secret between the watchmaker and his customer.' He smiled. Behind his glasses, his eyes were shining. 'These watches are rather an obsession for me. Perhaps that is odd, but we all have our passions.'

Natalie smiled back. Did she have a passion? She hadn't really thought about it. She resisted the urge to reach out and remove a small, white thread clinging to his dove-grey shirt, instead retrieving Floella's envelope from her shoulder bag. Eraldo took it from her, carefully prizing off the sticky tape.

'*Grazie*! Ruby friction jewels, winders and tourbillons – and what other parts, I can only guess! But I will look through all this later; if I start now, you will not get a word of sense out of me.'

'Well, I will leave you to your work.' Natalie reluctantly made to get up.

'Please, do not go yet. I cannot believe I have not yet offered you a cold drink after you are so kind to bring this to me. It is such a warm day, especially up here. I would have a ceiling fan but I cannot risk having tiny springs and collets being blown all over the room.'

'Thank you. I would like that very much.' The glories of St Mark's Square could wait a little longer.

'I have a small fridge in the back; is lemon iced tea okay? Or perhaps mineral water?'

'The iced tea would be nice, thank you.'

'Please make yourself comfortable on that old couch in the corner.'

Natalie moved a paint-stained apron and a folded-up copy of *La Repubblica* onto a low coffee table and sank down onto a three-seater settee tucked against the far wall. She nudged a cushion out of the way, her fingers making contact with something beneath it. Her hand wrapped around an ivory-coloured, empty-eyed mask, its long, curved nose shaped like a parrot's beak. She leapt from her seat, letting out a scream before she could stop herself.

Eraldo dropped the two glasses onto the coffee table, brown liquid sloshing over the sides. 'Natalie, what is it? Are you all right?'

'It's that... thing. That mask, it was under the cushion. It gave me quite a fright.' How silly she must seem. She sat back down gingerly.

He dried off the bottom of one of the glasses with the edge of the blue apron and handed it to her. 'That is the mask of the Plague doctor; it is rather sinister. Do you know the history of these things? Originally, the beak was stuffed with medicinal herbs to protect the wearer against the noxious fumes of the Plague but it must have been very frightening when a man turned up at your door cloaked and masked like that.' Eraldo took the offending object from the couch, positioning it halfway down the table.

Natalie shifted slightly so that the hideous mask was no longer in her line of sight.

'Tell me how you know Flo,' she said. Anything to change the subject.

'Ah, Floella.' His face broke into a smile.

She sipped her drink, trying to concentrate on what he was telling her, but she could only process a fraction of what he was saying. He'd met Flo on a design course at London's Goldsmiths College. They'd both been involved in an amateur dramatics performance – Floella in a starring role of course – but what the show was called or what part Flo had played went straight over her head. Whilst reaching for the iced tea, Eraldo had inadvertently knocked the mask further towards her. Despite the cold drink, her face was hot, sweat running down her neck. The memories were closing in.

'I'm sorry... I can't...' She scrambled to her feet. 'I can't stay.'

'Natalie?'

She bolted for the spiral staircase, clattering down the metal rungs, her bag banging against her side. 'Thank you for the drink,' she shouted upwards, half-tripping over the last step.

The mask maker looked up from his cash desk. '*Che c'è?* What's happening?'

She blundered through the shop, past a woman holding a harlequin mask to her face, past a table piled high with cat-featured *Gnaga* masks, out onto the street.

She took the steps up and over the bridge two at a time.

4

'Natalie!' Eraldo called.

She did not turn around, hurrying over the bridge without a backward glance at the mask maker's shop. She couldn't bear to spend another moment with that thing – that creepy, nightmare mask with its hideous curved beak, sucking her back to the night she'd tried so hard to forget.

She found herself walking down a narrow *calle*; in her haste, she'd turned the wrong way. At the end stood a courtyard flanked by two churches. A man sat on a bright-red bench smoking, a sad-eyed dog at his feet. She exited the square by a hexagonal newspaper kiosk, arriving on the side of a small canal, no longer caring where she was going; she just needed to put one foot in front of the other until she'd cleared her head. She followed the *fondamenta* until it met a wide walkway lined with cafés and restaurants buzzing with life. Across the water, she recognised the grand Palladian church of Il Redentore erected by the Venetians in thanks to the Lord for delivering them from the Plague. She had reached the promenade separating the Dorsoduro region from the long sliver of land known as the island of Giudecca.

Chatter rose from the table behind her: two women eating forkfuls of coiled *bucatini* pasta, drinking white wine from large goblets. On an adjoining chair, a terrier poked its nose out of a logoed carrycase. Natalie couldn't help but smile. Her heart rate gradually returned to normal, her breathing now slow and steady.

'You have a reservation?' A voice interrupted her thoughts. She hadn't realised she was standing right next to a vacant table.

'No, and I don't want to eat… *grazie.*'

The waiter shrugged, clearing away two unused glasses from another table where an elderly couple shared a bottle of wine, forking up a saffron-yellow risotto. The scent of the sea mixed with garlic stopped Natalie walking away. It had been hours since she'd eaten breakfast: a quick cappuccino and pastry standing at a bar, Italian-style.

'Please may I have a table? I've changed my mind.'

She expected a sigh or a raised eyebrow but the waiter merely gestured to an empty seat and departed with a cheerful, '*Subito* – I'll be back.'

The menu was already lying open, a slim, oxblood leatherette with gold lettering, but she didn't need to read it. When the waiter returned, she tilted her head towards the adjacent table.

'I'll have that risotto please and a glass of white wine.'

She spread out the city map her hotel had given her, waiting for her risotto to arrive. Eraldo's voice came back to her, calling out to her as she hurried down the stairs. Floella's old friend had been welcoming and kind. He must have been so bewildered when she jumped up and left. But she couldn't have explained; she wanted to push the memories aside, not relive them. And it didn't matter what he thought. She'd never go back to the mask maker's shop, never have any reason to see him again. She shook her head to dispel the memory of dark, dark eyes looking out from behind tortoiseshell glasses, the passion in his voice.

The waiter set a bowl in front of her, a glorious heap of fragrant rice crowned with a pair of langoustines. She pulled back the head on one, dug out the pale-pink flesh, swallowing it with a sigh of pleasure before dipping her fingers in a small glass water bowl. She ate the rest of the risotto, fork in one hand, tracing a route on her map with the other.

Leaving the last few drops of wine, she took the bill inside to pay at the counter. She slipped her corporate credit card back into her red leather purse, stowed it in her tan bag and strode determinedly down the waterfront. By a white stone church, she took the turning into the slightly scruffy Campo Sant'Agnese cutting across it into a street lined with small trees. As she walked towards the brick bell tower on the horizon, the vista opened up, revealing the curve of a wooden bridge. She felt a tightening in her stomach but she walked on. They'd be filming on that bridge in a few days' time; the view towards the iconic church of Santa Maria della Salute was one of the best in the city. When she went there with Cate and Phil, she'd have to be poised and professional. She couldn't mess up. She couldn't let Floella down.

Natalie gripped the handrail of the Accademia Bridge, put her foot on the first step. She was back in the spot where it had all begun.

5
———

Beautiful filigree balconies enlivened the soft apricot façade of the count and countess's palazzo. Their four-storey home was one of the most splendid buildings that lined the Grand Canal. Natalie knew from her internet research that the magnificent properties rested on thousands of wooden pilings driven into the bed of the Venetian lagoon, but she still couldn't wrap her head around it. Water lapping at the front wall of your house just seemed plain wrong, though it made for a great spectacle.

Lucia, *Luxe Life Swap*'s Italian fixer, gestured to the pointed archway over the front door. 'That's the entrance where Philip and Cate will arrive this evening on the private water taxi I've booked for them. You and I will be using the other entrance that can be reached from the *calle*, around the side. All these properties that face the canal have a second entrance, although you might not spot it immediately.'

'Of course,' Natalie said, as if she had expert knowledge of the palazzi of Venice.

'See the carving of the leaping goat? That is the symbol on the count's family crest. And of course, the striped poles outside the entrance – *pali di casada*, we call them – are painted in the family colours of peach and gold. I think the contestants, they will like it?' The young fixer furrowed her brow. 'They have a big house in England?'

'Yes, an old, restored vicarage outside Sevenoaks. Period features, a huge terrace on the back, a large pond and a weeping willow tree. I'm sure the count and countess will find it charming. But this...' Natalie broke off, mentally listing all the superlatives she could reach for during filming over the next fortnight.

Lucia's serious face brightened. 'Just wait until you see inside. Shall we go in?'

Natalie followed her down the steps from the bridge, around a corner and through a maze of streets and over a narrow *rio* barely wide enough for a gondola to pass to the side of the property. Lucia produced a hefty iron key with a faded, red tassel to unlock the wooden door.

Natalie ascended a flight of stone steps to the first floor, stepping into a magnificent rectangular entrance space. Cherubs and lute players frolicked across the ceiling. On the far wall, an oil painting showed two women in long, velvety robes below a sky of gathering storm clouds, their faces glowing with a divine light.

'A Titian, one of the finest in private hands.'

Natalie let out a breath. 'Quite an entrance hall.'

'This floor, the *piano nobile*, is where the original owners would have entertained, so the most dramatic and expensive decorations are here.' Lucia gestured at a hefty, gilded chandelier hanging by a long chain from the frescoed ceiling. 'The lower floor would have been used for the family's business, offices and so forth. The bedrooms were above, and of course the attic would have housed the servants.'

Natalie nodded, mentally adding Lucia's comments to all the other information the young woman had imparted over the course of the morning.

'I thought we would use the *Camera Rossa* – the Red Room – for some of the filming.' Lucia turned a handle hidden within the wooden panelling.

Natalie stepped onto a terrazzo floor shimmering with a dozen different coloured stones: shades of terracotta, caramel, cocoa and copper. Deep fringed sofas flanked a rococo fireplace, heavy, ruby-coloured damask curtains fell to the floor; the dark-red, silk-covered walls had a depth of colour only the finest cloth could bring. This room alone would have the show's advertisers purring. *Luxe Life Swap* would be a sure-fire hit, another series a foregone conclusion. As long as Natalie didn't mess up.

'Are you okay?' Lucia's eyes were concerned.

'I'm just trying to take it all in... and hoping someone has told Cate and Phil about Mandy's health scare.' She didn't want the cameras capturing the contestants' crestfallen faces when they realised they'd be spending a fortnight with Natalie 'Nobody' Spencer instead of Mandy 'National Treasure' Miller whose blend of old-fashioned factual reporting and breezy, best-friend charm had won her a devoted following.

'Ahh! You are a little worried because this is your first big show.' Lucia frowned. 'Perhaps you are thinking that I have not prepared everything. I know I am young, but I have worked on many productions.'

'These Venice episodes are vital to the show's success but it's not you I'm worried about, it's me. Mandy is so popular.'

'Mandy, she is a star who everybody loves; even in Italy we know her. So, if you are unsure, just ask yourself: what would Mandy do?' Lucia beamed as if her words were enough to sweep away all Natalie's doubts. 'And what will go wrong? Venice, this palazzo, all is *perfetto, sì*? Now we will go upstairs, I have a special secret to show you. And afterwards, I take you to Da Andrea near the Palazzo Fortuny: the best coffee in my city.'

Lucia led her through double doors up more stairs to a portrait-lined corridor and into a high-ceilinged room lined in a shimmering eau-de-nil damask dominated by a carved wooden bed piled high with sumptuous cushions.

'The contestants will be sleeping in the Gold Room but this one is interesting for you to see, I think. It is similar to the other rooms except for one special trick.'

Natalie scanned the panelled walls, expecting to see another carefully concealed door, but Lucia dropped to the floor, crouching on her heels and began to roll back a patterned runner near the foot of the bed.

'Look!' Lucia lifted up a small, diamond-shaped floor tile, revealing a grill set into the marble floor.

Natalie knelt down, peering through the gaps in the curled metalwork. The shimmering floor, the edge of a crimson sofa: there was no doubt about what she could see. She was looking directly down into the Red Room.

'Clever, do you not think?' Lucia said. 'A person can look and listen to what is going on below. The owners could overhear their guests' private conversations before they came down to greet them. To succeed in commerce like the Vicenzi family, one had to have as many advantages as possible.'

'Keep your friends close and your enemies closer.' Natalie grinned.

'And now we will have that coffee.' Lucia straightened up. 'Ah, my phone, I have a call.'

'Please, take it.' Natalie wandered across to the wide window. She dug out her own phone and checked an app. Cate and Phil's flight had taken off; it was due to arrive on time. She had one less thing to worry about.

'No! This is not possible!' Lucia's voice was shrill.

Natalie swung around. 'What is it?'

'*Sì, sì*... she is here.' Lucia crossed the room. She held out the phone. 'It is Floella, Natalie. You need to speak to her. One of your contestants has gone missing.'

6

Cate stepped out of the taxi. The driver plonked their cases down on the pavement with a thump. Phil put his wallet back in his inside pocket. The cab driver pulled back into the traffic. By this evening, they'd be in Venice.

'Departures are this way.' Phil marched ahead.

'*Italia*, here we come!' Cate cringed at the false note of gaiety in her voice. She followed her husband towards the entrance, having to half-run to keep up with him. 'Slow down! I know you're keen to go back to the place we first met but the plane won't take off any earlier,' she joked.

'We need to go up a level.' Phil manoeuvred their cases into the tightly crammed lift. Cate squeezed in, her face inches from a thin man in giant headphones nodding along to a silent beat; a red bag containing some sort of sports equipment jabbed into her thigh. A little boy banged his sandals against his ride-on case.

Cate caught Phil's eye. 'Isn't he just like our Oli was?'

'Yes, he was so cute at that age.'

The doors slid open. They stepped aside to let everyone else out first.

'This way.' Phil set off towards the Flight Information screens, pulling his giant case, his knuckles white on the handle of his carry-on.

'You're worrying about something, aren't you?' Cate said, hurrying to keep up. 'The business will be fine. Caspar will look after the showroom; you keep telling me he could do with some more responsibility. The Italians will take good care of the house and I've got an agency to send in a cleaner twice a week. This is a big opportunity for the business and think of everything you'll see in Venice; you'll come back bursting with fresh ideas for all those new customers who've seen the wonderful things you make.'

'A real-life Italian count eating at one of my tables, hanging his linen suits in my wardrobe; that's advertising money can't buy.'

'You see, it's a fabulous opportunity,' Cate said firmly. 'Look, our flight's on time and there doesn't seem to be too bad a queue at Bag Drop. Let's get rid of this lot. We'll be sitting in the lounge before we know it. I could murder a glass of champagne.' Perhaps it would help Phil to relax; she couldn't remember when she'd last seen him so tense.

The line for the bag-drop machines moved painfully slowly, a family with a pile of huge, monogrammed trunks causing a commotion in front of them. At last, a woman in a short-sleeved shirt beckoned them forwards.

'You first.' Phil heaved Cate's case up onto the belt. She scanned the boarding pass on her phone and attached the luggage tag, amazed the bulging case was several kilograms under the limit. It wobbled slightly as the conveyor belt carried it out of sight.

'Now yours.'

Her husband didn't seem to hear her, his eyes roaming an area beyond her head.

'Phil?'

'Just hold on a moment. I've got a message.' He pulled out his phone, an odd look crossing his face.

'What is it? Can't you check that once we've found the lounge?'

'No, no, I can't... This is important. I'm sorry, Cate. I can't come with you right now. You'll have to go on ahead.'

She bit down her impatience. 'It's okay, I'll wait. But let's get rid of your case.' She sensed the stares of the queuing families boring into the back of her head.

Phil slid the phone back into his pocket. 'You don't understand. I can't come with you to Venice today. There's something... a problem at the workshop.'

'Phil, what the heck! I'll have to get my case back. Where's one of the airline staff when you need one?' Cate swivelled her head.

'No, Cate, you have to go on ahead. We can't let the TV company down; think of the bad publicity. I'll get a flight out tomorrow. I can't hang around here; I'll have to go and find a taxi.'

'Phil! Where do you think you're going?' Cate's voice rose. 'You can't go back to the house; the TV crew is due any minute. The count and countess are arriving tonight.'

Phil threw his hands up in the air as though she were the one causing the problem. 'I'll get a hotel somewhere... There's one two streets from the office.'

'But that's a Premier Inn!' She couldn't remember Phil ever booking anything less than a four star in all the years they'd been married.

'Who cares? That's not important.'

'I'm coming with you.' Cate waved at a passing air steward. 'Please, are you with BA?'

'Cate!' Phil actually shouted at her. He never shouted.

'Is everything all right, madam?' The steward's brow wrinkled.

'Err, yes, thank you, it was nothing.' Cate would try and retrieve her suitcase as soon as she'd calmed Phil down.

'Phil...'

'Please, Cate. This is just one day, I promise you. Your seat's booked, your case is on its way, the TV people are meeting you at the other end. Go and buy yourself something nice in Duty Free, have a glass of champagne in the lounge, read a book. You're always saying you don't have enough "Me Time".'

Phil pecked her on the lips, grabbed the handle of his suitcase and headed towards the yellow sign for taxis.

She stood watching his departing back, aware that her mouth had literally dropped open.

'Are you sure you're okay, madam?' The steward had reappeared. His brass-buttoned blazer and polished shoes emitted a calm authority.

Cate smoothed down her dress, flicked a strand of Ted's hair off her sleeve. 'Yes, I'm quite all right, thank you.' The sooner she got moving, the sooner she'd be sitting down with a much-needed glass of champagne.

She walked briskly across the tiled floor, made her way through security and headed for the lounge, ignoring the bright lights and alluring scents wafting from the World of Duty Free.

The young woman behind the desk swiped Cate's card with the minimum of fuss. She sank down onto a comfortable leather seat, still seething with irritation. She'd spent weeks getting everything ready for their trip – not to mention organising their summer party – so that all her husband had to do was jump in a car to the airport. But she wasn't going to waste her energy on righteous anger; she was going to enjoy a cold glass of champagne and then she was flying to Venice. This was just a blip. Tomorrow, Phil would be getting on a plane. They'd meet up at the palazzo on the Grand Canal and everything would be fine. She wouldn't let her mind wander back to her conversation with Lucy, nor think of her neighbour Kiran alone in her big house whilst her husband was away. Phil's message was from work. It had to be. And now she'd use this sliver of 'Me Time', as he called it, to sit and think. To decide once and for all if she had the courage to sneak away during a break in the filming to do what she'd been putting off for the best part of twenty-five years.

7

'In the event of landing on water, please remove all high-heeled shoes.'

Cate automatically glanced down at her trainer-clad feet. Across the aisle, a bald man in a grey suit turned the pages of his newspaper. Cate's copy of *Hello!* poked temptingly from the mesh pocket on the back of the seat in front but she kept her eyes on the immaculately made-up stewardess as she completed the safety briefing. It seemed rude to ignore the woman's unappreciated commentary and she couldn't help thinking that the way today was going, she wouldn't be surprised to find herself bobbing in the ocean trying to top up her life jacket through its little plastic tube and blowing on her whistle.

'Thank you for choosing to fly with us today. We hope you have a pleasant journey.'

Easier said than done. Cate was sure to have a comfortable flight with no arguments over the armrest, but it was hard to chill out and enjoy her unscheduled 'Me Time' when her thoughts were fixated on Phil's out-of-character dash from the airport.

The plane climbed higher. Cate opened her copy of *Hello!*, closed it again and slipped it back into the seat pocket. What was going through Phil's head? What had happened that had escaped her notice? She stared out of the window. Nothing but blue sky.

'Madam?'

Cate turned, surprised she hadn't noticed the rattle of the trolley. 'A mini bottle of Prosecco and some pistachio nuts – just a small bag, please.' She shouldn't really drink on top of the champagne she'd enjoyed in the lounge, but today she needed it, deserved it, dammit, for getting on this plane and facing the embarrassment of turning up in Venice alone.

The bottle opened with a satisfying pop. The man across the aisle raised his own glass of red with a grin and a wink. Cate's cheeks heated. It always took her by surprise if anyone saw her as anything other than a wife and mother. She picked up her magazine pointedly and opened it at random. The glossy, double-page spread showed a stately home in Northamptonshire, the newly installed third wife of Lord Somebody-or-other posing in a purple ballgown in front of a vast marble fireplace. The caption said:

Lady Petronella successfully blends old and new

To one side, a blousy display of roses stood on an inlaid, crescent-shaped cabinet: one of Phil's most iconic pieces. He'd be so proud to see it there. He'd worked so hard to revitalise the business he'd taken over from Evan's uncle, and she'd been behind him all the way. With both their boys at boarding school, she'd been able to devote a couple of days a week to helping in his office. Had she lost sight of their marriage, become more of a colleague than a wife?

She took a sip of Prosecco, the little bubbles fizzing pleasantly on her tongue. She thought back to their last dinner party with Kiran and Mark. Cate's new neighbours were the perfect couple, always gazing at each other adoringly, touching each other when they thought nobody was looking, making Cate feel a little bit jealous of the way Mark so obviously adored his wife, even though she'd accepted years ago that Phil didn't believe in public displays of affection.

Her husband wasn't good at expressing his emotions, full stop. After they'd met at university, it had taken him almost a year to say those three little words: *I love you*. But she hadn't minded; she'd seen them forming on the tip of his tongue often enough. Her husband loved her. He showed her that, and sometimes even told her that, when they were home alone. Together. Safe. Phil and Kiran having an affair? It was laughable. But something was up with Phil and by the end of this trip to Venice, she would find out what it was.

She passed the rest of the flight leafing through her magazine, snapping open the fresh, green pistachios, gathering quite a pile of hard little shells in her paper napkin.

The seat belt signs went on; the plane began to descend.

They touched down smoothly, the pilot earning a splattering of applause. Despite the still-illuminated seat belt signs, the aisle began to fill up with passengers, cramming themselves into the narrow space, snapping open the overhead lockers. Cate stayed in her seat, her phone pinging with notifications: *Welcome to Italy*; a roaming charges update; a message from Phil that simply said:

> At hotel, sorry about today, don't worry.
> Love you.

There was a message from Evan's wife, Lucy, too. Surely she couldn't have got wind of Phil's vanishing act and popped up to commiserate? Or dig for gossip, more like.

Cate sighed. People like Lucy didn't just disappear if you ignored them. She clicked on the message.

> Thought you should see this.

A link to a news item:

Mandy Miller Lucky to Survive.

The accompanying photograph showed the popular TV presenter propped up in a bed against an improbable amount of pillows. Cate skimmed the article, trying to home in on the facts behind the sensationalist story: *emergency operation... out of danger... Mandy refused to let us issue a statement until the operation was pronounced a success; she didn't want to worry her fans*, a spokesperson said.

The steps cranked into position; the mass of passengers shuffled a few inches forward. Cate re-read the article, this time more slowly. Mandy was out of the woods but she clearly wasn't going to be jetting off to Venice any time soon. When had this story been released? When had the TV company planned to tell *her*? The message from Lucy had been sent less than half an hour before they landed, moments after the news broke. She checked her emails. There it was: an email from Flo-Go Productions sent just after take-off.

'Madam?' The steward was hovering by the end of her row,

his colleague clearing up discarded newspapers and magazines into a large, see-through sack. He had a ginger beard but still looked young, not that many years older than her Oli.

'Sorry, just one moment, please.' Cate's finger hovered over the message.

'I'm afraid I am going to have to ask you to leave this aircraft.'

Cate looked around. The seemingly unmoveable blockage of bodies and hand luggage had miraculously cleared. She was the only passenger remaining.

'Of course, I'm so sorry, I hadn't realised.'

'And try not to leave anything behind.' The steward scooped up a small, pink teddy from the row of seats on the other side of the aisle.

'No, I won't. Sorry to hold you up.' She took her small carry-on from under the seat in front and stood up.

'No problem.' The steward smiled. 'Have a lovely time in Venice.' He waggled the bear's arm to make it look as though it was waving.

Cate smiled weakly. She walked briskly down the aisle, stepping carefully onto the top rung of the aircraft stairs. Warm air hit her. The sky was clear blue. Venice. She was here. Without Phil. And without Mandy. *Come on, Cate, pull yourself together*. She was nearly forty, she'd raised two children, helped run a successful business, she was living a life she could never have dreamt of the last time she was here. She was a different person now, wasn't she?

* * *

Phil smacked his hand against his forehead. Poor Cate – she'd looked so bewildered. How could he have bolted from the airport, leaving her like that? He knew his hastily concocted lie about the crisis in the office hadn't fooled her, but how could he explain why he couldn't get on the plane? If he told her about what had happened in Italy all those years ago, she'd be sickened. She wouldn't look at him the same way again; she might even leave him, and he couldn't live without her. When the TV company told them they'd be swapping lifestyles with a couple from Venice, why hadn't he pulled the plug straight away? He could have made up an excuse, any excuse. Now it was too late. He was only putting off the inevitable; tomorrow, he would have to get on a plane. He just needed one more day. To be alone. To think.

'Is it here, mate?' The taxi driver's voice cut in.

'Yes, thank you.' He paid the man and stepped out, slamming the cab door too hard. The driver yanked Phil's suitcase out of the boot, dumping it on the wet pavement. It had started to drizzle again. Phil grabbed the handle, thrust his other hand into his pocket. He'd find a pub and drink until he'd blocked out the guilt and the shame. The way he always did when the memories taunted him.

8

Cate started reading the rest of the email from Flo-Go Productions, one eye on the luggage belt:

> Please be assured Mandy's unfortunate absence will not impact the filming schedule for *Luxe Life Swap*. Our local representative, Lucia, will meet your flight as planned.

Her smart, chocolate-brown, leather-trimmed case emerged from the top of the luggage chute. She shoved the phone back into her bag.

'Excuse me, umm, *permesso*?' She stepped across a harassed-looking mother. The woman didn't respond, too busy trying to comfort one wailing toddler whilst grabbing the legs of a slightly older boy determined to hurl himself onto the luggage belt.

Cate wrestled her overstuffed case to the floor. The luggage label was still attached, all zips safely done up; at least one part of her increasingly fraught trip had gone to plan. She clutched the handle, negotiating her way through the somewhat chaotic atmosphere out to the Arrivals area.

A young woman, chic in a simple, orange blouse and coffee-coloured skirt, was holding up a card with the Flo-Go Productions logo and *Mrs Cate Beresford* written in large letters. Cate's apologetic message about Phil's absence had clearly been received.

'Cate, *piacere*!' The woman pushed her hexagonal sunglasses up into her long, black hair. 'I am so happy to meet you. My name is Lucia.'

Cate felt the tension in her shoulders ebb away. She took the woman's dainty hand. 'Pleased to meet you.'

'Travelling can be tiring, a coffee or perhaps a drink? The camera crew are by the water taxi, but they can wait. Or would you prefer to go straight to the palazzo?' Lucia continued, taking hold of the handle of Cate's case and heading in the direction of the exit at a rate of knots that defied her high heels.

Cate strode beside her. 'I'm happy to go straight there. I can't wait to see where we'll be staying for the next fortnight.'

'Mandy was so happy when we sent over the pictures of the count's house. Your husband will love it when he arrives. He comes tomorrow, yes?'

'I'm so terribly sorry...'

Lucia waved a dismissive hand. 'It is no problem; we adapt, create a few, how you say, filler scenes. We will visit some of our best Venetian boutiques, show you some of our Italian fashions. The countess shops in the streets around St Mark's. All the big-name designer brands are there but we will visit the smaller boutiques she favours. You can see a unique selection, the best of Italian designers from the Veneto region. It will be fun, *si*?'

'Thank you, I would love that.'

It would be interesting to experience shopping Italian-style, and it wasn't something Phil would mind missing at all. It sounded terribly spoilt but she'd got bored with London's designer stores. At first, the doors held open by uniformed staff, complimentary champagne, soft music and hushed voices had made her feel like royalty but after a few visits, the novelty of being handed a box-fresh blouse to try on had worn off. And although the scent of the floral displays in Christian Dior was far more pleasant than the aroma that had hung around the changing rooms of Oxford Street on late Saturday afternoons, shopping in Bond Street wasn't half as much fun as the days when she and Natalie had illicitly shared a changing room in Topshop, snorting with laughter as they tried on armfuls of clothes before skipping off to Primark for something cheaper they'd take it in turns to wear on Saturday nights.

'Cate, meet our television crew.'

Cate snapped back to the present. They'd reached the landing stage. She tried to take in the names as Lucia introduced the make-up girl, the director, and the camera crew led by a burly fellow sporting a red, padded gilet, despite the warm evening, and his achingly cool female assistant whose sleeveless, khaki shirt revealed brown shoulders and arms, strong and sinewy from lugging equipment around.

After a brief conversation in Italian that went straight over her head, a dusting of face powder and the application of a rather vivid lipstick she was too overwhelmed to protest about, Cate was deemed ready. She stepped into the sleek, white water taxi, holding the arm of the driver for support.

Lucia sat down beside her. 'We will not begin filming until we are nearer to the Grand Canal. Do not worry if you cough, or sneeze or are not always smiling. We will only use a few small clips of this journey, just enough for the viewers to see you on the water. It is the shot of you arriving at the palazzo that is the important one. But if it is not right... pfft! We film it again.' She paused and spoke to the driver before turning back to Cate. 'Franco, he knows we may have to approach the palazzo's canal front entrance several times if the director is not happy. Now please sit back and enjoy the journey.'

Cate leant back and relaxed as Lucia chatted knowledgeably about the floating city she called home. There was something calming about being out on the water.

'We will focus on the intimate moments as you contemplate your new surroundings,' Lucia explained. 'And then a door from the library will open and Natalie will come out to meet you.'

'Natalie?'

Lucia frowned. 'You did not receive the email from us about poor Mandy?'

'Yes, I did but I had only read part of it when my case appeared on the luggage carousel. It was almost the first one off; that never happens.' Cate laughed. 'But Mandy, how is she doing? I should have asked straight away...'

'Do not apologise. It is overwhelming arriving in a new place, especially under these circumstances: passports, luggage, customs, remembering where you are going...' Lucia smiled. 'Mandy is doing well, but of course this is a serious operation; the poor woman's plans for the next months have been, as you say, turned inside out. Luckily, Flo-Go Productions has acted swiftly. Within a few hours, they arrange everything. They sent out this replacement lady, very nice, Natalie Spencer.'

'Natalie Spencer?' Cate's stomach lurched as though the Venetian lagoon had been replaced by the rolling waves of the Atlantic Ocean. In a storm.

This had to be a bizarre coincidence. It couldn't be *that* Natalie Spencer from school. Cate had seen Nat once and only once on television, many years before. She'd turned on a new afternoon children's show and when the camera closed in on Nat's face, she'd jabbed poor baby Oli in the face with a spoonful of banana puree. For a second or two, Cate had sat mesmerised by her old classmate's hideous dungarees, the smiling face made up with lots of pink blusher for a child-friendly look. Then she'd snatched up the remote control and changed channels. She'd concentrated on mopping squelchy pudding off Oli's puce-red face, hushing his cries before adding *Panda's Place* to the list of unsuitable TV shows she left with the au pair. And, despite Nat's fancy media studies degree, Cate had never seen her on television again. So how could she possibly be presenting a super successful, prime-time show, stepping into the towering heels of national treasure, Mandy Miller?

'*Sì*, Natalie Spencer.' Lucia beamed. 'You have heard of her? I think she is not so well known.'

'No, I...'

The producer gave a hand signal.

'We are about to start. It is best not to speak,' Lucia said. 'The camera will pan the whole area, lingering on you just for a few seconds at a time. A smile is all we need, although a look of awestruck wonder would be perfect.'

Cate nodded. 'Awestruck, got it.'

The driver turned into the Grand Canal, the scene instantly recognisable from a thousand photographs. And from her school trip. But she couldn't think back to those days if she had any hope of composing her features into a natural-looking smile.

A gondola glided past, the gondolier sporting the iconic

striped top of his official association. His two passengers were cosied up on the red leather seat, the girl clutching a fan, obviously bought as a souvenir, gazing at her lover as though all the wonders of Venice could not compare. Cate felt a pang of envy. She needed Phil here, someone to walk through the city with, to talk to over breakfast, to hold her at night. What if he missed more than one day? What if he didn't turn up? She gave herself a ticking off. She must stop being so negative. Phil would be here tomorrow; they'd go riding in a gondola of their own. And he would love this city. She could hear him now, rhapsodising over the architectural beauties that surrounded them.

Out of the corner of her eye, she noticed Lucia subtly motion towards the shimmering mosaics on the front of a grand, white palazzo. The sun was getting lower, the light changing, bathing the waterfront properties in an ethereal, golden glow. Cate flicked back her white-blonde hair and turned her elegant neck, conscious again of the camera on her. She thought of her two boys, Oli and Max; they always made her smile. Her life was perfect, like nothing she could have dreamt of back at St Margaret's. She would not allow anyone or anything to wreck her happiness. Certainly not Natalie Spencer, the girl whose careless words had torn Cate's world apart.

9

The make-up woman had been and gone. Natalie paced the entrance hall, catching sight of her newly sculpted face in the extravagantly framed, Venetian mirrors. According to Lucia, Cate was aboard the taxi-boat; all had gone smoothly. Natalie could only hope the same was true of what was going on in the Red Room where a second camera crew, sound technician and assorted burly men carting cables, reflective panels and other paraphernalia about had made it clear her presence was undesirable. She had to trust them to know their jobs but it was hard to concentrate on memorising her opening lines when raised voices, thumping, banging and something that sounded worryingly like a box full of broken crockery being scraped across the palazzo's polished floor emanated from the other side of the wall.

She stepped out into the corridor. The door closed with a click behind her. She took the steps that led to the upper floor. Taking a closer look at the ancestors whose portraits she had seen this morning might help while away the time until the taxi-boat pulled alongside the landing stage. She strolled the corridor, admiring the oils: a previous Count Vicenzi, splendid in a red dressing gown, a spaniel at his feet; a long-deceased great, great aunt, hair coiled and powdered, reflected in a looking glass.

It was no use; Natalie was still feeling jumpy. It was all very well Floella telling her she could pull off her audacious attempt to step into Mandy's shoes but when it came to the countdown to Cate's arrival, Natalie felt as helpless as the weak-looking kitten in the corner of the portrait in front of her. Somehow, she had to channel her inner Mandy Miller and make this work. So much was at stake. And she didn't want to disappoint her mum and dad either. They were so excited about the prospect of watching her 'on the box' in their little retirement flat down in Devon.

She wished she knew what Cate looked like. Natalie's email to Bettany reminding her to send over the missing file of photos had received only a bounce back telling her Flo's PA was out at an industry event, and there had been no point bothering the girl again at this late stage, when she'd be seeing Cate in real life soon enough.

It didn't feel right snooping about in the Gold Room where the couple would be staying. Instead, Natalie opened the door to the eau-de-nil bedroom and strode towards the full-length windows. A taxi-boat was approaching the peach and gold poles outside the palazzo, the driver turning the prow towards the landing stage. They were several minutes early; at any moment, Cate would enter the building. It was too late for Natalie to descend the stairs without colliding with the film crew. She'd have to wait up here, chancing that she chose the right moment to make her entrance.

Of course! How could she have forgotten? She crouched down at the edge of the patterned runner and rolled it back.

She removed the diamond-shaped stone. Peering through the grill in the bedroom floor, she could see right down onto the Red Room's dazzling terrazzo floor. Now she would be able to check everything was in place before she descended.

Lucia's disembodied voice floated upwards, giving the camera crew last-minute instructions. Someone outside Natalie's field of vision was entering the room below.

'Welcome to Venezia!' The housekeeper, Nunzia, stepped forwards, holding out a flute of Prosecco on a silver tray, exactly as they had rehearsed.

An elegant arm encased in a toffee-coloured jacket reached forward, taking the glass in a manicured hand. Natalie could see the top of her contestant's white-blonde hair.

'Thank you, *grazie*. I am so happy to be here.'

A cold hand crept up Natalie's spine. That voice. It sounded just like her ex-school friend, Cathy. A posher version, but even so. But it couldn't be. Scruffy little Cathy couldn't have bagged a millionaire husband whose high-class, handmade furniture was rumoured to grace the private bedrooms at Buckingham Palace.

Natalie crouched lower; she was almost lying down now, getting as close to the metal grill as she could without imprinting a geometric design on her forehead. She narrowed her eyes. Her old classmate's features came into view. Cate Beresford and Cathy Laidlaw were one and the same. There was no mistaking it.

'What beautiful frescoes!' Cate's head tipped back; her brown eyes stared straight up at the ceiling.

Natalie froze but the hidden spy grill was well concealed in the dense foliage surrounding the fresco's dancing nymphs. Her heart was racing; beads of sweat prickled on her cleavage. She tried to swallow but her mouth was dry. How could she cope with meeting the woman whose betrayal had started the chain of events that had wrecked her life? But she had no choice. Lucia would be consulting the time, glancing at the double doors, wondering where Natalie had got to. If Mandy Miller could smile her way through the agonies of endometriosis, Natalie could play the professional. She would walk tall and greet Cathy – oops, Cate – without batting an eyelid.

Natalie stood up and smoothed down her dress, thankful she hadn't worn linen. She tiptoed across the room, opened the door to the upstairs corridor and crept down the stairs, shoes in hand. Slipping into the library adjoining the Red Room, she steadied one arm on the back of a low sofa to put on her heels.

She squared her shoulders, flung open the double doors and advanced on her old school friend, head held high, arms stretched out. Their eyes locked. Cate took a step backwards. Natalie stepped forward. She swept Cate into a warm, Mandy Miller-style hug.

10

'Cate! What a pleasure to meet you! I'm just so sorry that it can't be Mandy who's here to welcome you,' Natalie said.

Cate steadied herself. She knew instantly that Natalie recognised her but if Natalie could play this silly game, Cate could too.

'It's such a shame about Mandy but it's lovely to meet you. It's a privilege to take part in *Luxe Life Swap*. I can only hope that the count and countess are having as wonderful a time as I am. Venice must be the most beautiful city in the world and this... this palazzo is magnificent. My husband, Phil, will be so excited to join us tomorrow. I can hardly believe this is to be our home for the next two weeks.'

Natalie forced a smile. She had to hand it to her old classmate; Cate was sailing through their awkward encounter like a true professional. Only the most eagle-eyed viewer would notice the white knuckles gripping her glass of Prosecco.

The director nodded his approval before requesting several more sequences, repositioning Cate and Natalie around the room, moving a vase of flowers here, a plump cushion there.

Natalie's face ached from the effort of smiling. At last, it was time to take the viewers upstairs. The camera crew disappeared to set up in the Gold Room. Natalie sat down on one of the crimson sofas; Cate had already perched on the edge of a chaise longue cradling her drink, her legs crossed neatly at the ankles.

Natalie waited for Cate to say something, to show some sign that she knew who Nat was, but Lucia jumped in.

'I thought we should run through our revised schedule for tomorrow.' The young Italian opened her leather folder and turned to Cate. 'We were going to film you eating breakfast here, served by the housekeeper, but for that, we will wait for when your husband is here. Instead, I have arranged for you to enjoy a traditional Italian breakfast along the Fondamenta Misericordia. The canal side in Cannaregio is very picturesque; it will make nice television.'

'That sounds perfect.' Cate smiled. Her teeth were very white, she must have had them lightened professionally, but her eyes were tired. Natalie hoped it wouldn't take the guys too long to set up for the next shots.

'*Allora*...' Lucia consulted her folder. 'After breakfast, we will visit the boutiques; the viewers will love to see the fashions.'

'About 70 per cent of the viewers of the last series were female,' Natalie added, trying to keep her voice as normal as possible.

'I have made arrangements for you to visit places where they know the countess very well; they will be delighted to help.'

'You have done this already?' Natalie said. 'Thank you, *grazie*, Lucia.'

'Lucia has made everything run so smoothly; she put me at ease the moment I arrived,' Cate said.

'Oh, it is nothing. It is so nice that you are here in my beautiful city.'

'I can't imagine anywhere better.' Cate said. She fiddled with the stem of her near-empty glass of wine. Natalie shifted on her seat.

Lucia beamed, oblivious to the tension between the two women. 'I will go upstairs and check on the camera crew.'

The door swung shut behind her. Neither Natalie nor Cate spoke, both waiting to see if the other would crack first. There wasn't just an elephant in the room, Natalie thought; this was a whole Kenyan safari park.

Lucia re-entered the room. Natalie let out a breath.

'All is ready upstairs,' Lucia said. 'We will film you entering the bedroom, Cate. There is no need to rehearse; we want to catch your expression as you see it for the first time and then Natalie will enter. They call your room the Gold Room; you will soon see why. I do not think you will be disappointed.'

'I'm sure I won't,' Cate said brightly.

She and Natalie followed Lucia up the stairs. Natalie waited outside on the landing, glad that the Italian production company had not chosen the room with the secret grill in the floor, where she had been hiding out earlier. She was sure she wouldn't be able to carry on a conversation in there without flushing.

A gasp from the Gold Room told her Cate was suitably impressed. Natalie counted to twenty as planned. She entered the bedroom, reciting the lines she'd rehearsed as the camera panned the gold, damask walls, sumptuous, golden drapes and high bed piled with cushions. Afterwards, a brief conversation was filmed by the windows that overlooked the Grand Canal. The sun had now set; the sky glowed blue.

The director put up his hand. '*Basta* – it is enough.'

'*Brava*! Cate, you have been a true professional,' Lucia said. 'Let us leave the crew to tidy up. We will go back downstairs and make a final check over tomorrow's arrangements before I leave you both.'

They trooped back down the stairs into the Red Room.

Cate took her phone from her bag. 'Oh, I have a message! Good, it's Phil, he's booked on a flight for tomorrow, arriving late in the afternoon. I can forward you the details, Lucia.'

'*Fantastico*! He will be in time for *La Traviata* at the opera house. So, tomorrow, everything is good. I will meet you and Natalie here at eight thirty in the morning to film in Cannaregio.'

Natalie nodded. 'That's all clear.'

'Tonight, we had booked a meal for Cate and Philip away from the cameras, at a small, traditional Venetian trattoria.'

'I can eat something here; I'm sure the housekeeper wouldn't mind fixing me something in the kitchen. I'm not fussy.'

'That won't be necessary,' Lucia said. 'You and Natalie can take the reservation. It will be good to get to know each other better before your trip to the fashion boutiques tomorrow. It will create a nice chemistry for the viewers.'

'Of course, that makes sense,' Cate said smoothly. 'But I do believe Natalie and I may have met before. You went to St Margaret's, didn't you, Natalie?'

Natalie winced. 'How clever of you to remember.'

'How beautiful that you should meet again!' Lucia said. She checked her folder. 'The reservation has been made at *Osteria Le Pistole*, on Rio Terrà dei Assassini.'

'*Le Pistole* – does that mean what I think it does?' Cate asked.

'The pistols. It is a strange name perhaps but it is appropriate. The name of the road means the street of the assassins.'

'Street of the assassins,' Cate repeated. 'It sounds like a place for old enemies to meet.' She looked at Natalie and raised an eyebrow.

A bark of laughter escaped before Natalie had time to stop it. Cate's lips began to twitch; her shoulders shook.

'I miss something? What is funny?' Lucia said.

Cate let out a strange noise, somewhere between a giggle and a hiccup.

'It's rather too difficult to explain.' Natalie avoided Cate's eyes, pressing her lips together to try to keep a veneer of professionalism.

Lucia frowned as though she were puzzling over another English peculiarity like Marmite or instant coffee.

'Well, I will leave you both to enjoy your meal. *A domani! Buona notte.*' She picked up her folder.

'Allow me to show you out, Lucia.' The housekeeper, Nunzia, had materialised as if from nowhere.

The door clicked shut behind them.

'Are you ready, Cate? Or perhaps I should call you Cathy.'

Cate smirked. 'For the street of assassins? Sure, I'm ready!'

11

Cate placed her quilted handbag on the empty chair beside her. Natalie instantly regretted chucking her tote bag onto the floor. Cate's aura of sophistication had her feeling as though she were still an unworldly schoolgirl. She found it hard to tear her eyes away from her ex-classmate's silky, white-blonde hair, line-free forehead that attested to a top cosmetic surgeon on hand and quietly luxurious clothes, all creams and golden browns. Cate Beresford was a far cry from the lanky Cathy Laidlaw whose single-parent dad had battled to get her to school fed and dressed and didn't have the time or money to worry about fraying cuffs or unpolished shoes.

'I can't believe it's really you! This is just so weird. It must be nearly twenty-five years,' Cate said. She shrugged off her gold-buttoned blazer. It wasn't warm inside the trattoria; perhaps Natalie's old classmate wasn't feeling quite as cool as she looked.

'I know! After all this time!' Natalie opened one of a pair of leather-bound menus. The sooner they ordered, the sooner she'd be out of this awkward situation. 'Shall we take a look at the menu? What do you fancy?'

The tension in Cate's jaw almost imperceptibly softened; it seemed she too was glad to steer the conversation to a nice neutral subject. Natalie dropped her head to scan the short selection of *antipasti*, *primi* and *secondi*.

'*Risi e bisi* – rice and peas; that sort of risotto usually has pancetta in it, doesn't it?' Cate gave the impression she ate out all the time. She probably did.

'I'll have the *spaghetti al nero di seppia*,' Natalie said, glad of the English translation. It sounded delicious but she hoped the squid ink wouldn't stain her teeth; they already didn't bear comparison to Cate's top-class dentistry. 'Then I'll have the seabass; it says it's cooked in a rock-salt crust.' She snapped shut the menu, twisting her neck to look for a waiter. A cold glass of something from the extensive wine list might help calm her. And she needed a drink *right now*.

'Meat for me, after the *risi e bisi* but definitely not the liver. I don't care how much of a speciality it is here; that's one thing I won't touch. Do you remember that time Mrs Nickson forced me to eat some?'

'She stood over you, making you finish every morsel to teach you a lesson after she'd caught you flicking a lump of mash at Julie Paine.'

Cate laughed. 'I used to hate Julie. I don't know how she and I ever ended up as friends.'

By ganging up on me. By deserting me when I needed you most. Did Cate really not know what she'd done?

Natalie turned to the hovering waiter, his electronic tablet an incongruous sight amidst the traditional, white tablecloths, glowing wall sconces and old wood panelling.

She ordered, as did Cate, who pronounced her choices like a born Italian.

'Did you keep in touch with her?' Natalie asked.

'Who, Julie?' Cate smoothed her hair over one shoulder. 'Not once I'd left school. I lost touch with everyone when I went to Durham Uni. But I did see Julie again once, though not to speak to. It was last Christmas. The big car park at Fernbank Shopping Centre was full so I parked up at Tesco. Julie was there, just outside the double doors, washing down the trolleys. It gave me such a shock to see her there. Not that there's anything wrong with working at Tesco but I expected her to end up doing something exciting: running a scuba-diving school in the Maldives, selling carpets in a souk in Marrakech. She seemed so daring...'

Natalie took a large gulp from her thankfully acquired glass of white wine. 'We were in awe of her. When she got those tickets to see the Spice Girls, we were so envious. She got her hair dyed like Ginger Spice, do you remember?'

'It didn't suit her at all.' Cate laughed.

'You're right, but that didn't seem to matter back then.'

'Julie seemed so important, the queen bee of the school. But she was just a stupid little girl, we were all silly... immature, I guess.'

Natalie drank her wine, not sure of how best to respond. Were Cate's words a half-baked apology for how she'd behaved back then?

The arrival of the waiter bearing two steaming bowls saved her from the need to reply. She dug into her black spaghetti, trying to focus mindfully on each bite. They'd both moved on, she told herself firmly. She couldn't let the past derail *Luxe Life Swap*'s crucial Venice leg.

'When did you stop calling yourself Cathy?' Natalie savoured another mouthful of pasta.

Cate rested her fork on the side of her bowl. 'As soon as I got to Durham. It was such a change for me, living up north – I'd never been much beyond the M25. A different set of people, a new start...'

'And your husband calls you Cate?'

'The only person who ever calls me Cathy is my father.'

How formal she sounded.

'Did your father,' she deliberately used the word Cate had chosen, 'ever remarry? I thought he was old back then, everyone's parents seemed old, but he was really young, wasn't he?'

'He was eighteen when I was born; both of my parents were just teenagers. He never remarried and now he never will. He's in a nursing home: early onset Alzheimer's. I didn't even know it was something people could get in their fifties.' Cate's voice was as emotionless as if she were reciting the bus timetable but her fingers worried at the button on her silk cuff.

'I'm sorry,' Natalie replied automatically.

'Just one of those things. The Evergreens is very good. I see him twice a week, not that he always knows who I am. But we were never close. Not after that trip to Venice.' Cate pushed the last grains of rice around her bowl, took a sip of wine. 'Maybe you did me a favour that day, Natalie, by telling me what my father was really like. Because now I can deal with this. If Dad and I had been close, seeing him like this would rip me apart.'

'I—' Natalie began.

'No! Don't say anything. I needed to know what Dad had done. I was naïve before then, thinking he loved me and wanted the best for me.' Cate gave a bitter little laugh. 'I would have found out the truth eventually; you just helped me to find it out sooner.'

Cate signalled for the waiter, tapping lightly on her empty wine glass. 'Another one of these, please... Natalie, anything for you?'

'No, I'm fine, thanks,' Natalie lied. She prayed her fish would come soon, then she would be one quick coffee away from leaving the restaurant, getting away from Cate. This trip to Venice was going to be the longest fortnight of her life. Natalie had been wrong to say the things she'd said that night but if Cate hadn't ganged up with Julie, Natalie would never have slipped away by herself. And everything would have been different.

12

Natalie's fish appeared, surrounded by herbs on an oval platter. The flesh was cooked to perfection, but it was hard to savour the subtle hints of thyme and rosemary whilst the careless words she'd uttered so many years ago were going round and round in her head.

She speared another piece of fish, biding her time, wondering what she could possibly say to lighten the atmosphere. Suddenly, something caught in her throat: a piece of bone, perhaps. She coughed but nothing happened. She coughed again more violently but still it didn't dislodge. Her eyes began to water.

Cate looked up from her veal. 'Are you okay?'

Natalie shook her head, tried to cough into her hand so the whole restaurant wouldn't hear.

'You have a fish bone?'

It was an Italian voice, male and strangely familiar. She looked up into the concerned face of the white-haired mask maker.

'*Sì*, a bone,' she spluttered.

'Allow me.' The sharp thump of his hand on her back took her by surprise.

The bone shot onto the tip of her tongue. She discreetly removed it. 'Oh, thank you, *grazie*!'

'*Di niente*, it was nothing. I could not have you choking to death; it would be bad for business.' He had a twinkle in his eye.

'You own this restaurant?'

He spread his hands. 'Alas, no. But my younger son, he is the chef here and I could not afford to support him if this place closed down.' He gave a little chuckle. 'But I will have to complain to the kitchen; this dish should be filleted, should it not?'

'No, please… it was my fault for eating too fast.'

'Do you do everything fast? You departed my shop in a big hurry yesterday. Whoosh…' He flung out an arm. 'And you were gone!'

Natalie's face burned.

'You two have met before?' Cate said.

'I'm so sorry, how rude of me, I must introduce you. This is Cate; she and her husband, who arrives tomorrow, are appearing in the television show I am presenting… Cate, this is Pietro, a very talented mask maker, he has a shop and workshop in the Dorsoduro area of the city.'

'Pleased to meet you.' Cate held out a slender hand.

He took it in his large, hairy paw. 'Enchanted. Please excuse my appearance; I assure you my hands are clean, just stained by the dye I have been using. And now I must leave you to enjoy your meal. I did not wish to interrupt. Ah, there he is! Eraldo!' He raised a hand towards the doorway.

The watch restorer let the osteria's heavy door swing shut behind him. Natalie felt the tail end of the draught. Eraldo signalled to the waiter that he was in no need of assistance and approached Natalie and Cate's table, running a hand through his dark hair, his expression somewhere between surprise and pleasure.

'*Buonasera*. Natalie, what a coincidence! I did not think... but now... *allora*, we meet again.'

'You are lucky Eraldo is looking more presentable.' The mask maker grinned. 'Earlier today, he was not fit to be seen!'

'I have been working too many hours. I have barely left my workbench.'

'I found him upstairs asleep when I unlocked the shop this morning.' Pietro laughed.

Eraldo gave a rueful smile. 'I am a little obsessive, what can I say.'

'I went out and brought him *cornetti* for breakfast but he cannot live on those and coffee. I had to bribe him to leave the workshop and have a proper meal with the promise of this fine food. But first, I had to send him home to shower and change.'

'And I am now glad that I did... I mean... well, it is a smart restaurant; I do not like to look out of place.'

'Eraldo, this is Cate,' Pietro interrupted, making the introduction Natalie had failed to. 'And now, if you excuse me a moment, I will go into the kitchen to greet my son.'

'*Piacere*, pleased to meet you, Eraldo.' Cate smiled.

'And you.' Eraldo's eyes landed on Cate's eternity ring, the row of emeralds glittering in the candlelight. 'That is a beautiful piece of jewellery.'

'My husband had it made for me at a little workshop in Hatton Garden.'

'I studied gemmology, but I rarely use precious stones in my work.' Eraldo's eyes stayed on Cate's ring.

'What exactly do you do?' Cate asked.

'I am a watch restorer. I like to take unwanted or broken antique timepieces and give them a new life, to add my own twist, to create something unique.'

'How talented you must be.'

Cate was probably just making conversation but the way she beamed at Eraldo made Natalie determined to butt in.

'Eraldo is working on a secret watch,' she said. 'The face is hidden beneath a rotating pyramid.'

'Thanks to you bringing me the watch parts I have been waiting for.'

Natalie wished she'd accepted Cate's suggestion of a second glass of wine; the combination of Eraldo's dark-chocolate eyes and the passion in his voice was making her feel unusually flustered.

'You take commissions, I imagine,' Cate said. 'I've been wondering what to get for my husband's birthday. He is so hard to choose presents for, but he collects watches and a restored antique watch would be perfect. Phil has an appreciation for fine things and he's such a wonderful man, he deserves something special.'

'Phil's company creates incredible furniture; he has a royal warrant.' Natalie could relax now Cate was gushing about her husband. She didn't know why the thought of her ex-classmate flirting with the handsome Italian should bother her. It wasn't as if Natalie was interested. She wasn't here to look for a partner; she wasn't even here to make friends. She was in Venice for one reason only: to work. And that was a good thing. People always let you down in the end. Especially the ones who meant the most.

'Ah, Pietro is back from the kitchen at last, and I must join him,' Eraldo said. 'The delicious smells in this osteria are making me very hungry.'

'Of course. It was so nice to see you again,' Natalie said.

'A most pleasant surprise. And lovely to meet you, Cate. Do visit my workshop if you find the time. Come tomorrow if you like and we can talk about a commission.'

'Thank you, I will, if that's okay with you, Natalie?'

'Of course.'

'I look forward to meeting you again, Cate,' he added. 'And Natalie, of course.'

'Me too.' She just wished she could meet him again without crossing the mask maker's floor.

* * *

'I do hope you had a lovely evening.' The housekeeper ushered Cate into the palazzo.

'Yes, thank you, Nunzia.'

'May I fetch you a drink?'

'That is so very kind but I think I will have an early night,' Cate said.

She just wanted to be alone, to unpack her things, and to send a goodnight message to Phil. She wouldn't phone him; she knew he'd catch something different in her tone of voice and before she knew it, she'd be spilling the whole story of her soured friendship with Natalie Spencer. And she wouldn't be able to do that without letting slip the secret she'd kept from him.

She climbed the stairs, turned the handle on the bedroom door. The Gold Room seemed marginally more homely now that her perfume bottle and hairbrush stood on the marble-topped dressing table, her travel alarm clock and the new Marian Keyes novel on her bedside chest.

The housekeeper had unpacked all Cate's belongings, her

suitcase squirreled away, out of sight. She opened the doors on the triple wardrobe; the aroma of cedar wood mingled with the fragrance from the vast vase of fresh flowers set on the tallboy. Her clothes had been hung on wooden hangers, arranged by colour, accessories stashed in cubby holes.

She stepped out of her dress, hung it up carefully and shrugged on the sumptuously soft, oversized robe left out for her on the chaise longue by the window. The thick, white material brushed against her ankle bones; the cuffs nearly reached the tips of her fingers. Reflected in the dressing-table mirror, her head looked tiny, as though it had been photoshopped onto the body of a polar bear.

She wished she felt tired enough to climb into the great high bed, lean against the painted headboard, read for a few moments then drop off. But she was wide awake, with nothing to distract her mind from harking back to the night of the school trip that had upturned her world.

She sat down on the velvet-topped dressing-table stool and opened her travelling jewellery box, a clever fold-up design given to her by Lucy. A slim compartment lay beneath the orange, velvet lining. 'I use mine for hiding my lover's letters,' Lucy had said. Cate wasn't quite sure if Lucy was joking; even after years of mixing with Phil's upper-class friends, she didn't always get their sense of humour.

She slid out the photograph and the torn scrap of brown paper she kept hidden there. Cate didn't recognise herself in the picture but she could tell this was her christening day. Mum and Dad, barely more than children themselves, looked as though they'd raided the dressing-up box, her mother Lina in a polka-dot blouse with huge shoulder pads.

Cate smoothed out the piece of old envelope. She'd unearthed it from the bottom of Dad's sock drawer when she'd been packing up his belongings to take to The Evergreens. A moment's inattention and the paper would have gone straight in the bin. But her eye had recognised the handwriting, identical to the message inside her book of nursery rhymes.

Just a few words were written in the smudged, blue-black ink. A return address in Burano, Venice.

13

Natalie had to admit, Cate was a pro. Despite being asked to take her 'first' sip of cappuccino three times and to eat a breakfast that consisted of three bites of four different identical *cornetti*, her smile didn't falter. Her no-make-up make-up was flattering and sophisticated, her spun-silk hair glowed in the morning light, not a single buttery flake had fallen on her white shirt. Natalie's hastily eaten *cornetto* had left a sticky film on her fingers, a blob of the apricot *marmellata* marred her thankfully patterned dress and only a discreetly raised eyebrow from Lucia alerted her to the dusting of icing sugar clinging to her lipstick.

'It's a wrap.' The director was satisfied. The crew started packing up; curious onlookers began drifting away. Natalie let out a breath. They'd been filming a simple sequence but she knew how much could go wrong. Today, it had all gone smoothly; she could set Floella's mind at rest. For now. Flo had said she had every faith in Natalie, but her frequent messages and emails told a different story.

'Now we will go to the San Marco district where the

countess likes to shop,' Lucia said, tucking her dark hair behind her ears. 'We will go to the exclusive small boutiques. That will be enjoyable, *si*?'

'Perfect,' Natalie said.

Cate pulled down her sunglasses. 'You and me shopping together – shades of Lakeside.'

'Lakeside, what is this?' Lucia broke off from glancing around the café, making sure neither they nor the crew had left anything lying around.

'A shopping centre, a mall, I suppose you'd call it,' Natalie explained. 'I used to save up my birthday and Christmas money to go there. Those branches of Claire's Accessories and Dotty Ps seemed the most thrilling places in the world.'

'I got my ears pierced in that branch of Debenhams,' Cate added.

Natalie remembered it well. 'Are we okay to go, Lucia? Have we got everything?'

The young woman peered beneath their table. 'Yes, I have checked everywhere but I must thank the owner... ahh, Bianca, *grazie mille*, thank you so much. I hope we were not too much trouble.'

'Not at all.' The woman patted a chair back as if assuring Lucia that everything was quite in order. '*Arrivederci*, Lucia, give my love to your mamma.'

'*Grazie, arrivederci*.' Lucia tucked her leather folder under her arm. '*Allora*, Cate, Natalie. The crew will meet us at the boutiques. They have a barge to transport their equipment most of the way. We three can walk, if you like.'

'Sure. I need to keep up my steps,' Cate said.

They set off along the canal front.

'I do like this area; it's got a different, quieter neighbourhood feel,' Natalie said.

'That will change as soon as we get to the Strada Nova. We will meet the crowds going to and from the railway station. Tourists everywhere.' Lucia shrugged.

'The lady who owned the café where we had breakfast, was she a friend of yours?' Cate asked.

'Yes, I know Bianca well; she is a family friend.' Lucia's face brightened. 'Perhaps it was wrong of me to choose her café for the filming this morning, but it is a nice place.'

'Don't worry, it was perfect,' Natalie said. 'Now, which street do we need to take?'

'Follow me. Be careful of the suitcases.' Lucia cut a path through the wheelie-case-wielding groups across the wide Strada Nova into a shady *calle* which brought them out right by the vaporetto stop.

'We have private water taxis booked for most of your stay, but we will take the vaporetto today. We need the Number One. It is a fun way to travel the Grand Canal, zigzagging – I think you say – between a stop on one bank and then the other.'

'Of course, that does sound fun... You have the tickets already, Lucia?' Natalie asked.

'Yes, *certo*.' Lucia opened her enviably organised folder. 'You must validate them by tapping here and that will open the gate.'

'The vaporetto is coming, that's Number One, isn't it? And look! There's some outside seats free!' Cate sounded more like a child queuing up for a Florida theme park ride than a designer-clad grown-up with a goodness-knows-how-much-that-cost bag and a swishy blow-dry. Natalie couldn't help smiling.

The three of them squeezed their way through the inside cabin and out of the rear door to the open-air deck. Lucia managed to grab three spare seats all squashed up together, so close Natalie caught a waft of Cate's warm, floral fragrance.

The vaporetto pulled away from the mooring, moving slowly through the green water. A sleek, black gondola with cherry leather seats glided past carrying a Chinese couple cuddled up together, its gondolier's traditional straw hat and striped polo shirt a far cry from the baggy shorts and logoed T-shirts of the crew of the workaday barge piled high with reels of electrical cable heading in the opposite direction.

Neither Cate nor Natalie spoke, content to listen as Lucia pointed out the baroque façade of the Ca' Pesaro, the gothic Ca' d'Oro and the bustling fish market. Cate took photo after photo on her phone. Perhaps she was planning to send them to the absent Phil.

The canal swung to the right, bringing the elegant arch of the Rialto Bridge into view. A couple were leaning against the white, stone balustrade, kissing, wrapped in each other's arms. A little girl in a floppy, yellow sun hat, held high in her daddy's arms, waved as they passed underneath. Cate waved back enthusiastically, ponytail bobbing. She'd had the sense to tie back her hair as soon as they'd sat down on the exposed deck. Natalie pushed her fringe out of her eyes, hoping Lucia had a hair stylist on standby for when filming recommenced.

'Simona Rinaldi is one of the most exclusive boutiques in the city,' Lucia explained as their vaporetto continued its journey along the winding canal. 'The collection she has is incredible! The cuts are exquisite, the fabrics of the highest quality. And she is renowned for her expert eye. The way she puts an outfit together has her customers walking out feeling several centimetres taller.'

'Really? I never seem to know what suits me.' Cate glanced down at her narrow-legged trousers.

'I would not say that; your style is quite chic.' Lucia smiled.

The vaporetto slowed to a halt on a sharp bend, waiting as vessels criss-crossed this way and that. A few moments later, they were on the move again.

'There's the Palazzo Grassi, now used for art exhibitions.' Lucia pointed. 'And on the other side, Ca' Rezzonico, once the home of the poet Robert Browning.'

Natalie knew what was coming next. She didn't need Lucia's help to identify the wooden bridge curving over the canal in front of them, and neither – by her sharp intake of breath – did Cate.

The vaporetto passed under the Accademia Bridge.

'After the old masters in the Accademia gallery, we pass the *Collezione Guggenheim*, where they hold the American heiress's famous modern-art collection.' Lucia continued her commentary, oblivious to the tension Natalie felt so strongly. It was hard to believe the rest of the passengers were able to talk or fiddle with their phones as if today were like any other.

'We are here.' Lucia consulted her smartwatch as the vaporetto nosed towards the landing stage. 'Perfect. We will arrive exactly when Simona is expecting us.'

Cate pulled her ponytail out of its half-moon clip. Natalie stood up, ready to disembark. She had a job to do. And she was determined to do it professionally.

Cate walked beside her, up the *calle* that led to Simona Rinaldi's shop, shoulder bag clamped to her side, dark glasses obscuring half her face. It was impossible to know just what she was thinking.

14

VENICE, TWENTY-FIVE YEARS EARLIER

Miss Morrison led the way, striding across the Accademia Bridge in her sensible, lace-up shoes.

'Look over there, girls. That's the church of Santa Maria della Salute!'

'It's really beautiful,' Natalie piped up, aware that no one else was paying attention to her favourite teacher's enthusiastic pronouncements. Every head had swung round to gawp at the group of boys behind them.

Even at this distance, Natalie could tell these boys were a different breed from the slouching, mumbling pupils at the boys' school round the corner from St Margaret's. These fine specimens swaggered, chins up, across the wooden bridge as if the iconic views on either side were something they'd seen a hundred times before. At their head marched a golden-haired youth, as handsome as any statue they'd seen in the Doge's Palace.

'Keep moving, no loitering on the bridge.' Mrs Nickson glowered.

Several of the girls began giggling. Natalie's best friend

Cathy yanked at her lank fringe, desperately trying to obscure her pimple-strewn forehead. Julie Paine arranged her features into an expression of casual disdain. As the blond boy drew nearer, she accidentally on purpose let a packet of chewing gum fall from her fake Burberry handbag like the heroine of a period drama dropping a handkerchief at the feet of an eligible squire. Mrs Nickson gave her a look that would dry up the Grand Canal.

The boy picked up the gum and handed it back, letting his fingers brush against Julie's. The other boys sniggered, striking confident poses, all except two, who hung back awkwardly. One fiddled with the edge of his shirt; the other stared down at his super-cool trainers with bright-yellow laces.

'Come on, girls!' Miss Morrison said gamely, trying vainly to separate the two school groups, now merged on the bridge, blocking anyone else's chances of coming or going.

'Stop messing around, Upper Fifth!' a man's voice commanded. The boys sprang to attention. 'Ladies first,' he added, poking one of the boys in the back to allow Mrs Nickson and Miss Morrison a clear passage. Natalie's school party moved on towards the Accademia.

They'd only got as far as the first of the display rooms before the two school parties crossed paths again. Natalie tried to concentrate on what Miss Morrison was saying despite the nudging and giggling. Close up, the boys were far less interesting than the three-dimensional faces carved into the gallery's coiffured ceiling.

Julie Paine burst into snippets of songs from Madonna's new *Ray of Light* album whenever they passed another depiction of the Holy Mother. Cathy laughed loudly even though it had only been funny the first time. Natalie peered at the white labels by each painting as they moved from room to room:

Titian, Veronese, Carpaccio. She hung back as her classmates moved on, fixing her gaze on an oil painting of Mary in a blue robe and faded-red dress flanked by two serious-looking young women. Her classmates' voices drifted away.

She felt someone come up behind her. She turned, expecting to see Cathy, imagining her best friend, bored of Julie's japes, would have come back to find her, but it was one of the schoolboys. The one with the fancy trainers.

'Oh, you gave me a fright.'

He took two steps back.

'Sorry,' he mumbled to the floor. 'I just... just wanted to... you know, get away from the others, look at these paintings properly.' His voice was friendly; he didn't speak with a posh, Prince-William accent like most of his classmates did.

She moved aside to let him read the label.

Madonna with the Child between Saints Catherine and Mary Magdalene

'Yeah, Giovanni Bellini, I thought it was.'

'How did you guess?'

'I just like art: the old stuff anyway.' He shrugged.

'Same here.'

'What do you like about this one?'

'The fabric of their clothes. How do they make it look so real?'

'Dunno... the brush strokes?' He lapsed into silence.

The peace was broken by the squeak of shoes on the gallery's terrazzo floor.

'There you are!' Cathy's voice was cold. She grabbed Natalie's arm. 'Come on, everyone's wondering where you went.'

'Err, bye, see you.' Natalie let her friend drag her away.

'What were you doing with him?' Cathy hissed.

'Nothing, just looking at the pictures.'

'Yeah, right.'

They slipped back into her school group, now several rooms ahead.

'I found her,' Cathy said rather loudly.

Julie Paine sidled up. 'Did you really go off with one of those boys?'

'I didn't go off with anyone.'

'She was with that boy with the Nike trainers.'

'Bet you fancy him,' Julie said.

'Of course not! Don't be so stupid.' Natalie forced herself to keep her voice down. She didn't want Mrs Nickson standing nearby to hear anything, let alone the boy's friends, some of whom were looking over at her with interest. She tried to move away towards where Miss Morrison was pointing to a giant painting covering an entire end wall and holding forth about the genius of Veronese but Julie blocked her, arms akimbo.

'Yeah, you do.'

'No, I don't.' She longed to smack Julie's smirking face.

'Nat never fancies any boys,' Cathy said, like it was some sort of character flaw. It wasn't true, Natalie did like some boys, but so what if she did or didn't?

'I know why,' Julie said. 'I reckon you've got a crush on Miss Morrison.'

'No, I don't; she's nice, that's all. You tell her, Cathy.'

Cathy said nothing, just smirked.

'Let's go and talk to that really good-looking blond boy.' Julie grabbed Cathy's arm and steered her away.

Miss Morrison tapped Natalie on the shoulder. 'Next, we're going to look at Tintoretto's *The Removal of the Body of Saint Mark*; you'll like that one.'

Natalie tried her best to look interested as Miss Morrison waxed lyrical about the artist's use of colour but all she could think about was Julie's stupid false laugh coming from the far side of the room, followed by Cathy's giggles.

At last, the visit was over. The girls filed back across the Accademia Bridge, leaving the artworks and the pupils from the boys' school behind.

* * *

'This is Simona Rinaldi, our first boutique,' Lucia said.

Natalie snapped back to the present. She had to put the school trip out of her mind but she could still recall the hurt she'd felt back then. Julie and Cathy skipping off arm in arm had seemed like the biggest betrayal. But it was nothing compared to what happened next.

15

Another boutique, another fake smile. Natalie was sure she was doing a poor job of aping Mandy Miller's unfailingly sunny disposition. Floella had assured her she should just be herself and let her natural personality shine through, which would be perfect if the viewers wanted to see an increasingly grumpy presenter humiliating herself in a variety of just-able-to-close-the-zip outfits whilst Cate preened for the camera in a super-sleek, ice-blue all-in-one.

'The style of Alessandro Valentino's designs is quite different from those you tried in Simona Rinaldi's boutique earlier but here again we see the quality, luxe fabrics and attention to detail for which the Italian fashion industry is known,' Natalie said, trying not to sound breathy as she held her stomach in.

'I've never found such a flattering jumpsuit before.' Cate twirled like a gameshow hostess.

'So, you will take this. A good choice. And perhaps this.' The spaghetti-slim shop girl draped a floor-length cape fashioned from layers of acid-yellow feathers around Cate's shoulders. Natalie coughed back a laugh she hoped could be attributed to the pungent smoke rising from the oil burner on the heavily veined, marble mantelpiece. 'And for you, Natalie,' the salesgirl purred, 'this satin bomber embroidered with eagles.'

'How unusual.' Natalie shrugged on the cropped jacket. Three-dimensional metallic thread and sequined wings protruded above each of her breasts. Lucia's expression was unreadable. Natalie had to hope this would be edited out but if it wasn't cut, at least it would give her mum and dad a good laugh – if Mum hadn't fainted at the sight of the sky-high price tags.

'I'll just take the jumpsuit, please. Anything for you, Natalie?' Cate's eyes were as innocent as the Madonnas' in the Accademia.

'Not for me, unfortunately.' Natalie smiled at the camera. 'I'm here to report on the luxury lifestyle of Venice's elite, not to live it... Are you sure there's nothing else for you here... This, perhaps? Furs are very much part of the Italian look.' She picked up a strange oval bag that seemed to have been stitched together from the skins of a dozen small rodents.

'The embroidered evening purse we found earlier will be quite sufficient,' Cate replied smoothly.

The camera crew began packing up. Cate helped Lucia to gather up the half-dozen ribbon-tied bags from Simona Rinaldi they'd left discreetly out of camera shot.

The assistant handed Cate a single dayglo orange bag containing the gold tissue-paper-wrapped jumpsuit and wished them a formal goodbye.

The glass door swung shut behind them. Natalie breathed in a great lungful of unperfumed fresh air. 'What a place!'

Lucia shook her head. 'I cannot imagine what the countess buys in there. But the jumpsuit you found, Cate, it is very beautiful.'

Cate laughed. 'It was the only wearable thing in the shop. Do you think they ordered it by mistake? I suppose we'll need to go back to the palazzo now; we won't be able to carry all these bags around with us.'

'Oh, no,' Lucia interrupted. 'I will take these bags back; the housekeeper will have everything hung up for you. You are free to carry on shopping. I will pop my folder in with this dark jacket, if you don't mind, Cate; it will do it no harm.' Lucia undid the ribbon on one of the logoed carrier bags.

'More shopping, Cate?' Natalie couldn't face another boutique but she thought she'd better offer.

'Only one. Salvatore Ferragamo – I'd like to choose Phil a new tie.'

'*Certo*! I will show you both where that is.' Lucia set off briskly, leading them through the narrow *calle* until they came to a wide street of designer shops. 'There on the end, right by the small canal.'

'Thank you, Lucia. I will see you later.' Cate bent to kiss Lucia's cheeks.

'Have a lovely day. We will not need you until tonight, Cate, when we film you and Philip arriving at *La Fenice* for the opera. Your husband's flight was due to leave on time, I believe.'

'Thank goodness,' Natalie added.

Lucia gathered up all Cate's purchases and set off in the direction of the vaporetto stop.

The search for Phil's new tie took no more than ten minutes. Cate and Natalie stepped out of the air-conditioned shop. The day was getting warmer. Shorn of Lucia's presence, Natalie felt stripped naked.

'Well, what now?' Cate said.

Natalie racked her brain for an idea. But how could she choose what to do today when all she could think about was the past?

16

VENICE, TWENTY-FIVE YEARS EARLIER

Eight beds were crammed into the dormitory. Julie Paine stood slap bang in front of the only mirror in the room, wielding a pink hairdryer she'd pinched from Shy Kelly. Natalie sat on her narrow, metal-framed bed fiddling with the broken elastic on the mask she'd so carefully created. She tied the two ends back together; it made the mask fit a bit too tightly and some of the glitter had dropped off. But she didn't care. Everyone was looking forward to tonight, apart from her. Over breakfast, she'd tried to ask Cathy what she'd done wrong at the Accademia gallery but her old friend just shrugged and went back to sucking up to Julie and her new mates.

'I can't believe we're going to a party,' Tall Polly squealed for the umpteenth time.

'A masked ball isn't a party, it's a cultural event, and you will behave appropriately,' Natalie said, mimicking Mrs Nickson's haughty tones. She hoped Cathy would laugh the way she always did when Natalie did one of her impressions, but Cathy just peered into her hand mirror, dabbing at her spots with a grubby-looking sponge caked in Maybelline concealer.

'Do you think those boys from the posh school will be going tonight? Do you think they'll recognise us when we're wearing our carnival masks?' Shy Kelly fretted.

Julie smirked. '*You* don't need to worry; they'll recognise your mousey hair and big conk anywhere. And they'll all recognise me.' She tossed the hairdryer onto Kelly's bed, flicking back her hair. '*Tell me what you want, what you really, really want,*' she sang into the mirror, gyrating her hips, hips that sported Cathy's prized chain belt. The one she'd never lend anybody, not even Natalie.

Julie sprayed on an ozone-obliterating blast of Impulse, blew a kiss at the mirror and span around to face her audience. 'I reckon those boys *will* be going and that blond, tall, good-looking one is mine.' Julie's eyes narrowed. 'So, don't any of you lot think for a minute you're going to get near him. At least I won't have to worry about you, will I, Natalie? You'll be snogging that boy you were flirting with yesterday.'

'I don't know what you're talking about.' Natalie wouldn't even speak to any boys tonight, not even the harmless, nerdy one with the trendy trainers. She already felt enough of an outcast without deliberately courting evil looks from Julie and her mates.

* * *

'Goodness, girls, isn't this splendid, and so many schoolchildren; there must be nearly two hundred of you here!' Miss Morrison beamed, flinging her arms wide but still cutting a tiny figure in the grandeur of the ballroom. 'It's such a privilege for our school to be invited here. Just look at the frescoes on the ceiling.'

Natalie found herself standing up a little straighter; it

wasn't a room that called for slouching. Only Tall Polly hunched her shoulders in a vain attempt to appear shorter than the group of boys – the boys from the art gallery were here! – who were strolling across the terrazzo floor as though they owned the place.

'Look what they're wearing,' Shy Kelly whispered. No homemade masks paired with ordinary clothes for those top-notch students and their teachers; they must have splashed out in one of the city's hire shops for they were decked out from top to toe in authentic Venetian costumes. Some had chosen colourful carnival masks, others traditional white *bauta* face masks paired with long, black cloaks, strutting around like sinister penguins. A handful even wore the creepy, long-beaked mask, hat and gown of the Plague doctor.

A live orchestra started to play; the musicians dressed in pastel-coloured frock coats and breeches, their hair covered with curled, white wigs. Waiters carrying fancy silver-plated trays circulated the room, serving *cicchetti* to the assembled throng. Natalie tried an oval slice of toast topped with creamy-white *baccalà mantecato* which Miss Morrison explained was cod whipped into a fluffy mousse. Cathy and Julie giggled in the corner.

The musicians stopped for a break, replaced by chamber music piped through the loudspeakers. Miss Morrison was talking to one of the boys' teachers; Mrs Nickson was studying a painting of a hawk. Natalie moved quickly. She pushed open the great wooden door that led to the hall. A few strides across the chequerboard floor and she was outside.

The *campo* was quiet; the church of Santa Maria Formosa was closed up for the night, the fruit and vegetable seller gone. No tour groups gathered in the corner by the entrance to the Querini Stampalia museum where just a few days ago, Mrs

Nickson had gone purple with rage when Julie plinked a key on an antique piano.

Natalie walked past the church, her mask dangling from her wrist. The street ahead was quiet, lamps glowing in the window of a trattoria. Beyond that, a row of shops selling stationery, chandeliers and artworks. She kept walking, not caring where she was going. Across a small bridge, the road widened. The wall of a church seemed to check further progress but she found a passageway to her left.

The route became busier, with diners clustered at outside tables; Natalie strode with greater confidence. A lantern hung from an archway ahead of her. Beyond a crush of people, she glimpsed a lion on top of a soaring pillar. She had reached St Mark's Square. She pushed her way into the piazza through a gaggle of tourists.

A clanging sound startled her. She swung around, stepping back to gaze up at the tower behind her. Above the royal-blue zodiac, the Virgin Mary nestling in a nook and the winged lion of St Mark, the two bronze Moors were striking the hour.

She turned away from the clock tower, walking ever so slowly around the basilica, craning her neck to look up at the colourful mosaics of turbaned men, the horses over the main door that looked as though they might gallop off at any moment. Her class had come here on their first day in Venice but the basilica was such a riot of arches and columns, statues and carvings, that she'd barely had a chance to take in a fraction of its riches before they'd all been ushered inside the famous church to marvel at its golden mosaics and marble floor.

Eventually, she got tired of looking. She strolled along the covered arcade of the Doge's Palace towards the twin pillars at the edge of the piazza. She passed between them. How tall they were! How dramatic everything was compared to back home! There was now nothing ahead of her but the end of the Grand Canal, widening here into a bigger body of dark water, the passing craft providing dots of light. Across the way, she could make out a spur of land, a white church glowing almost ghost-like. She followed the sound of music back across the piazza. Outside the Caffè Florian, an orchestra was playing. The tiny audience of café patrons wore pashminas and jumpers around their shoulders against the slight chill of the evening. She shivered in her thin dress.

With one last glance back at the basilica's façade, she crossed out of the piazza into a street she didn't recognise. The beautiful, sapphire sky had faded away, replaced by dark, gathering gloom, but she'd be okay if she kept to the main streets, avoiding the deserted, narrow passageways and the dark *sottopassaggi* that ran under the buildings. She kept on walking; the streets became quieter. She was conscious of footsteps behind her speeding up and slowing down to match hers but when she glanced over her shoulder, no one was there. Every so often, she swore she could hear a muffled cough, spied the movement of a black cape swishing out of the corner of her eye, but it was just her imagination.

A theatrical supplier, its windows filled with feather headdresses, hats, masks and curious puppets, intrigued her enough to stop and look. Her own reflection stared back from between the puppets' wooden faces. A dark, cloaked figure loomed over her shoulder: a man, dressed all in black, hat pulled low, his face hidden behind the unmistakeable mask of the Plague doctor. She tried to scream but all that came out was a strange gulp.

'It's Natalie, isn't it? Don't be scared.' The voice was quiet, as though speaking from behind a velvet curtain.

She forced herself to turn around, searching for clues in the parts of his face that weren't covered by his hat and mask. His skin was plump and pink, belonging to a young man or a teenage boy. It was then that she noticed his trainers, the dayglo yellow laces incongruously paired with the seventeenth-century costume. It was him! The boy from the gallery who had shared her love of Giovanni Bellini's painting. The fear slowly began to subside.

'Oh, it's you! Why is your voice so strange? You sound different.'

'I sound strange because I am the Plague doctor.' He made his voice even more sinister.

'Oh, that's creepy.' She gave a nervous giggle. 'Why are you here? Why aren't you at the party?'

'I saw you go.'

'You were following me all this time?' Her whole body tensed.

'I was worried about you. You're safe now. I'll walk you back to the party. It's this way.' He gestured to a dingy *sottopassaggio* leading off to one side.

'Are you sure?'

'You do trust me, don't you?' His gloved hand closed over hers. He gave it a comforting squeeze.

'Of course I do.' She wasn't sure if she did but at the Accademia, he'd seemed so nice, so ordinary amongst his swaggering classmates. And she was lost.

The passageway was narrow, gloomy. On one side, rusted grills were set into boarded-up windows. If she stretched out her arms, she could touch both of its rough stone walls.

'Are you sure this is the way?'

He kept hold of her hand and started to walk faster. She hurried along beside him. The passageway darkened.

'I... don't like this. I want to go back.'

The boy gripped her hand tighter. Fear walked down her spine like a cold hand.

'Let go!' She tried to pull away from him.

He cupped his other hand under her chin, twisting her head, shoving her up against the rough wall.

'Stop! No!'

He clamped his hand over her mouth; she tried to bite his palm, her attempts feeble. He pressed his body up against her, the hard beak of the papier mâché mask pushed against the side of her cheek, minty-chewing-gum breath in her face. His hand lifted the hem of her dress, probing fingers working their way up her thigh. She writhed and struggled but he was too strong.

A dog barked once. Barked twice, louder. Footsteps in the alleyway.

Out of one eye, she could see a big man with a shaved head, a pointy-nosed white bulldog trotting by his side, approaching from the other end of the narrow passage.

Her attacker must have spotted him too. He loosened his grip slightly, stroking Natalie's hair with one hand, perhaps to give the man the impression they were two young lovers, overcome by passion on a magical, Venetian night.

The man drew level, his inquisitive dog pausing to sniff at the boy's trainers. The boy froze, his hands dropped to his side. She had seconds to act. She shoved him in the chest as hard as she could. Surprised, he stumbled backwards. The dog yelped in pain.

The man swore loudly, grabbing hold of the boy and shouting right in his face. Natalie ducked around them, out the way the man had come in. A small bridge at the end of the passageway led over a narrow canal. She was up and over it in a trice, running as fast as her feet would carry her. Running and running, her breath loud and fast, heart hammering at her chest. A dead end forced her down another *sottopassaggio*. Emerging on the other side, all was quiet. Neither the boy nor the man nor the dog had followed her.

She took out her phone; the battery was dead but her fingers caught the edge of something tucked into its leatherette case. An unused vaporetto ticket. A sign high on the wall pointed the way to the Rialto Bridge; she clasped her hands together in thanks. A few stops along the canal and she'd be back at the hostel. The masked ball would be over, the girls getting ready for bed. She no longer cared what Cathy had said or done; she just wanted to tell her what had happened. They'd hug and make up. They'd be best friends again.

* * *

Natalie pressed the buzzer. The night porter barely glanced up from his copy of *La Gazzetta dello Sport*. Not bothering to wait for the lift, she climbed the three flights of stairs. The corridor was dark but strips of light glowed beneath the doors of the girls' two dormitories. She hesitated outside the small room that her teachers shared. Had they noticed she was missing? Were they waiting up for her to come back? She pressed her ear to the door. No sound, no light shining through the lock. She let out a breath. Miss Morrison sleeping soundly was some comfort. Natalie couldn't bear to think of her favourite teacher's shocked face and her guilt – for she knew Miss Morrison would blame herself.

Quietly, she pressed her room key to the dormitory's door; it opened with a click. All eyes turned towards her.

'Where the heck have you been?' Julie Paine looked Natalie up and down as if inspecting her for clues.

'Sit down.' Shy Kelly patted the end of her bed and budged over a bit. 'Don't worry, you're not in trouble; Tall Polly told Mrs Nickson you'd got your time of the month and gone off to bed with a bad stomach. What's happened? You look all upset.'

Natalie couldn't hold it together any longer. She burst into noisy, gulping tears. Kelly handed her a tissue. She took it gratefully, even though it was none too clean and covered in lip-gloss prints.

'What happened?' Julie demanded.

Natalie sniffed. She didn't want to tell the whole room but if she confided in one person, everyone would know soon enough anyway.

'I... I went for a walk... I was, umm, hot so I went outside. I walked to St Mark's Square then I sort of got lost and this boy, one of those boys from the posh school, he was following me. He spoke to me and he grabbed my hand...'

'Yeah, right!' Julie sneered.

'Yeah, those boys aren't interested in us,' Tall Polly said. 'That blond one wasn't even interested in Julie.'

'Shut up.' Julie threw Polly such a death stare, Natalie was surprised she didn't spontaneously combust.

'It wasn't like that; it wasn't cos he liked me. He wouldn't let go; he took me down an alleyway. He pushed me up against the wall. He tried... he tried...' Natalie curled up in a ball, sobbing.

Julie yawned. 'You're such a big, fat liar, Nat. You went for a boring old walk by yourself and now you're trying to make it sound like some big drama.'

Natalie shot upright. 'I'm not lying. Why would I?'

'You're always looking for attention. Look at the way you

hang around Miss Morrison, trying to come out with clever comments.'

'I just like her. So what?' Natalie wiped her eyes. 'I'm not lying. Everyone else believes me. Cathy believes me, don't you?'

'You always have to be the centre of attention,' Cathy mumbled, fiddling with her lank fringe. 'You're just making it up. Who goes for a walk when there's a party on? It's just boring, isn't it?' She glanced at Julie for approval.

'Maybe I didn't just go for a walk. Maybe I went to visit your mum.' The words were out of Natalie's mouth before she could stop them.

Cathy started. 'What do you mean?'

'Your mum lives in Venice, didn't you know?'

'No, she doesn't.' Cathy's chin was raised but there was a tremble in her voice.

'No one knows where Cathy's mum lives, not even Cathy's dad,' Julie chipped in but she didn't sound too sure.

'I do; I've known for months,' Natalie pressed on. 'I overheard my dad talking to your dad. Your mum was born in Venice and that's where she went to live after she left you.'

'Dad doesn't know what happened to her after they split up. Mum went off travelling; they never kept in touch. No one knows where she is, no one.' Cathy sniffed, tears gathering in her eyes.

'Your dad's been lying to you. He didn't want you to know where she was. He didn't want you to find out. He doesn't want you to meet your mum cos he wants you all to himself.'

Cathy's face crumpled. She let out a big sob. Tall Polly put her arm round her and Shy Kelly stroked her hair.

Natalie thought she'd feel triumphant but she just felt slightly sick.

'Cathy, I didn't mean...'

But there was no taking the words back. She'd lost Cathy's friendship for good.

17

'Well, where to now?' Cate repeated the question. She tightened the ribbon on the bag containing Phil's new tie.

'We could get something to eat, I suppose,' Natalie said.

'I'm not hungry, are you?'

'Not really.'

'Then why suggest lunch?' Cate realised she was sounding a little impatient, but Natalie was supposed to be in charge, wasn't she? Cate was a guest on *Luxe Life Swap* – albeit an unexpected one.

'I thought you might want something.' Natalie shrugged.

'I do. A drink. According to my app, we're right near Harry's Bar.'

'We'll be filming there another day but I guess there's nothing to stop us going there now.'

'Come on then. This way.' Cate strode on. Nat was dithering; someone had to take charge. And Cate needed one of Harry's famous bellinis. Right now.

They didn't have to walk far; her app hadn't lied. She

pushed open the frosted-glass door, pushing her sunglasses up into her hair.

'Looks like a couple of free seats over there,' Natalie said.

Cate headed for the end of a row of round tables. Plain walls, simple, curved, wooden chairs with tan leather seats: there was nothing intimidating about the famous bar where Charlie Chaplin, Ernest Hemingway and Truman Capote had all hung out. But she would never have had the nerve to poke her nose round the door the last time she was here. These days, she comfortably mingled in the Royal Enclosure at Ascot and ate at the smartest of restaurants. But sometimes, she still glanced down, half-expecting to see a hole in her tights, a pair of scuffed, down-at-heel shoes.

'And for you, *signora*?'

The waiter and Natalie were looking at her expectantly.

'The same for me, please,' Cate said quickly. She assumed Natalie had ordered one of the bar's iconic white peach bellinis. But who knew? Perhaps Nat had developed a taste for neat whisky. She had no idea what her old friend liked or didn't like any more.

The man removed the list of drinks. No glass to fiddle with, no menu to flick through, no sunglasses to hide behind. Cate felt uncomfortably warm, the atmosphere heavy with words unsaid. Natalie regarded her with a half-smile. Cate had to break this weird standoff.

'Nat, can you believe we're really having cocktails together in Harry's Bar?'

Natalie stiffened. Maybe no one called her Nat any more.

Cate waited for the waiter to set down their drinks. Bellinis, thank goodness.

'You bought some beautiful clothes this morning,' Natalie said.

'Simona Rinaldi's was out of this world. Those Fortuny pleats! The sheen on that silk dress! I hope Harrods lives up to the countess's expectations.'

'There's no need to worry about the Italian couple; Floella tells me they're thrilled with everything. And Harrods stocks every style of outfit the countess could possibly want... but perhaps not a yellow, feathered cape.'

'That cape! I was desperately trying to keep a straight face. I didn't dare catch sight of myself in the mirror; what on earth did I look like?'

'Big Bird from *Sesame Street*?'

Cate smacked her hand to her mouth. 'That's it! I knew it was some sort of cartoon character. And that dreadful furry bag – you were wicked to suggest I buy that. Didn't it look like Julie Paine's nan's hat? The one she used to wear on Sundays, do you remember?'

'You're right! How could I forget? Julie used to boast it was made from real squirrels.'

'Roadkill, more like.'

'Stop it!'

'Or rats?' Cate's shoulders began to shake.

Natalie's laugh sounded more like a huge snort. Two women at the next table turned around. Cate tried to stop laughing, but looking at Natalie just made it worse. She stared intently at a spot on the wall until their giggles gradually subsided.

'Maybe we should go back to that shop again,' Cate said.

'What for? The rat bag or the cape?'

'Not those. Maybe I should get that bomber jacket with the bird wings you tried on, oh, I don't know.'

'You *are* joking!'

Cate ran a hand down her caramel, linen, cigarette pants.

'Sometimes, I think I should be more adventurous. Like you: look at the colours on your dress.'

Natalie gave her a strange look, almost as if she thought Cate was taking the mick. But she genuinely loved the multitude of little turquoise and purple diamonds that formed the pattern on Nat's midi dress. 'You were always good at choosing things when we went shopping together. Do you remember when you found me that great sweatshirt in Lakeside?'

'The day you got your ears pierced – you got the tiniest studs cos you knew your dad would go mad.'

Cate fiddled with the end of her cocktail stirrer. 'We had such fun, didn't we? All these years, I've never had a friend like you. Maybe it's fate we've met like this. I'd love it if we were friends again, wouldn't you?'

Natalie didn't respond. Surely she couldn't still be mad at Cate for her clumsy attempt to ingratiate herself with school-queen Julie and her daft pals? Not after all these years. Maybe Natalie still felt guilty about spilling the truth about Cate's mum.

'I *have* forgiven you,' Cate assured her.

'For what?' Natalie snapped. Her face had gone a strange colour.

'For telling me about Dad,' Cate ploughed on. 'I told you last night, I would have found out soon enough. And I understand why you said what you said. You just lashed out because you were embarrassed when nobody believed that silly story.'

'What story?' Natalie's voice was icy.

'That daft stuff about some boy in a Plague-doctor outfit following you down an alley and molesting you!' Cate laughed. 'I don't know how you came up with it. I knew you had a wild imagination but really! It was so obviously a cry for attention. Gosh, we really were stupid young girls back then.'

Natalie drained her drink in silence.

Cate started to get a bad feeling. A very bad feeling right deep down in her gut.

'Nat?'

'I didn't make up a story.' Natalie's white knuckles gripped her empty glass. 'Everything I said in the dormitory that night was true.'

Cate gasped. 'Nat... oh my God, Natalie. How awful! Why didn't I realise? I never meant... I mean... Oh, Natalie, I am so, so sorry.'

Natalie turned away. She signalled for the bill.

18

'Let's go,' Natalie said. The feeling of joy she'd felt drinking cocktails in Harry's Bar had vanished with the last drop of her bellini. She paid quickly and picked up her bag. Cate followed her out onto the street in silence.

Natalie consulted the map on her phone, not bothering to ask Cate where she wanted to go.

Cate stood in a patch of shade, knees pressed together, hands thrust into her pockets, ruining the line of her beautifully cut trousers. Natalie wanted to grab hold of her shoulders and yank them upwards the way she'd yanked up Tall Polly's as they stood queuing for St Mark's. Polly had blushed beetroot, tears in her eyes. Natalie had been thoughtless, insensitive back then. They all had. But what Cate had done was worse than thoughtless and Natalie wasn't going to forgive her. But she couldn't let it show. She couldn't let the past derail the filming, couldn't let Floella – or herself – down.

'Let's go to the Guggenheim Collection; we could see the Picassos and the Dalis,' she suggested.

'No, I can't face any crowds. Let's just walk, get away from these people.' Cate flicked a dismissive hand at a meandering tour group.

'Sure, we could walk straight along the canal side out towards the old shipyard at the Arsenale.' Natalie didn't care where she went as long as Cate perked up before her trip to the opera that night. Some television shows delighted in building people up to knock them down but *Luxe Life Swap* pedalled an unashamedly aspirational dream. Their viewers didn't want misery; they wanted to escape to a fantasy world of super-privileged people with happy faces.

Natalie forced herself to try and lighten the atmosphere, commenting on this and that. Cate trudged along beside her with all the enthusiasm of an old lag taking a turn around the exercise yard at HMP Wandsworth.

As they walked eastward, the crowds gradually thinned. The activity on the far reaches of the Grand Canal slowed down. The sky was a cloudless blue. Cate slowly thawed. It was easier to talk walking side by side, as long as Natalie kept to neutral topics like Cate's beloved dog, Ted. By the time they reached the far end of the *riva*, the frown that had been threatening to burst through Cate's botoxed forehead had disappeared; the bloom had returned to her cheeks.

They turned up the canal side path leading to the Arsenale. The old shipyard area was quiet, the vast industrial site now out of bounds. The two great towers either side of the sealed entrance looked as though they'd been plucked from a medieval castle. Natalie blinked as if by looking again, she might conjure up the thousands of men who once toiled in the great shipyard and the sounds of hammering, shouts and cursing as huge girders were manoeuvred into place. Had those workers been conscious of their place in history, aware that Venice's wealth and power was dependent upon its ability to trade with the world? She'd never know; they'd vanished into the past. Now the loudest sound was the clink of crockery and the voices of tourists coming from the café by the great stone lions.

'They had so many workers, they say they could turn out three whole ships in a day,' Cate remarked.

'You certainly read up before you came.'

'Phil told me; he's fascinated by any sort of craftmanship.'

'Of course, that would make sense with his line of work. Handmade furniture's quite a niche area to get into these days.'

'He got lucky; the uncle of one of his old school friends gave him a paid internship. He worked his way up from there and once Seb retired, Phil took over the business. He's always been interested in art and design; he'll be in his element once he gets here.'

'It will be nice to meet him.' It would be easier to keep up a professional façade when it wasn't just the two of them.

'I'm so relieved he's on his way,' Cate said.

'So am I, but at least one of you arrived on time. Although we like to see the couples together on screen, we can always use a few extra shots of the wives. Our viewers love to see all the different outfits the women wear; the men can look a bit samey.'

'Good thing we went shopping; my wardrobe's not very colourful.' Cate chewed at her bottom lip.

'You're fine, honestly, just as you are.' Natalie reassured her. Just as Cate had reassured Natalie in the changing rooms in Topshop twenty-five years ago. She pushed away the memory. 'Have you seen enough? Shall we go? We can take a waterbus back.' She started to walk off down the side of the café.

'Natalie! You're going the wrong way!'

'Of course, how stupid!' Even with a headful of memories –

and a blindfold – she should have been able to retrace her steps to the Grand Canal.

'Looks like I'll have to navigate our way to your watch restorer's workshop,' Cate joked. 'Don't forget, I've got a commission to discuss.'

'*My* watch restorer? I've only met him twice!'

'Sometimes, just once is enough.' Cate's face broke into a smile for the first time in hours. 'You like him, don't deny it. I can still tell what you're thinking; you haven't changed that much, you know!'

'I'm not sure we'll have time to go there; you'll want to be waiting at the palazzo when Phil arrives.'

Cate pulled out her phone. 'It's fine, we've got hours; Phil's only just about to go through security... I hope nothing goes wrong.'

'Why should it?'

'No reason, I suppose.' Cate's face told a different story.

Natalie bit back the question on the tip of her tongue. She couldn't help wondering whether it was really a work crisis that had prevented Phil from flying out with his wife.

19

The San Marco vaporetto stop was swarming with tourists heading towards the great basilica. Natalie already missed the wide-open space of the Arsenale, the feeling of insignificance as they'd looked up at the soaring towers.

'I'm really not sure we'll have time to go to Eraldo's workshop,' she said.

Cate peered at the app on her phone. 'We've only got to hop across to the San Salute stop and take a short walk. Come on! I really want to talk to him about creating something for Phil. Look, there's a Number One coming now.'

'Okay.' Natalie sighed. She tapped her pass on the reader and waited whilst the passengers emptied out. A young woman ushered them on.

Cate leant against the side of the vessel. 'Let's stand here; it's fun to look out.'

'Sure.' Natalie squeezed past a huge, yellow suitcase into a neat gap. Across the water loomed the great dome of Santa Maria della Salute, familiar from every website she'd skimmed on the journey over.

'Beautiful.' Cate's elbow brushed Natalie's as she raised her phone to take another photo.

Natalie tried to focus on the waterfront, pushing down the nerves she felt at returning to the mask maker's shop she'd so hurriedly exited just days before. It would be so much easier to take herself off for a tour of Santa Maria della Salute and leave Cate to make her way to the workshop. She took a deep breath. 'We'll be getting off in a minute. Have you worked out the route? I took the traghetto over last time.'

'Yes, it's easy. Don't look so nervous, Nat!'

'I'm not nervous,' Natalie lied.

'When you like someone, it's only natural.'

'I'm not interested in Eraldo. He's just a nice guy; he's a friend of Floella, that's all.'

Cate raised her eyebrows.

The vaporetto inched towards its floating dock. A young woman began untying the rope. They squeezed their way off. Cate marched confidently ahead, across a square, over a bridge and down a *calle* lined with craft shops and small galleries and over another bridge, Natalie trailing behind her. The scent of rose and patchouli wafting from the perfumery confirmed Cate had led her to the right place.

'What a gorgeous shop!' Cate exclaimed, coming to a halt. 'Look at the quaint glass bottles; they've even got a gentleman's range! Now, where exactly is this watch place? Oh, there it is: just on the other side of that cute little bridge above that mask shop. Do you remember that mask making? What a mess we made! Glitter everywhere and no one was brave enough to tell Mrs Nickson she had a great lump of glue stuck in her hair.'

'Complete chaos.' Natalie had to laugh.

She turned away from the perfumery towards Pietro's window. And stopped. The harlequin costumes and carnival masks had been joined by rows and rows of white *bauta* masks like an installation at a trendy Shoreditch gallery. But that wasn't what was making her palms sweat. It was the unmistakable cloaked figure of the Plague doctor, hat pulled low over hollows for eyes, a curved beak protruding from its sinister mask.

Natalie swallowed. She took a step back. *Come on, Nat. It's only a mannequin. There's no one behind it.*

'Natalie? Nat, are you okay?' Cate's voice was soft.

'Yeah...' She would be all right in a minute; she just needed a moment to bring her heart rate back down. She swiped the beads of sweat from her upper lip, glad that the pattern on her dress would hide the damp patches spreading beneath her arms.

'You poor thing; does that monstrous costume bring it all back?'

'Yes,' she croaked.

'Look at me.' Cate's eyes were sincere. 'You've got this, Nat. There's nothing to be scared of. That creepy guy's long gone. You're not in a deserted alleyway; you're not alone any more.'

'I know. Thanks for trying to make me feel better.'

'I'm so sorry I didn't believe you that night. I'm going to do everything I can to make it up to you. I'm your friend, whether you like it or not.'

'Thanks,' Natalie mumbled. She pushed open the door. The bell tinkled.

'*Buonasera*! Good afternoon!' Pietro wiped his hands on his brown apron and polished his glasses on a purple handkerchief before popping them back on his nose. 'So nice to see you both again. Have you come to purchase traditional Venetian masks? Or perhaps you are here to see my younger and more handsome friend?' He chortled.

'I am hoping to commission a watch for my husband's birthday.'

'Eraldo!' Pietro boomed. The pink feathers quivered on a mask hanging on the wall just behind his head. 'Two ladies to see you!'

'*Avanti!*' Eraldo called from above.

'After you.' Natalie followed Cate up the spiral staircase, trying not to dwell on the strange thrill she got from the sound of Eraldo's voice, deep and warm as a sheepskin rug.

Eraldo emerged from behind his workbench. 'Natalie, Cate, so nice to see you. I am glad you have found the time to come by. Please, take a seat over there.' He waved a hand towards the couch where Natalie had previously sat. Her cheeks heated at the memory of her untimely departure.

Cate popped her handbag on the seat beside her. Eraldo cleared a space on the table with a sweep of his hand.

Natalie sat down gingerly.

'I tidied earlier. I can assure you there will be no unwelcome surprises under the cushions.' Eraldo smiled.

'Sounds intriguing.' Cate crossed her slender ankles.

'Pietro has a habit of leaving things lying around when he comes up here. Last time, poor Natalie was almost sitting on the mask of the Plague doctor. It was not such a warm welcome.'

'She must have been terrified!' Cate exclaimed.

Natalie shot her a look.

'Terrified? That would be a rather extreme reaction, though they are a little creepy and…' Eraldo stopped mid-sentence, frowning as though something was beginning to make a little more sense. He stroked his hand across his dark stubble. '*Allora*, you have come to discuss a possible commission.'

His question was addressed to Cate but his eyes swept Natalie's face. She glanced at the floor.

'Yes, I have come to discuss a watch, something special.'

'Of course. You have a strong idea? Or perhaps a theme, a mood we can explore.'

Cate twisted her diamond-studded wedding ring. 'Something traditional. Roman numerals, a second hand of course, perhaps the date. Understated but different, unique.'

Eraldo removed the lid from his fountain pen and jotted a few words in a leather-bound notebook. 'Traditional but different. You are looking for – how we say – classic with a twist.'

'Exactly.' Cate smiled expectantly.

'I will show you something I have recently completed. I am just waiting for the customer to come and pick it up.' He rose from the couch. Natalie couldn't help noticing the snug fit of his dark jeans as he crossed the room, his muscular arms, the way the sun from the small attic windows picked out silver streaks in his black, curly hair.

Cate nudged her gently. 'Like what you see?' she mouthed. Natalie tried to look cross but judging by Cate's wry smile, she hadn't succeeded.

'Here.' Eraldo returned holding out a small, velvet-lined tray. 'I make this for a well-known actor – I cannot say who – created from an old watch he remembers his *nonno* wearing when he was a small boy. I have restored it, identical in every way except this blue face.'

'It's gorgeous.' Natalie admired the contrast of the steel numerals against the rich blue.

'I am pleased with it. The depth of colour, it really is something and of course, if I tried to reproduce this exactly – which I assure you I would not – it would never be exactly the same.'

'It's stunning,' Cate said.

'Yet I feel that you hesitate. This shade is particularly bold but a coloured dial need not be quite such a statement. A softer tone would work as well: a pearl grey, lavender, perhaps. And we would personalise it further, engraving a name, perhaps a special date upon the back... I can work up a few sketches, email you some costings.'

Cate fished a Duty-Free leaflet out of her handbag and jotted her email address on the back of it. 'Thank you, that would be perfect. I am so glad we could come to see you today before my husband arrives. I can't wait to show him the palazzo where we're staying, and we're off to the opera tonight.'

'*La Traviata* at La Fenice?'

'Yes, that's right.'

'That should be marvellous. I hope you enjoy it very much, and you too, Natalie.'

'Oh, Natalie isn't coming; it's just my husband and me – well, apart from the camera crew.' Cate laughed. 'I'm afraid Natalie is spending the evening alone.'

'Ah.' He placed the watch back on the velvet tray, fiddled with the end of his pen.

Natalie made to pick up her bag.

Eraldo cleared his throat. 'If you have no particular plans tonight, Natalie, perhaps you might allow me to introduce you to a rather charming *bacaro*. They serve the finest *cicchetti* in Venice, at least in my opinion. And the wine, too, is very good.'

Natalie felt Cate's eyes boring into her. 'Yes, thank you, that would be lovely.'

'I look forward to it. I hope it will make up just a little for missing the opera.'

'I'm sure it will.'

'Thank you, Eraldo. I do look forward to receiving your ideas.' Cate hitched her bag on her shoulder and stood up.

Natalie followed her down the spiral staircase, keeping her eyes firmly on Cate's back as they made their way out through Pietro's shop.

Natalie waited until they'd crossed the mini bridge to the perfumery. 'That wasn't very subtle.'

'No, the blue was a bit bright, but a pearl grey would be perfect.'

'I wasn't referring to that watch and you know it.'

'Don't get cross with me.' Cate pulled a comically sad face Natalie recognised from long ago.

'I suppose I should be thanking you.'

'No problem.' Cate flipped her hair over one shoulder. 'That's what friends are for.'

'Hmm,' Natalie said. 'I expect you'll want to get back to the palazzo now, have a chance to relax before your husband arrives.'

Cate gasped. 'I was so caught up with planning his present, I quite forgot to check his plane did take off on time.'

'Hold on a moment, Cate.' Natalie could feel her phone vibrating. 'It's Lucia calling... Hi, Lucia, what is it? Slow down!'

Natalie could hardly believe what Lucia was saying. She took a deep breath. She had to channel that inner Mandy Miller; she couldn't let herself panic. 'No, no, don't worry, we'll work around it somehow. We'll pick up again tomorrow. *Ciao, ciao!*'

'What is it? You look so worried.'

'It's Phil. I hate to break this to you, Cate, but he won't be arriving in Venice tonight.'

Cate grabbed her phone from her bag. 'I've got a missed call. I can't believe it! How could he do this to me?' She sounded so angry, a woman peering in the perfumery's window picked up her little boy and gave him a comforting cuddle.

'What do you mean?' Natalie couldn't believe Cate was losing her cool like this. 'Phil can't help it, it's—'

'Work, I suppose he says,' Cate cut in. 'Oh, I am a fool; maybe Lucy *was* right.'

'Who's Lucy? You're not making any sense.'

'The wife of Phil's best friend. She tried to warn me but I wouldn't believe her. But now he's left me here alone, humiliated me like this.' She yanked at her hair.

'Cate!' Natalie gently held her wrists. 'I don't know what you think is going on but Phil couldn't board the plane. Nobody could. There won't be any planes leaving London tonight nor from Paris, Frankfurt or Rome. It's environmental protestors, hundreds of them all over Europe; they've chained themselves to the control towers and glued themselves to the runways.'

Cate clapped her hands to her face. 'Oh, I'm so relieved!' She laughed. 'To think for a moment I believed that gossipy Lucy! Oh, it was awful; she told me she thought Phil was having an affair. I knew he wasn't the type but when he didn't get on the flight out with me, acting all weird and when you said he wasn't on the plane... oh, I just couldn't bear it if she'd turned out to be right.'

'I'm so glad it's nothing like that.' Not just for Cate's sake: Floella would go spare if she thought one of her perfect couples was on the verge of divorce.

'Is Phil not getting here going to make things really difficult?' Cate asked.

'A little but we'll do tomorrow's filming on the Rialto Bridge as planned even though there aren't two of you. Then I guess we'll keep the afternoon free, get Lucia to sweet-talk the crew into doing a few extra hours on the days after Phil arrives. Everything will work out.'

It was a pity 'everything' didn't include her date with Eraldo. She couldn't leave Cate to go alone to the opera tonight; she'd have to go back to the shop or call him. Either way, she'd be letting him down. She couldn't understand why the thought made her feel so wretched. His smile made her heart leap, but starting a new relationship was the furthest thing from her mind.

Reluctantly, she turned around.

'You're going to go the wrong way again, Nat!'

'I have to go back to see Eraldo, tell him in person I can't see him tonight.'

'Not so fast, hang on a mo! Let me check this message first; looks like it's from Lucia.'

'Probably telling you everything she told me just now.'

'Not quite,' Cate said. 'She's just confirming the arrangements for the opera tonight.'

'Better tell her I'm going with you.' Natalie tried not to sound as though it were the last thing she wanted to do.

'No, you're not.'

'Okay, go by yourself if that's what you want.' It seemed Cate's commitment to rebuilding their friendship was over already.

'I decided my Dior handbag deserves its own seat.'

Natalie stared at her.

'I'm kidding you; I'm not that precious! I'd love you to come with me but the moment you told me Phil was stranded, I texted Lucia to check she was free. She's so happy; she's been desperate to see *La Traviata*. Now I get someone to go with and you'll still have your hot date.'

'Hot date? What a lot of rubbish you talk!'

'Whatever!' Cate grinned.

'Lucia works so hard, it's nice she's getting the chance to dress up and go out tonight.'

'Even nicer, you get to see Eraldo and have a few glasses of wine and make eyes over a bowl of spaghetti.'

'I don't think *bacari* serve pasta,' Natalie said primly.

'Well, whatever you do eat, I can't wait to hear about it. Now let's get a move on. I want to call Phil before I sink into that ridiculously over-the-top bath in my en suite.'

'I'll let you know how it goes with Eraldo,' Natalie said, surprising herself. She had plenty of people in her life: her lovely parents – but they were so far away – people she knew in the TV business, acquaintances and neighbours. But she hadn't had a real, close, gossipy girlfriend in years. She'd never been as close to anyone as she'd been to Cathy. She hadn't realised how much she'd missed her.

20

Eraldo patted the top of an oak barrel. 'We are lucky we got this before anyone else spotted it.'

Natalie shimmied up onto one of the wooden bar stools. There were just three outside tables squeezed into a corner by the entrance to Il Turacciolo; the rest of the patrons stood shoulder to shoulder on the strip of paving or crowded inside the tiny *bacaro*, pressed right up against the long, marble counter half-obscuring the glass-fronted displays of Venetian snacks.

Natalie peered around Eraldo's shoulder. 'I guess there's just no room for more seating.'

'We are used to doing it this way but I thought you would like to sit for a while after walking all over the city today. It must have been tiring.' His dark-brown eyes met hers.

Natalie's cheeks warmed; she wasn't used to people looking out for her. 'That's kind,' she mumbled.

'Now, what to drink? It is traditional to pair the *cicchetti* with a tiny glass of wine we call an *ombra*; it means "shadow". I usually leave it up to the waiter to recommend the best *cicchetti* then let him pair it with a wine.'

'Sure.' Natalie hoped she sounded casual. She didn't like the thought of anyone else choosing her food. She was sure she'd read somewhere that Venetians ate horsemeat and considered cartilage a tasty snack. But there was no time to backtrack. Eraldo was already chatting with the bearded waiter, who was running through the list of today's *cicchetti* at a bewildering rate. A few more nods and hand gestures and the man vanished back into the throng crowding at the door.

'*Allora*, so tell me, Natalie, how long have you been in television? Floella tells me this is your first time in front of the camera for many years. You presented a television programme for children a long time ago, I believe.'

'Oh, *Panda's Place*! That was rather embarrassing.'

'No! That cannot be. But even if you think that, it is part of your journey, your story, that brought you here. So, tell me, how was the world of talking bears and musical slides?'

Natalie hesitated. Had Floella given Eraldo the low-down or had he been googling her? She cringed at the thought of the handsome Venetian finding pictures of those hideous dungarees, the haircut she'd copied from Rachel in *Friends* that didn't suit her at all.

'Perhaps you do not want to share these experiences?' There was a note of disappointment in his voice.

'Oh, no, it's not that.' She searched for an amusing anecdote. 'Live television was quite an experience. The producer decided to use real animals on our Christmas nativity special instead of kids dressed up but they didn't anticipate the donkey lifting its tail and adding an extra gift alongside the gold, frankincense and myrrh…'

Eraldo let out a laugh.

'That's not all. One of the little boys with a tea towel on his head was too shy to ask for the toilet so a moment later, a great puddle spread across the studio floor.'

Eraldo wiped a tear from his eye. 'What a disaster! But funny also, *sì*?'

'The producer didn't think so, not even after the audience rated it their favourite episode. We were pre-recorded after that. At the time, I felt humiliated, as if I was somehow responsible, but it *was* funny. I'd almost forgotten that.'

She'd been so focused on using *Panda's Place* as a stepping stone to a prime-time adult show, she hadn't appreciated how liberating it was to perform for an easily pleased audience who rolled about clutching their sides every time a man in a giant panda bear suit got stuck halfway down the musical slide. Which happened every week. She hadn't had to worry about the cut of her dungarees or whether her hair was bouncy and her eyebrows shaped to perfection. The audience of *Luxe Life Swap* would be a lot harder to please. She could already envisage the disparaging comparisons between her Primark bargains and Cate's designer threads. Not to mention her failure to live up to Mandy Miller's virtuoso talents.

'Are you okay, Natalie?'

She realised she was frowning. 'Yes, of course.'

'Ah, good, that looks like our food arriving.' Eraldo flashed a smile in the waiter's direction. The man put down a plate of snacks: crispy rings of what she assumed was calamari and oval crostini smeared with black-olive tapenade.

Eraldo picked up a miniature triangular sandwich secured with a toothpick. It was made from the type of sliced white bread Natalie hadn't seen since Mum made her packed lunches. But these *tramezzini* weren't curling at the edges, and that filling definitely wasn't Tesco's own-brand sandwich spread.

'Tuna?' she guessed, biting into the soft, white bread. It *was* tuna, the flaky fish mixed with juicy, green olives and tart cornichons causing her to *mmm* with pleasure. 'This is delicious.'

'Just wait until you try the crostini and the calamari.'

A tiny, golden crumb clung to Eraldo's full top lip. His tongue ran across it; the golden speck disappeared. A strange liquid sensation filled the pit of her stomach. She bit into a ring of calamari, the crisp coating giving way to a melting taste of the sea. She'd always found calamari chewy in the past, and a bit greasy too, but not this time.

'Even better than the tuna,' she said.

Eraldo smiled. 'Then you must have the last one.'

'If you're sure.' She'd normally hold back but the nibbles had only succeeded in making her realise how hungry she was.

'The kitchen here makes a fresh batch of *cicchetti* every hour but the calamari are always the first to go no matter how many they make. We were lucky to get any at all.'

'As lucky as getting this table. It's the perfect perch.' She sipped her *ombra* of wine.

'Do not get too comfortable; we will be leaving soon.'

His words took the magic of the evening with them; the warm, fuzzy feeling vanished like the last piece of squid. She gulped down a mouthful of wine. Someone elbowed her in the back; her glass knocked against her front teeth.

Eraldo didn't seem at all bothered their evening was wrapping up so soon, signalling to the waiter and waving away her offer to pay. A quick bite, a tiny glass of wine and their night was over. And why would he choose to prolong it? She didn't have Floella's ebullient personality, Cate's ethereal beauty or Mandy's warmth. She slithered down from her stool.

'This way, Natalie.' He wove a path through the rest of the customers, steered her around a group of teenagers walking arm in arm. They turned the corner, emerging right by the opera house. Inside, Lucia and Cate, resplendent in one of her new gowns from Simona Rinaldi, would be listening to the soaring voices.

'La Fenice! I had no idea we were so close.'

'I took you to a *bacaro* nearby in case there was a problem with the film crew or something else needed your attention. But now the performance has started, I think it is safe for us to go somewhere else. If you would like to?'

'That was so thoughtful of you. Yes, I'd love to carry on. Lucia can deal with anything. I'm off duty this evening.' And now she was going to spend it with him. To think that a few moments ago, she'd believed he was trying to shake her off!

'Good.' He slipped his arm through hers as they continued to walk. A friendly gesture, no more, but her breath caught. 'I am glad you are able to relax but in a job like yours, you are always – how do you say? – on call.'

'Is that what Floella says?'

'Not just Floella. Also my wife.'

A wife. Of course. There'd been no reason to believe he was single. Just the feel of his arm against hers, the warm scent of his amber cologne, the softness of his brown eyes – they'd all conspired to send her daft imagination running off. What a fool! But perhaps she shouldn't be too hard on herself. It wasn't every day she met a handsome, charming man in the most romantic city in the world.

'My ex-wife nowadays,' he added.

Natalie bit down on a smile. 'Your ex was in television?' She tried to sound casual.

'Yes. A producer on *International Food Challenge*, one of Floella's first shows. Flo introduced us; that is how we met.'

'She was English?'

'No, Italian, from Vicenza, an hour's drive from here. It is ironic that it took a Londoner to bring us together.'

'Fate.'

'Yes, I suppose.' She could not read his tone.

'But you're no longer together.'

'No,' he said shortly. Why had she asked? Wasn't 'ex-wife' enough for her?

They kept walking in silence, cutting through narrow streets and across small *campi*.

'Stefania loved her job,' he said at last. 'I knew it was her passion but I did not realise what she would sacrifice to get on. That it was more important, bigger than anything else, bigger than us. I hoped we would stop renting and buy a place, have a family perhaps, but there was always one more project first. Every time, just one more. But reality shows were just a stepping stone to greater things. She is a film producer now; she lives in California.'

'You didn't want to go with her?'

'I did not fit into her new world... so she said. But enough about that. It is all in the past. And now we find our next *bacaro*.'

'If it's half as good as the last place...'

'Il Turacciolo has the best calamari but this little place behind the fish market has the best *polpette* – what you call meatballs. We will have to cross over the canal. This way...'

He weaved a practised path through the tourists massing on the Rialto Bridge, across the now deserted fish market, and steered her towards a green awning.

'This looks a cute place.'

'I hope you are ready for more wine, more *cicchetti*?'

'Yes, please.' She slipped into a seat at the table Eraldo had found, content to let him take charge of the ordering once more. Two *ombre* of wine appeared, red this time.

'After we stop here, we will go to another place just a few metres away and finally, we cannot finish the night without a visit to my favourite of all.'

'I'm glad these glasses of wine are so tiny. I hadn't realised we were having a sort of Venetian pub crawl.'

'Ah, the great British pub crawl: you need a lot of stamina for that! I remember the first time I went with my new friends from Goldsmiths. I had never even had an English pint before, only the little bottles of beer we have in Italy. And each pub we went to, we had to drink another. *Mamma mia*, so much beer and nothing to eat but these strange little snacks, pork scratchings. I thought this beer, it must be not so strong but the next morning, well! I felt as though the night before, I must have been banging my head against a big wall. Some of my friends, the next day, it was like they had drunk nothing at all. Ah, it was fun... but you know, I prefer to go out to have some nice, small things to eat and a little wine like this. *Cin cin!*' He clinked his glass against hers.

'*Cin cin!*'

Natalie bit into a crostino topped with something creamy and white – a taste strangely familiar. It was the *baccalà mantecato* Miss Morrison had made her try all those years ago. 'Mmm... this is better than a cider and a packet of crisps any day.'

'I am glad you approve.'

Natalie returned his smile. The evening was exceeding all her expectations. She could kid herself it was the tasty *cicchetti* that lit up her tastebuds like an explosion of tiny fireworks on her tongue or the colour and chatter of the diners but she knew it was Eraldo's company that was making the evening so special. She found it hard not to smile each time his nose gave a little twitch of pleasure as he sampled another snack. And it wasn't just his good looks that entranced her; it was the gratifying way he listened – truly listened – when she spoke and even seemed to find her feeble attempts at humour amusing, rewarding her with a smile that flashed even white teeth and lit up those dark, dark eyes.

It was so rare to find a man who found her assignments for Flo-Go Productions so enthralling but she soon switched the subject. She was far more interested in finding out more about the man sitting in front of her than discussing any new show Floella might have in the offing.

'Do you remember the first watch you worked on?' she asked.

'My *nonno*'s old watch; Papà had inherited it. The glass was cracked and the winder did not work. Papà took it to a local repairer who told him that for the money it would cost, it was not worth the trouble, so he put it in a drawer with his vests and underpants. I would take it out sometimes when he was not around and twist the winder, hoping somehow that it would spring to life. Of course, it never did.

'Then, when I was ten, I won a prize at school. I cannot remember what for even though it was the only one I ever won.' He paused to laugh and shake his head. 'Mamma gave me some money to spend on whatever I liked; she was so proud. I secretly took that watch and returned to the repair shop so that I might give it to Papà for Christmas. It had become a sort of dream of mine that it would work again. The same man was working there. He had small, round glasses and very little hair. I reached up to the counter – I was still very short back then – and laid Nonno's watch there and my small pile of coins. Of course, it was not nearly enough money, though to me, it seemed a fortune. When he told me so, I asked him to tell me how to fix it so that I could try to do it myself. He gave me such a strange look, for a moment, I thought he was angry and that he would throw me out of his shop...'

'But why? Did he think you were being cheeky?'

Eraldo ran his hand through his hair. 'Yes, I thought that for a moment but then I realised it was something else. That I had made him sad. Of course I did not know why; only later, I found out that I had made him think of the son he had lost, the son to whom he had hoped to pass on his craft. He agreed to start to mend the watch the next day if I came after school had finished and I sat with him and helped... I was too young to realise I could not possibly be any more than a hindrance. So, that was my first lesson and I was hooked. I went back there whenever I could. He always seemed pleased to see me and would let me sit there whilst he worked. He had a big, old cardboard box of broken spare parts he would let me rummage through and try to find bits and pieces that might go together; it was like a small puzzle for me.'

'And what about your *nonno*'s watch? Was your dad surprised? What did he say?'

'I never forget his face as he opened my present. He was so delighted but a moment later, his face changed. He was angry. He could not see how I could afford to get it fixed. He thought I must have stolen the money. But Mamma calmed him down and when I told him, he hugged me and told me how sorry he was to think such a thing. I asked if he was cross that I visited the watchmaker instead of concentrating on my studies but he gave me his blessing. He must have known of course about the terrible illness that claimed the old man's child. And he was pleased I was not hanging around after school on the streets causing all kinds of nonsense.'

Natalie smiled. It was easy to imagine Eraldo as a mischievous young lad with the sort of cheeky grin that could buy his way out of trouble.

He waved for the bill. This time, she didn't feel slighted; she knew the evening was far from over and just minutes would pass before they'd reach the next venue on their *bacaro* tour.

'I'll get this one.' She opened her purse.

'No, no.'

'Really, I insist.' She put a note on the small, silver tray.

'My mamma tells me, never argue with a woman.' Eraldo grinned. 'But the next stop, I pay.'

It was only a short stroll to the next *bacaro*, tucked up a narrow *calle*. This time, there were no tables to bag, just a huddle of locals clutching small beakers of wine and paper-napkin-wrapped snacks. Definitely not a place where an episode of *Luxe Life Swap* would ever be filmed.

'This is, how you say, rough and ready,' Eraldo said, squeezing into a gap in the throng. Natalie ended up wedged into a rather small space pressed up so close to Eraldo, she couldn't help examining the fine lines around his eyes, the tiny scar on his cheek.

'These *arancini* are the house speciality.'

His voice made her jump. What was the matter with her?

'They look fantastic.' And smelt even better. She bit into the crispy coating, the rice grains and cooked ham giving way to a melting middle of stringy mozzarella she had to wipe from her chin.

'If I could eat only one thing for the rest of my life, it would be Marco's *arancini*, but fortunately here in Venice, I do not have to make such a choice. My stomach is crying out for more of these but we have one more place on our *cicchetti* crawl.' He laughed as he said the last words. This time, after they'd finished eating, she did not attempt to help pay the bill. She was glad to make a move, to put a little distance between them. Sitting or standing where she was no longer able to breathe in the warm scent of his cologne might help rein in the inappropriate emotions that kept surfacing. This evening wasn't a date, she told herself, just a kind offer to spend the evening with a friend of a friend so she wouldn't be alone in the city.

They set off to their next venue, strolling side by side through quiet streets and vast *campi*, the only sounds a television burbling from a half-open window, the tap of an old man's cane. A Venice far from tour groups, logoed baseball caps and plastic replicas of St Mark's Basilica.

On the far side of a small bridge, a light glowed in a low window, an armchair just visible, a woman reading a book. Natalie rested her hand on the balustrade to steady herself. She hadn't envisaged walking quite so far when she'd chosen to sport her favourite heels.

A row of houses, most rooms in darkness, faced them, a dark *sottopassaggio* providing a route beneath.

'Not far, just through here,' he said.

'Great.' She faked a breezy tone. She tried to focus on the building at the other end of the passage as they walked along, a chink of light ahead. But the walls were closing in on her. The low roof of the passageway cast a dark shadow across Eraldo's face. Almost as though he were wearing a mask.

'Are you okay, Natalie?' He stopped walking, put a hand on her arm.

Instinctively, she flinched.

A tiny frown flicked across his face. 'Natalie?'

She took a breath big enough to make her shudder. 'I'm fine. I'm just a bit claustrophobic, that's all.'

'I am sorry I took you this way, but it was quicker. I did not think.'

'How could you know?' She managed a small smile. 'I'm okay now.'

'Good. I am glad that you will not miss the last place on our small tour… or perhaps you would rather I take you to the vaporetto stop. It has been a long day for you, I understand.'

'No, let's carry on, I'm looking forward to it.' She didn't want the evening to end. But she couldn't help feeling from the brief nod of his head that something between them had shifted.

21

Cate clapped so hard, her palms were stinging. Some of the audience had leapt to their feet.

Lucia wiped away a tear from her eye. 'That was marvellous!'

The company of singers finally left the stage, the switching on of the lights signalling that this time, there would be no further encore. Cate picked up her glossy programme and Dior bag which had in fact enjoyed a seat of its own up in their box. Slowly, they made their way back out of the theatre.

'Thank you so much for coming with me, Lucia.'

'No, thank you. It is my dream to see an opera here.'

'I can see why.' Cate had seen *La Traviata* several times but to experience it here in Venice was something else. And the tragic story of Violetta and Alfredo had taken her to another dimension where concerns about Phil's odd behaviour and worries about whether Natalie would truly accept her friendship didn't exist.

'You wish me to show you the way to the vaporetto?' Lucia's

face was earnest. It hadn't taken her very long to switch back to professional mode. Despite the carefully applied make-up, the young woman looked exhausted; she'd been up with the film crew since dawn.

'No, I know the way,' Cate said. Well, she could guess. 'I'll see you tomorrow morning at the Rialto Bridge.'

'I am so sorry that we start so early but the crowds...'

'It's no problem, really.' Cate planted kisses on Lucia's soft cheeks. 'Bye, Lucia. I will see you in the morning.'

Lucia crossed the *campo*; a quick glance over her shoulder, a wave and she was gone.

Cate stood outside the opera house trying to get her bearings. It didn't matter if she got a little lost; she'd still wake up early whatever time she got back to the palazzo. She never slept in. Back home, she'd come downstairs to the sound of claws on the front doormat, Ted waiting patiently, lead in his mouth. And even if she hadn't been an absolute pushover where Ted was concerned, she always woke when she felt the mattress shift very slightly as Phil got out of bed. Boarding school had instilled in him the habit of rising early as surely as it had created his drive for perfection, his need for success. And that had given them their wonderful old, rambling house, an enviable lifestyle mixing with the great and the good. But, Cate suspected, those years at Hillingdon had left another legacy. They'd taught her husband to seal his feelings away, encased in an outer shell of worldly success and bonhomie, his emotions carefully protected like the little, green kernel inside a pistachio nut. On very rare occasions, she'd sense that he was about to let her in but then the moment would slip away from her as though she had tried to nail a gelato to the wall.

But Phil wasn't the only one keeping his cards close to his chest. She hadn't been entirely honest with him either.

* * *

Natalie slid her card key into the slot by the door. Two wall sconces and the central chandelier sprung to life. She slipped off her shoes, rubbing the back of her heels and wiggling her feet. Her stomach felt uncomfortably full; the seafood snacks at Eraldo's last choice of *bacaro* had been an unnecessary burden on her digestive system. But she couldn't blame a single one of the delicious *cicchetti* for the way their perfect evening had turned into a dud. The easy intimacy between them had evaporated the moment she'd shrunk away from his touch.

* * *

Phil perched on the mustard-coloured bedspread, his case – which had been taken back off the plane – resting on the fold-out rack. The airport hotel's tiny room was a masterpiece of design in its own small way. Clean, an en suite bathroom, an incongruous mango fragrance coming from the plug-in air freshener in the corner. His parents would have been happy to stay in a place like this. They'd be all at sea in the swanky hotels he and Cate stayed in, walking around with invisible we-don't-belong-here signs.

Next-door's television hummed through the walls, men with American accents shouting over staccato gunfire, but it couldn't blot out the noise in his head. He'd been all set to get on the plane this time. He needed to feel Cate's arms around him, bury his face in her neck, inhale her soft fragrance that promised everything would be all right. Now, thanks to the eco-warriors of Europe, he was stuck in this hotel room, the only one *Luxe Life Swap* could secure in all the mayhem. They hadn't wanted him to go home and get driven back again, not with the police blocks holding up the traffic as they tried to tighten up security around the airport too little too late. They couldn't even guarantee his flight would take off as scheduled tomorrow. The planes were all out of sync and new cancellations were being added by the hour. Yesterday, he hadn't wanted to go back to Venice, the scene of his shameful secret. Now he just wanted to get it over and done with.

He took out his phone, clicked on the Facebook app and tapped in his eldest son's password. Oli wouldn't care, he didn't use the app any more; he said no one his age did. *Wrong password*. He felt a surge of panic. Oli wouldn't have closed down his account, surely? He couldn't have. Phil tried something else: Ted110378. Their beloved pet and the birthday of Didier Drogba, Oli's favourite footballer. Success! Phil clenched a fist. What a fool he must look if anyone were spying through the window.

His fingers shook as he typed in Raj's name, prayed he'd find a recent picture, something to show his old school pal was okay. And – yes! A beautiful photograph: Raj, his wife Neelam – still with that long plait that nearly reached her waist – and the three children. For once, he could see all their faces clearly; usually at least one child was half-hidden behind a huge puff of candy floss, buried under a pile of balls at a soft play centre, or bent down stroking a goat at a petting zoo. Raj – his blood brother (they'd pricked their thumbs with a compass in Maths class and rubbed them together) – was happy and well. Tears filled Phil's eyes.

He scrolled down the photos Raj had posted since Phil last dared to look. It seemed he was still running the Costless Coffee franchise, his sister had adopted another child, his parents were still alive. Phil's finger hovered over the phone. He couldn't help it. He had to look, had to torment himself. He scrolled all the way down to the pictures of Raj and Neelam's wedding day. Raj was wearing a white sherwani, his parents beaming with pride. The best man was someone Phil didn't recognise.

22

Cate and Natalie strolled across the Rialto Bridge side by side, backs to the camera. The morning's shoot was over; Natalie no longer had to worry about whether a shadow was creating a double chin effect nor whether the camera was zooming in on the fine hairs above her top lip. Presenting wasn't as much fun as Natalie remembered; perhaps she'd been less self-conscious in the days of *Panda's Place*.

Despite Phil's temporary absence, the Venice leg of the series was shaping up nicely. Cate was the perfect, camera-friendly contestant. The backdrop of the palazzo, not to mention the city itself, was advertising catnip and was certain to send their viewing figures soaring. The only thing preying on Natalie's mind was the fizzing out of her evening with Eraldo. Trying not to dwell on it was as futile as wishing she had Mandy Miller's natural warmth and charm.

'That is all for today.' Lucia glanced at her clipboard for confirmation, though she doubtless had the entire fortnight's schedule committed to memory.

'Thanks, Cate, you did a great job,' Natalie said.

'No problem, it was fun.' Cate smoothed her hair back, sending a waft of Chanel perfume Natalie's way. Today, she'd teamed a blush-pink blouse with an elegant pencil skirt and a dotty scarf tied just-so at the neck: a look that would scream cut-price air hostess if ever Natalie tried to emulate it.

'We are so lucky you persuaded the crew to take the rest of the day off and add a little time on at the end, Lucia. It will make it much less of a rush once Phil is here,' Natalie said. 'Poor fellow, it can't be fun being stuck at that airport hotel all day but at least he's not sleeping on the departure-lounge floor.'

'It is such a shame we could not book him on a flight today but he will be here by tomorrow evening,' Lucia said. 'Now you are free to explore our city. You are two old friends, so this will be fun for you, *si*?'

'Yes. It's so lucky we found each other again.' Cate's voice was genuine.

Natalie held back responding in kind; she didn't want Cate to think her apology had been accepted so readily. Instead, she just said, 'It's going to be a lovely day.' It was already warm, the sky the colour a paint company might suggest for a little boy's room.

'Then I will leave you to enjoy your day.' Lucia turned to the director, speaking in Italian.

'Well?' Cate said.

'Coffee next.' Natalie used her most decisive voice.

It didn't take them long to find a little place with empty tables to be had. It was still early; the day trippers had yet to descend on the city. The café's chairs were comfortable: rattan with round, red cushions secured to the seats and backs. Natalie stretched out her legs, the tension of the last few days beginning to drift away like stray strands of seaweed in the canal's green waters.

Cate didn't seem so comfortable, sitting ramrod straight as if afraid that the red cushion's vivid colour might rub off on her blouse if she leant back against it.

'Are you okay, Cate? You aren't worrying about Phil getting here, are you? I can't imagine anything else can go wrong.'

'Of course not. Third time lucky!'

Natalie ignored Cate's super-bright tone. 'There's no point worrying; there's nothing you or I can do.'

'I know.' Cate picked up her teaspoon, seemed to examine her reflection in its tiny bowl and put it down again. 'It's not that... I was wondering about today... if you had any thoughts about what we should do.'

'We could take a boat trip out to Torcello. That's one of the lagoon islands we won't get to film on.'

'Do you remember our trip to Murano where they make the glass? Julie Paine blew bubble gum balloons every time that fellow blew into his great long pipe.' Cate laughed.

'Shy Kelly bought that turquoise glass turtle for her mum and dropped it on the boat on the way back. She wouldn't stop crying.'

'Honestly, what a drama! Things seemed so important back then when really we had nothing to worry about.'

Natalie didn't reply. She waved for the bill.

'Oh, I am sorry. I didn't mean...'

'It's okay.' There was no point making Cate feel any worse.

'Nat...'

'What?'

'Could we take the waterbus out to a different island? I want to go to Burano.'

'The one where they have all the colourful houses? It's

already on our itinerary.' Natalie fished out her phone along with her purse to pay for the coffee. 'Yep, we're filming there in a few days' time.'

'I want to go there today.' Cate's voice was strange; all traces of her adopted 'to the manor born' confidence had vanished. 'I need to go to Burano before Phil gets here but I don't want to go alone. You will come with me, won't you?'

'Sure. We can stroll up to the Fondamente Nuove and get a boat to the island from there. Why do you want to go?'

Cate's eyes flicked from side to side. She snapped open the catch on her bag, removed a scrap of brown paper held together with sticky tape and smoothed it out on the table.

'What's this?' Natalie peered at the blurred ink.

Cate's forefinger stroked the curvy script. 'It's an address on Burano. The house where my mother, Lina, lives.'

'So, you're in touch now; that's fantastic!'

'No, we're not.' Cate's voice was bleak.

'You're not? After all this time, why not? Were you worried about upsetting your dad?'

Cate gave a strange sort of snort. 'Hardly. He wasn't worried about upsetting me.'

Natalie hastily ordered two more coffees from the confused waiter who'd appeared holding the card reader. Never mind the extra caffeine, she and Cate weren't going anywhere. Not until she'd got to the bottom of this.

'Why then? What's the big mystery?'

Cate sighed. 'I used to fantasise about meeting Mum, you know. I imagined her living in a grand palace or castle in some faraway place with a big doll's house in a pink bedroom just waiting for me. When Dad confessed he'd always known where she was, I wanted to get straight back on a plane. But I was just a school kid; how could I have afforded to get the money for a ticket? Dad wasn't going to give it to me, that's for sure, even if he'd had any spare cash, which he didn't.'

'But that's hardly a problem now.' Natalie glanced pointedly at Cate's handbag.

'No. Of course, you're right, that's not the reason. And even at uni, I could have lived on beans and gone to Italy. It's just...'

Natalie waited, glad that the swift arrival of the coffee gave her something to do other than watch Cate shifting awkwardly on her chair, playing with her gem-studded stacking rings.

'Dad and I never moved; he stayed in that council house where he and Mum lived until he had to go into the nursing home. He wouldn't even budge after I married Phil. He said he didn't want our charity. Mum knew where I was. She knew exactly where to find me. She could have come back to see me any time. Dad couldn't have stopped her. Not if she really wanted to.'

'Oh, Cate.' Natalie's heart went out to her. 'There could be any number of reasons why she didn't come back.'

'Dad never really explained why Mum went. I always thought they'd had a row and he'd told her to leave. I wish I'd pushed him for answers back then, but the way he is now, it's too late. Now I'm here, it feels like I've got to find out. But I'm scared. Scared that she won't want to see me.'

'What does Phil say about all this?'

'I haven't told him. I don't want to tell him unless she wants to see me.'

'Doesn't he think it's strange you'd come to Venice and not try to visit her?'

Cate chewed her lip. A couple sat down at the empty table next to them, dropping their shopping bags at their feet, discussing what they would and wouldn't have to drink whilst the waiter hovered. Natalie waited.

Eventually, Cate mumbled, 'He doesn't know she's still alive.'

'You told him she was dead?' Natalie's voice came out a little louder than she intended. The women on the next table, who'd finally decided on nothing more exciting than a couple of *caffè latte*s, turned and stared.

'Not exactly. I just never corrected him when he assumed that was the reason I'd never tried to make contact.'

'But why?' Natalie asked, dropping her voice this time.

'Phil's always got on with his folks; he struggles to understand why I didn't make up with Dad. I always get the impression he thinks it's a bit of a character failing though he'd never say so. He knows Mum left when I was a baby but when I told him she was no longer around, he misinterpreted what I said and it just seemed easier not to correct him. I knew he'd be nagging me to go and find her and I didn't know if I could. Phil's parents doted on him. His dad's passed away but his mum's house is full of family pictures. She's even still got one of his first day at school up on the mantelpiece looking all shy in his cap and a blazer that was way too big for him. I don't want him dwelling on why Mum left. I didn't want him or my boys to see me as someone damaged and unlovable.'

Natalie instinctively touched her old school friend's soft hand. 'I'm sure whatever the truth is about your mum, it wouldn't affect how your family think of you.'

'Maybe you're right but if Mum rejects me, I couldn't bear Phil to know.'

'This has been haunting you, hasn't it?' She couldn't imagine what Cate had been going through. Natalie had always taken her own mum and dad's love for granted; she supposed most people did.

Cate nodded. She looked close to tears. 'I've been terrified of the thought of sneaking off by myself. You will come with me, won't you? There's no one else I can ask.'

'Of course. We'll go now.' Natalie rooted in her purse to find some cash; she was too impatient to wait for the waiter to go off and fetch the card reader.

Cate picked up her bag, her second coffee untouched.

'Are you okay, Cate? Are you sure you want to do this?'

'Yes... but you won't put any of this in the programme, will you? Promise me.'

'Of course not, don't worry. *Together At Last* is a completely different show.' Flo-Go's other production specialised in heart-warming family reconciliations. The stories that ended in slammed doors and shattered dreams didn't make the screen. That wasn't what the gene-testing company who sponsored the show wanted their viewers to see.

Natalie forced a big smile. 'Everything will work out, you'll see.'

23

'That was quick!' Cate made to get up.

'This isn't our stop. This is Murano.'

Cate sat back down, shifting her legs to allow the family sitting opposite to get up in a kerfuffle of bags and dropped toys.

'Do they really make animals out of glass here, Daddy? Can they make Peppa Pig?'

The child's eager voice made Cate smile despite her worries. It hardly seemed any time had passed since Oli and Max were that age. How she'd treasured every milestone. But when she concealed a shiny pound coin from the tooth fairy under Oli's pillow or lifted up Max to blow out his birthday cake candles – all of them in one go! – it had only made her wonder more how her own mother could have missed out on doing all those things with her.

Cate's phone buzzed. A message from Phil. He'd already rung to tell her he'd had a decent cooked breakfast at the airport hotel, caught up on his work emails and started reading a thriller some previous guest had left behind.

> I miss you. Can't wait to see you tomorrow. I'll
> be on that plane even if I have to fly it myself!

The boat set off again, the water becoming choppier as Murano faded away. Cate turned her face to the window. The lagoon was far bigger than she imagined, a vast lake of green water spiked by the wooden stakes that marked the navigation channels. Natalie sat beside her, looking at her phone, though Cate suspected Nat was only pretending to be busy so that Cate didn't have to speak. She appreciated the kindness, but it didn't stop her half-wishing they'd jumped off at the last stop. How much easier it would be to join a tour of one of the glass factories and leave with her own colourful souvenir than search for her mother's house not knowing what, or who, she might find.

'We can get off the stop before Burano at the island of Mazzorbo and walk across the wooden bridge that links the two,' Natalie said. 'I've been reading up; they say it's lovely and peaceful there.'

'Yes, sure.' After all their time apart, it was extraordinary how Natalie could pick up on Cate's mood without her saying a word.

The waterbus cruised on. Cate closed her eyes, listening to the rattle of the engine, feeling the vibrations through the thin soles of her sandals. Phil's message had sounded perfectly normal. No hint that anything was wrong. But she couldn't shake off the feeling that something was troubling him.

'It's Mazzorbo; we're here.' Natalie's voice cut through her thoughts.

Only a handful of other passengers disembarked with them. No mass of sightseers here: just people in ones and twos strolling at their own pace, strung out along the waterfront like struggling no-hopers at the tail end of a horse race.

The absence of human voices and the tweet of the birds went some way to reducing the pounding in Cate's head. She was glad Natalie didn't bother her with comments or questions, just led the way, looping into a park past a small brick church along a path shaded by trees, heavy with leaves. Two women sat chatting on a lipstick-red bench, half keeping an eye on a little boy tottering on the grass brandishing a toy fire engine in the air. Another mum pushed a small girl back and forth on a swing, a white nappy sticking out below her cute pinafore dress.

Cate caught her breath. If Mum had taken her to Venice instead of leaving her with Dad, would she have played on those very swings or taken her first steps here on wobbly legs? Had Mum gone on to have other kids, sat on one of those benches gossiping with a friend, their pushchairs parked in the shade? She'd always thought of Mum as single, sad and lonely, missing her little Cathy, eating dinners for one in front of the TV. But maybe she'd built a whole new family, a house full of mess and laughter? Was baby Cathy just an unpleasant memory, an unfortunate consequence of a failed relationship she'd rather forget?

They exited the park. The lagoon was quiet, the peace disturbed only by the whirr of a single motorboat speeding by, a black and white dog balanced on the prow. Nat's voice was saying something about the specialist artichokes grown on Mazzorbo and the Prosecco vineyard behind the tall brick wall. Ahead of them lay a narrow wooden bridge.

'It will be okay,' Natalie said.

Cate inhaled a huge lungful of fresh air. She followed Natalie over the bridge onto Burano. It was busier here, but with a happy, holiday vibe quite at odds with her own feeling of dread.

'Ready?' Natalie asked. 'We'll just walk around for a bit first, if you like.'

'Yes, let's.' She'd put off searching for Mum for more than twenty years; another twenty minutes wouldn't make a difference.

She walked slowly past the market stalls, examining the lace tablecloths, napkins, skirts and simple dresses, fully aware she wouldn't buy any of them. Natalie let her dither for a while before leading her up a shopping street until they reached a narrow canal lined with boutiques and restaurants that forked off to the right and left. Cate had seen colourful buildings before, the vivid blue of Santorini, the pastel pinks and yellows of the street in West London where Evan and Lucy lived, but never colour combinations like this: brick red, primrose yellow, lime green and orange in one direction, vivid bluebell, apricot, terracotta and pink when she turned her head.

'I can see why you're planning to film here,' she said.

'It will make wonderful television. Mandy's notes say we might all like to wear white, to contrast with this rainbow of colours but now I'm here, I'm thinking we should wear the brightest outfits we've got, go the whole hog. If we put some stills out on our social channels, the engagement will be off the scale!'

'I knew I should have got that feathery cape.' Cate surprised herself with a quip. It was impossible not to feel a little lighter on an island where the colour scheme looked like it had been dreamt up by the audience of *Panda's Place*.

'We'll walk down to Piazza Baldassarre Galuppi; that's the main square. It must be this way,' Natalie said.

Cate followed her along the towpath, ignoring the entreaties from a rather dashing waiter to sit at one of his tables. On any other day, his promise of fish caught straight from the lagoon would be enough to entice her. It was definitely lunchtime but she couldn't face eating anything, not even the smallest cone from the gelateria on the corner.

The end of the canal met a wide piazza; it was clear this was the centre of the town. A rather plain brick church stood on one side, behind which a campanile rose at a decidedly odd angle. Not as dramatic as Pisa's famous Leaning Tower but certainly no longer as straight as the original architect intended.

'Look, that's the sign for the lacemaking school.' Natalie pointed to the other side of the square. 'Now it's just a museum but tourists used to be able to watch the women working away.'

'There's lots of lace for sale here.' Cate surveyed the boutiques dotted around the square, several with racks of clothing shaded by cream-coloured awnings.

'Most of it is machine-made nowadays with a hand finish; the real handmade lace is very rare. There are only a few people who still have the skills to keep their craft alive and they tend to be very elderly. We could go to the museum, if you like; they're said to have a fascinating collection upstairs.'

'Maybe afterwards,' Cate said, knowing that was exactly what Natalie knew she would say. 'It's time to go and find Mum's home.'

'I looked at a map on my phone on the waterbus. We're only a few minutes away.'

'It's a tiny island; they say less than 3,000 people live here... Oh, Nat, do you think she's still here?'

'There's only one way to find out.'

'I don't know if I'm ready.'

'You'll never be ready,' Natalie said.

'You're right.' Cate wiped her hands on her skirt. A woman struggled past, a cotton shopping bag hooked over a cracked elbow, skinny, brown arms sticking out of her cheap, sleeveless dress. Her mother, Lina, wouldn't be much older; at fifty-seven, could she look as downtrodden as this? Cate glanced down at the expensive-looking outfit she'd been wearing for the filming on the Rialto Bridge. Why hadn't she gone back to the palazzo and changed into a casual, summery dress? Oh, why oh why was she doing this?

'Cate.' Natalie's voice was as firm as Mrs Nickson's had been when Cate had a wobble outside the exam room just before taking her History GCSE. Chastened, she followed Natalie down a narrow passageway and through a network of courtyards, each small house a cube of colour. Terracotta pots brimmed over with fuchsia flowers, red-and-white striped curtains shaded the doorway of a turquoise house, buttercup-yellow shutters enlivened another.

And it was so quiet, not a tourist in sight, no comings and goings, no footsteps to break the silence. A cat stretched out on a well-scrubbed doorstep, ginger and white fluffy belly turned upwards. She could almost imagine the place was long deserted if the fresh paintwork and well-stocked window boxes hadn't demonstrated that a thriving neighbourhood existed behind the shuttered windows and closed front doors.

'Which number is it?' Natalie said.

'It's the orange one.' Cate's voice came out in a croak. She swallowed several times, trying to drum up some saliva. 'Will you wait for me over there?'

'Of course.' Natalie wandered away.

The orange house didn't appear to have a doorbell, just an iron knocker shaped like an upside-down horseshoe. Cate rapped the door twice and stepped back, looking up at the balcony running along the length of the upper floor, a checked tablecloth and striped towels pegged out to dry. A movement from behind a half-open shutter caught Cate's eye. A patch of bright blue – a woman's dress? It was hard to tell. Cate clasped her damp hands together, forced herself to be patient.

The front door slowly opened.

* * *

Natalie looked away. There was no point trying to read Cate's body language and guess what was being said. And it was no hardship to wait; it was a lovely day to drift aimlessly around the courtyard drinking in every little detail of the colourful houses, trying to identify their proudly displayed pot plants. The quiet was broken only by a man's voice reading the news – presumably on the radio – coming from an upstairs window. At this hottest time of the day, no one ventured out except for the tourists and those whose jobs depended upon them.

The cat that had been lying on its back padded past. Every so often, Natalie glanced towards the orange house, hoping that Cate was experiencing the happy reunion she'd dreamt of. It shocked her to realise just how much she cared.

24

A woman around ten years younger than Cate stood in the doorway to her mother's house. An aroma of something baking drifted from the end of the narrow hall.

'*Buongiorno*,' Cate said. Or was it now good afternoon?

The woman's eyes roamed over Cate's attire, widening slightly as they alighted on her Gucci bag. Seemingly satisfied that Cate was unlikely to be attempting to break in or trying to flog unwanted household goods, she wiped her hands on her patterned apron.

'*Posso aiutarla*?' she said.

'Sorry... do you speak English?' Cate said.

'No... my daughter... Pina, *vieni, vieni!*'

'*Subito!*' A young voice came from the same direction as the cooking smells. Pigtails flying, a girl of around seven or eight ran towards them, sending a pottery owl wobbling on the lace-topped console table.

'*Piano, piano!*' the woman admonished. She turned back to Cate. '*Dimmi!* Speak!'

Cate bent down slightly, trying to look friendly and relaxed, not panicky and on edge. 'Hello, I'm Cate. Do you speak English?'

The girl glanced at her mother for reassurance. The woman made an impatient hand gesture.

'*Sì*! I learn.' Her shy smile revealed a set of braces.

'I am looking for Lina; I think she is your grandmother?'

'No.' The girl shook her head. She stared at Cate with big, brown eyes.

'You have a *nonna*? She lives here?' Neither the woman nor the little girl were wearing the blue dress she was sure she'd seen through the upstairs window.

'*Sì*.' The little girl put her hands on her hips, twisting from side to side.

'What is Nonna's name? Is it Lina?'

'No.' The child, now bored, turned to go.

Cate's heart sank but she knew she was at the correct address. Perhaps her mother went by a different name as she now did.

'Has your *nonna* lived here a long time?' She tried another tack.

'*Sì*.' The girl looked at her mother, asked something in Italian then counted out thirty years on her fingers.

'I think your *nonna* is my mamma,' Cate pressed on.

'Nonna is mamma of Mamma.' The little girl glared.

The woman's eyes narrowed; perhaps she understood more English than she spoke.

'*Basta*!' She gestured with her thumb towards the door.

'Please! Please tell Nonna I am here. Tell her Cathy is here.' Cate tapped her chest. 'Cathy.'

The woman hesitated, perhaps moved by the desperation in Cate's voice. She raised her hand in a gesture that meant 'wait', took the child by the hand and climbed the stairs. Cate dared not move from her spot on the doormat. Her eyes searched the dingy space, scanning the glossy ceramic owl, the framed prints on the wall, the choice of tiles and rug, desperately hoping to find some hint of connection between her own life and the two Italians with whom she surely shared a common bond.

Voices drifted down. Every fibre in Cate's body strained to bound up the stairs two at a time. She forced herself to study a framed photograph on the wall but the picture of the two individuals who had stood in the hall with her just moments before didn't bring her any comfort. The woman's pinched face and the child's big, round eyes gave not the slightest suggestion that the three of them were related.

The child clattered down the stairs first, her mother following behind.

'*Mi dispiace.* I am sorry,' the woman said.

'Nonna not know Cathy.'

'If I could just see her. Please.'

'*Nonna è molto stanca.*' The daughter had exhausted her English vocabulary. She mimed a yawn.

'Please, just for a moment.' Cate moved towards the stairs.

The woman's face changed, all trace of empathy gone. She uttered a curse in Italian, advancing on Cate with an expression half-fearful, half-menacing. Instinctively, Cate stepped backwards. The woman kept coming. Cate backed off, hands up. The woman wasn't pacified. She shoved Cate in the chest; she staggered back onto the doorstep. Too late she tried to wedge her foot in the door. It slammed shut in her face. She reached for the horseshoe knocker, banged it hard against the wood, one, two, three times but the door stayed resolutely shut.

Cate stood rooted to the spot, her whole body trembling as though all the stress of the last few hours was trying to fight its way out. She looked up at the balcony. A flash of blue passed across the window as though the person upstairs had come to take another look at her before she walked away.

She felt, rather than saw, Natalie come and stand beside her. Without a word, her old friend pulled her into a hug. Cate buried her head into Natalie's shoulder, sobbing ugly, noisy tears. Natalie said nothing. Just held her like she'd always be there.

25

Natalie wrapped her arms around Cate's slender frame. There was no need to ask how the visit had gone; Cate's eyes met hers with the glazed stare of an earthquake survivor.

'I'm so, so sorry.'

Cate broke away. 'I'm fine. Let's get some lunch. I couldn't eat a thing but you must be starving.'

Natalie didn't move. 'You're not fine.'

'Don't tell me how I'm feeling! I've survived without Mum since I was six months old and I'll keep on surviving. If she doesn't want to see me, I'll just have to respect that.'

Natalie bit back the words she wanted to say, instead asking, 'Are you sure it was her? Did you get to speak to her?'

'No, she was upstairs; they said she didn't want to see me. But it *was* her. The little girl said her *nonna* had lived there thirty years. Look, Nat, we could dress this up any which way but I'm never going to have a relationship with Mum again. I don't want to talk about it any more. Let's go back to those eating places on the canal. I need a drink.'

'Okay, sure.' Natalie rather fancied a glass of something herself and her stomach was gurgling like an emptying drain.

They retraced their steps through the interlocking courtyards, down the narrow passage, emerging back on to the main square. Tourists smiled and laughed amongst racks of lacy clothes, groups of friends clogged the little bridges over the canal, voices rose from tiny tables crammed side by side. It was almost as if she'd imagined the silent square they'd left behind.

'Over there.' Cate marched towards a vacant table at the edge of the canal with the tread of someone used to getting her own way. Natalie took in the group of chic women drinking from long-stemmed wineglasses, the small blackboard chalked with the day's menu in Italian only: a proper, authentic trattoria; Cate had done well to spot this. And the scents, oh! Garlic and fresh herbs deliciously mingling. A memory of Eraldo's nose twitching with pleasure made her smile, then sigh as she recalled how she'd shied away from him.

Cate squeezed into a seat facing away from the canal, affording Natalie the view.

'A glass of Soave, a large one, please. Nothing to eat for me.' Cate addressed the waiter who'd sprung from his post by the door at the sight of his chic, blonde customer. Natalie didn't need any more time to decide, ordering the same to drink and the *bigoli con le sarde*, a local dish of pasta and sardines she'd been longing to try.

The wine appeared in oversized glasses but that didn't stop Cate from glugging back half of hers the moment the waiter had set it down. Natalie forced herself not to put out a restraining hand. This was half her fault. *Luxe Life Swap* was responsible for Cate's trip to Venice and without Natalie urging her on, Cate might never have had the courage to visit her mother's house. She sipped her wine: cold and crisp.

'Cate...'

Cate raised her hand. 'Don't! I'll be fine in a minute. Please don't fuss.' She sniffed, took another great mouthful of wine. 'I'm lucky. I've got a wonderful life whether Mum's in it or not, Phil's a great husband and we've got two healthy, kind, bright boys who I adore. Really, I'm blessed.'

'Have you got any pictures? I don't know why I didn't ask you before.'

'Probably still in shock from running into me again. I didn't offer to show you before...' Cate paused.

'Because you didn't want to rub your perfect life in my face?'

'Well, now you know it's far from perfect. But I've no reason to feel sorry for myself, especially since I've found you again. I can't tell you how good it feels to have an old friend.' Cate swiped roughly at her eyes.

'Aww! Stop it, you're making me all embarrassed. I'm glad I found you too. It's like all those years in between never happened.'

'If anything goes wrong again, we will talk it through, won't we? I couldn't bear it if we fell out now. I keep up with a couple of girls from uni and go out with a few of Phil's friends' wives but there's no one like you, no one who really gets me.'

Natalie raised her glass; she clinked it against Cate's. 'Same here. There's no one like an old friend. Nothing will come between us again, I promise.'

Cate fished into her bag. 'Here, you drink your wine, let me find some photos. I've got lots of cute ones from when the boys were small but they're going through those self-conscious years now. They have a magical way of vanishing whenever I try to take their picture and when I do get some, they insist on inspecting them and making me delete the ones they don't like. I've got far more pictures of the dog!'

'Ted?'

'Yes, look, isn't he adorable?' Cate's face softened, all traces of her earlier anguish gone.

Natalie took the phone. A rather scruffy mutt, white save for a black splodge over one eye, stared back at her, one ear cocked; the other appeared to be half-missing. She'd imagined Cate owned a sophisticated Afghan hound or a silky, super-slim whippet.

'Oh, he is cute!'

'Swipe along if you like; I've taken rather a rather a lot of him.'

Cate wasn't kidding; there were an awful lot of pictures: Ted in a blue, quilted coat outside the old vicarage front gate; Ted lolling in a rather fancy woven basket; Ted in the garden; in the park; by a lake with a yellow tennis ball clamped in his jaw; by the sea putting a tentative paw in the surf. After showing a suitable level of enthusiasm, she handed the phone back. Her meal had arrived and she feared it would be stone cold by the time she'd worked her way through every image of the pampered pooch.

'Ted's the best,' Cate cooed. 'Every time I work at the shelter, I want to bring some sad puppy home with me but I wouldn't want to upset him; I think he likes being an only dog.'

Natalie supressed a smile. She twirled a few strands of the spaghetti-like *bigoli* around her fork. It wasn't the most photogenic of dishes – she made a mental note not to eat it whilst they were filming – but the mixture of sardines and onions cooked until they were translucent and meltingly soft was something else.

'You volunteer at the dog shelter?'

'Yes, a couple of days a week when I'm not helping in Phil's office or visiting Dad. Sometimes, I get lucky and answer the phone; other times, I'm cleaning out the cages.'

'Not dressed like that.' Natalie raised her eyebrows.

'I'll have you know I wear a very fetching navy-blue boilersuit.' Cate laughed. 'What's your food like? It smells divine.'

'Tastes amazing.'

'I'll get one too; I'm ravenous.' Cate waved over the ever-helpful waiter and ordered a plate of *bigoli* and another two glasses of wine even though Natalie had barely started to drink hers. 'Let me find some pics of our boys whilst I'm waiting... Oh, here's one of Max by a Spitfire at the air museum. We went there for his last birthday. He's still determined to be a pilot when he's older even though we've tried to persuade him it won't be half as exciting flying a Boeing for Ryanair.'

'But it will be a lot safer.' Natalie studied Max's freckled complexion, mop of red hair and confident air.

'Yes, but I'd still rather he stayed on solid ground. That's typical of all mums, I suppose... well, some of them.' A cloud crossed Cate's face.

'What about Oli, your older boy?'

'He wants to be a furniture designer like his dad; he's very artistic. I'll try to find you a decent snap.' Cate frowned down at her phone. 'To think once upon a time I could take as many as I liked: on the climbing frame, at the zoo, even in the bath! Ah, here's some where he's playing cricket. I usually get away with taking a few then; he's secretly rather proud of being on the team. Max looks like me apart from the red hair but Oli takes after his dad.'

'Let's see.' Natalie laid down her fork. It was hard to make out the boy's face, his ill-defined features thrown into shade by his white cap, but he shared an upright bearing and confident aura with his younger brother.

'Swipe along – there's probably two or three.'

'This is a good one.'

Oli was holding some sort of trophy, looking straight at the camera. There was something oddly familiar about the older brother's face. Something that made Natalie feel as if invisible centipedes were crawling over her skin. Oli's face was the face of the boy from her school trip: the face of the boy who'd attacked her. But that was ridiculous. It had to be a strange camera angle, a trick of the light. She swiped to the next photo. Now she could barely discern any resemblance between Cate's son and the youth who'd followed her the night of the masked ball. Venice, with its years of history, its myths and shadows, was sending her imagination into overdrive.

Cate smiled expectantly; she'd been too busy thanking the waiter and digging into her newly arrived *bigoli* to spot Natalie's temporary unease.

Natalie handed back the phone. 'They look like two lovely boys.'

'They are.' Cate wiped a tiny smear of olive oil from the side of her mouth. She dug her fork back into the pasta. 'Sorry I don't have a decent one of Phil; he's even worse than the boys when it comes to getting his photo taken. Actually, I couldn't believe it when he agreed to apply for the show, but I suppose the possible boost to his business overrode everything. And I guess being filmed is easier than posing for photos, not knowing what to do with your hands or the rest of you!'

'Mandy Miller makes it look so easy.'

'It's smiling and looking natural all at the same time that's hard.' Cate pulled a face.

'You're a pro.'

'I hope Phil won't look and feel too awkward. I'm beginning to wonder if that's what's been bothering him lately: worrying about how he might come across.'

'He is okay, isn't he?' Natalie tried to sound casual. *Luxe Life Swap* didn't deal in stress and marital strife.

'Oh, I don't know.' Cate rubbed her hand across her forehead. 'He's never been good at showing his feelings. But let's not talk about that. Let's get the bill. I know we talked about going to the Lace Museum but I've seen enough of Burano to last a lifetime.'

'I suppose we could try to change the filming schedule,' Natalie said, although Floella would probably kill her.

Cate smiled brightly. 'It's okay. We'll come back here for the filming; I won't let you down. Look at the colours, the quaint little houses; your viewers will love all this. And Phil knows it's on our itinerary. I don't want him questioning why things have changed. I can't have him worrying about me. You won't tell him about today, will you? Promise me.'

'No. I promise. Shall we go?'

'Coffee, ladies? Some dessert, perhaps?' The waiter, as if sensing a shift in mood, had reappeared.

'Just the bill please. This one's on me, I insist.' Cate opened her wallet. 'Here, this will more than cover it; keep the change.'

'*Grazie.*' The waiter slipped the cash into the pocket of his apron.

'Thank you, that was kind.' Natalie stood up.

'Wait a moment.' Cate rooted in her bag. She scrunched up the piece of brown envelope with her mother's address and dropped it into the aluminium ashtray. 'I won't be needing this any more. I think the vaporetto stop is over that way. Come on, let's go.'

'After you.' Natalie hung back, just for the split second it took to palm Cate's cast-off scrap of paper into her bag.

26

A three-foot-wide chandelier suspended from the frescoed ceiling hung over the breakfast table.

'So, this is how the other half lives,' Natalie joked.

The housekeeper set down a basket of pastries, filling the air with the sweet scent of vanilla.

'*Grazie*, Nunzia,' said Cate. 'I could get used to these breakfasts. I'm a cornflakes and apple girl back home.'

'I'm a grab a bit of toast whilst running out the door kind of girl.' Natalie grinned.

Cate laughed. She seemed lighter that morning, all the cares of yesterday set aside, or else she was wearing some super effective new foundation that Natalie really needed the name of.

'You're looking... rested.'

'I don't know what Nunzia sprayed on my pillow but it smelt divine; I slept like a baby. And Phil messaged me; he's in the airport lounge already, far too early of course but it's a weight off my mind.'

'I'll be excited to meet him now he's finally arriving.'

'Barring engine failure, a volcanic ash cloud or a hijacking.'

'Or an air traffic controllers strike! But, seriously Cate, that's not going to happen; you've had enough bad luck on this trip.'

'And plenty of good. Look at this place.' Cate waved a hand towards a fine marble statue of a magnificent doe and stag. 'And, I don't want to keep going on about it but us becoming friends again, it means a lot to me.'

'And to me. But I'll have to put my professional hat back on when we're filming. So if I start bossing you about, don't take it personally.'

'Okay, but only if you let me take charge today before Phil gets here. It's my last chance to do exactly what I fancy before you and Lucia take over again.'

'So, what are we doing?' Natalie stirred a lump of sugar into her cappuccino, disturbing the pretty leaf design etched onto the surface.

'First stop: Eraldo's workshop. I've had a good look at the suggestions he sent me so I'm ready to commission Phil's watch.'

'You could just send an email.'

'I could but then *you* wouldn't get to see him.'

'*I* don't need to see him.'

'But you want to. Your cheeks have gone as pink as the serving girl in that picture over the fireplace.'

Natalie rubbed the back of her neck. 'I'm a bit warm, that's all.'

'It's not exactly stuffy in here.' Cate surveyed the huge, high-ceilinged room.

Natalie sighed. 'Okay, I like him but what's the point? He lives in Venice, I hardly speak a word of Italian, we've nothing in common...'

'Right now, you're also in Venice, he speaks near-perfect

English, you're both friends with Floella and you're going to have a lot of fun finding out what you do have in common – apart from a tendency to gaze at each other when you think the other one's not looking... If you've finished that coffee, we'll get going. I can't sit here looking at the rest of those pastries.'

Natalie stopped herself reaching for a second. 'You're the boss.'

'I am.' Cate turned to the hovering housekeeper. 'Thank you, Nunzia, *grazie mille*.'

Natalie followed her out of the property's side entrance and round to the walkway. The Grand Canal was busy, a barge loaded with brown cardboard boxes passing one way, the Number One waterbus packed with people going in the other.

Morning in Venice was a sight she could never tire of, the vista before her barely changed since Canaletto had picked up his brushes. It was a shame that almost all his paintings had left the city. Just two remained in the Ca' Rezzonico but the count and countess were proud owners of a series of his sketches displayed in gilded frames on the second-floor landing.

'Shall we walk?' Cate asked. She was wearing a pair of trainers – designer, naturally – and a floaty dress more suited to strolling than the stiff pencil skirt of the day before.

'Sure.' Natalie was equally comfortable in denim shorts, knowing Lucia's camera crew wouldn't be following them. Now they were friends, it didn't bother her as much that her stubbier legs couldn't compete with Cate's honeyed limbs but if she'd known they'd be heading for Eraldo's workshop, she would have done more than slick on a bit of mascara and run a comb through her hair.

Cate strode on. 'I feel like I'm getting to know this city, at least a little bit.'

'Same here.' Learning to navigate her way from A to B without peering at an app on her phone gave Natalie a chance to spot numerous little gems: the lion of St Mark's on a lintel over a door, a curvy flourish carved into an old stone well, a plaque of St George slaying his dragon high up on a wall. And it was fun to people-watch, trying to pick out the native Venetians from amongst a population swelled by the summer crowds.

Neither of them referred to their school trip as they crossed the Accademia Bridge, though Natalie knew the night of the masked ball must be playing on Cate's mind the way it was on hers.

A few minutes later, an intoxicating mix of floral scents told her they'd reached the perfumery. In a few moments, she would see Eraldo again.

'Wait a moment!' Natalie took her powder compact from her handbag and dabbed her shiny nose, ignoring Cate's smirk.

'Ooh, they do perfume-making courses here; I didn't notice that before.' Cate read from a notice pinned in the window. 'I took a scented-candle-making workshop once but I've never done anything like this; balancing all those oils is a real skill.'

'That's an idea! Floella did ask me if I could think up some sort of activity or challenge for you and Phil to try.' She didn't mention she'd squashed Flo's suggestion of mask making straight off the bat.

'It's a tiny place, though.' Cate peered through the window.

'You're right. There's no way we could get a camera crew in there. And I think Lucia's gone ahead and arranged a traditional Venetian cooking class already.'

'I'm not sure Phil will be keen on that. He can't boil an egg without burning the pan and turning the air blue.'

'Apart from the swearing, that sounds ideal. The viewers

want to see that perfect people aren't naturally good at everything.'

'Perfect people?'

'People who are living lifestyles our audience can only dream of.'

'I guess that *is* me. Sometimes, when I wake up, I have to pinch myself.'

'At least you appreciate what you've got. Most don't.'

'I do. I don't know how I got this lucky.'

'*Buongiorno!*' A booming voice made them both jump.

'*Buongiorno*, Pietro!' Natalie shouted back.

The mask maker beckoned from the doorway of his shop. Natalie and Cate crossed over the humpbacked bridge.

'Come in. I suppose you are here to see Eraldo, not to purchase one of my beautiful creations.'

'I am afraid so,' Natalie said.

'Oh well.' He rubbed at his beard. 'You are very welcome; please go up.'

'I messaged Eraldo just before we left,' Cate said.

'Good to know he's expecting us.' Natalie headed straight for the spiral staircase, careful not to glance right or left.

'Wait!' Cate's hand was on her shoulder.

'Natalie, Cate, is that you?' Eraldo's voice came from above.

'Yes, it's us; we'll be up in two minutes,' Cate said.

'What's going on?' Natalie turned to see Cate holding a golden mask in front of her face. Her eyes gleamed through the oval slits. She replaced it on a shallow display shelf.

'Or how about this?' Cate held up another, all purple glitter and shocking-pink feathers. 'Try it.'

'Okay, boss.' Natalie carefully secured the elastic around her head.

'Look in the big mirror, over there,' Cate commanded.

The gilt-framed glass hung over the far wall above the white *bauta* masks and the glass-topped drawers where the Plague-doctor masks lived.

'No, I can't. I can't go near them.' Natalie snatched off the mask.

'Just a few steps nearer; we're going to count to ten.'

'No.'

'I'm in charge today. Ten seconds, that's all, I promise.'

Natalie swallowed hard. 'Okay.'

'You're not allowed to close your eyes. Now count backwards slowly.'

Natalie clenched her fists. 'Ten, nine, eight…' The shop lights seemed brighter, mesmerising her, as though she were staring into the candles on a birthday cake, the aroma from Pietro's small cup of espresso like plunging her nose into a bag of ground coffee. 'Seven, six, five, four…'

'Three, two, one. Well done. Now we climb the stairs.'

Natalie needed no encouragement, gripping the metal handrail with her now sweaty hands. 'What the heck was all that about?'

'Desensitisation. It's a good way of tackling phobias,' Cate said, briskly bounding up the stairs behind her. 'Max had to see a therapist once; he had a terrible fear of spiders.'

'Hello, Natalie, Cate.' Eraldo greeted them both with kisses. 'What is all this about spiders?'

Cate looked at her.

'I have… a fear of those Plague-doctor masks. Cate thinks it's a phobia like a fear of spiders.'

'Of those masks? That is why you were terrified? Why you left so suddenly the first time you were here?'

'Yes, it's silly, I know...'

'Not at all. Those masks would have struck fear into the hearts of the very people the Plague doctors were trying to help but you know they have no power, they cannot hurt you.'

Natalie stiffened, but she understood he was clumsily trying to reassure her, not belittle her.

'But I am glad that is the reason you scarpered,' Eraldo continued. 'I thought it was something that I said or perhaps you found my company so dull, you could not wait to get away from me.'

'Not at all. But still, you invited me out for the evening when Cate went to the opera.'

'It was the least I could do for a friend of Floella.'

So, he had invited her out of politeness. The sensation of an invisible thread pulling them closer as they'd shared *cicchetti* under a darkening sky had been nothing more than the magic of Venice bewitching her as it had bewitched thousands before. She had to forget her foolish imaginings. She hadn't come here to progress a relationship that hadn't even begun; she was here for Cate, who was already sifting through the pile of drawings Eraldo had fanned out across the coffee table.

'Do sit down, Natalie,' Cate said.

'Coffee?' Eraldo said. 'It will concentrate our minds for the important decisions.'

'Please,' Cate said.

Natalie nodded. 'Yes, thanks.'

'Sit, relax, I will attend to the drinks.'

He was back with a tray of cups in a matter of minutes.

'Now, Cate, tell me about this commission... that is, if you have not changed your mind.'

Natalie hadn't realised how many details had to be considered when rebuilding and reconfiguring an old watch but the ensuing conversation was anything but dull. Eraldo's enthusiasm was contagious, his voice full of passion. And Cate, surprisingly, had such an innate understanding of style and colour, it seemed a pity that her role in her husband's company seemed limited to administration and charming the clients.

The coffee had long gone cold by the time the discussion wrapped up.

Eraldo tied the cords that closed his leather-bound notebook. 'So, everything is decided.'

'The deposit?' Cate was reaching for her bag.

'Ah, no, not for friends. Besides, I am so happy with our proposal if you do not purchase the finished watch, I may be tempted to keep it for myself. Except – oh, I quite forgot – the engraving on the back: have you decided what you would like? Your husband's birthday or the date you were married, perhaps?'

'Yes, I have decided. The day I first set eyes on Phil; that will make him smile.'

'How romantic.' Eraldo re-opened his notebook. 'Write it here for me so there can be no mistake.'

Cate added a date in her neat hand.

'That can't be right, that's...' Natalie began.

'When we were on the school trip,' Cate cut in. 'At the Accademia gallery.'

'But... I don't remember you meeting anyone there.' A horrible suspicion was beginning to form.

'I didn't meet Phil exactly. We didn't actually speak... Oh, I know it sounds crazy but when I saw him, I just knew...' A big smile lit up Cate's face. 'I just felt that this was the boy I was going to marry. I was buzzing; I couldn't wait to tell you. I sneaked looks at him whenever I could but I couldn't make it too obvious; I didn't want Julie Paine to notice and make everyone laugh at me, so I tried to concentrate on the paintings but then I turned around and he was gone, separated from the rest of his group. I sneaked off to try and find him.'

Natalie knew what was coming. But she was wrong; she had to be.

'I found him soon enough, talking to you. I know how childish this sounds but I was so upset. That's why I flounced off. I hated you that day; I was so jealous of you. I couldn't bear to talk to you in case you told me that you liked him or he liked you. And when Julie started being snide, it was so easy to gang up on you. Pathetic, wasn't I! When I found out that the boys' school were going to be at the same party as us, I couldn't wait but I was far too cowardly to go up and talk to any of those boys with all Julie's mates looking. When we met four years later at Durham, it's no wonder he couldn't remember me!'

'And yet, here you are, married. A beautiful story,' Eraldo said.

'So, Phil was one of those boys from that posh school?' Natalie tried to keep her voice steady. Deep down, she'd known the moment she'd zoomed in on the photo of Cate and Phil's son holding his sporting trophy.

'Yes, they seemed such an arrogant bunch but I could tell straight away that Phil was different from the others. There was something about him; he looked more approachable, less sure of himself, perhaps because he was a scholarship boy. And he was wearing these really cool trainers,' Cate blathered on.

'With bright-yellow laces.' Natalie had to check, had to be sure.

'How on earth do you remember that? He really must have made an impression. Perhaps I was right to be jealous of you!' Cate laughed.

'It's just one of those odd things that sticks in your mind,'

Natalie said. Like the swish of a cape, a mask pressed up against a face, the stench of raw fear. She felt the bile rise in her throat. Cate was married to the boy in the alley, but this time, Natalie couldn't run. In a few hours, Phil would be arriving at the palazzo.

27

'We could have stayed longer; I didn't want to tear you away from Eraldo,' Cate said.

'I didn't want us to be late; you booked timed tickets.' Natalie tried not to look at Cate as they strolled along the *fondamenta*.

'I'm glad we're squeezing in Peggy Guggenheim's collection before Phil arrives; modern art isn't really his thing. He always says he'd rather look at a thousand Madonnas than some faceless woman or surrealist nightmare!' Cate laughed.

'*Luxe Life Swap*'s viewers aren't keen on anything later than the nineteenth century, at least that's what the focus groups tell us.' As long as Natalie fixed her mind on her job, she'd be okay. She'd been handed a once-in-a-lifetime opportunity. She couldn't let Cate's revelations about Phil derail her even though the thought of meeting him made her stomach heave. In less than a fortnight, she'd be back home. And she'd never have to see Venice or Cate ever again.

'That must be the entrance to the gallery down there:

where there's a bit of a queue. I know this is going to be amazing… Are you okay, Natalie? You seem a bit quiet.'

'I'm fine.'

'I can't wait to see the Kandinsky and Picasso, and of course there's lots of Jackson Pollock too. I read that Peggy was collecting a painting a day at one point. Can you imagine!' Cate walked on briskly, obviously energised by the thought of immersing herself in paint-dripped canvases and depictions of two-headed women.

Cate showed the ticket codes to a woman at the entrance. 'I'd like to go round the sculpture garden first, if that's okay with you.'

'Sure.' Natalie followed, thankful they would be out in the fresh air. Somehow, it felt easier to cope outdoors than cooped up inside with her erstwhile friend, who was already exclaiming over a red, metal sculpture.

'Oh, isn't it fun doing things together! I almost wish we had another day before Phil arrives even though I miss him so badly. I know he's going to love the palazzo; it's like something out of a fairy tale. Phil will just adore the Red Room, and the ancestors' portraits on the landing will blow him away.'

Every mention of Phil's name went through Natalie like the squeal of a dentist's drill. She wandered past the pagoda to the far wall, pretending to examine two rectangular plaques fixed to the bricks whilst sending an upbeat reply to Floella's latest anxious message.

'Peggy's ashes are buried here.' Cate's voice was soft. Natalie could feel her warm breath on her ear, caught a waft of her floral perfume. 'And look, on that other plaque, those are the names of all Peggy's dogs. She had these cute, silky Lhasa apsos she took everywhere with her. White Angel and Madam

Butterfly – they're pretty names! And Foglia, she didn't live long, poor little thing! How sad. I can't imagine losing dear Ted.' Cate sniffed. 'Sorry, sometimes I can be so sentimental. Phil says—'

'Let's go into the main gallery,' Natalie said quickly.

'Of course. I don't know why I'm babbling on when there's so much amazing art to look at.'

'I know you want to see the Kandinsky.' Natalie followed Cate inside, trying to keep a distance between them. She feigned a particular interest in a mesmerising, black and white mobile flanked by two Picassos until Cate wandered away down one of the corridors. But her wished-for solitude didn't last long. Cate was soon back, uttering exclamations of delight at every painting and regaling Natalie with snippets she'd apparently gleaned on a history of art course she'd once taken.

'Look at the Andy Warhol,' Cate said. 'Evan – that's Phil's best friend – has a marvellous Warhol, one of his screen prints of Marilyn Monroe. His wife Lucy's father was quite a collector. I always admire it when we go round for supper. Phil says...'

Natalie tried to switch off. Her neck and shoulders felt stiff and heavy. Glancing down, she noticed her fists were clenched. She put her hand to her forehead; it felt all scrunched up like discarded wrapping paper.

'What's wrong?' Cate gently touched her arm.

'Get off me!'

Cate snatched her hand away as if she'd touched a hot pan. Her eyes clouded with confusion.

'Sorry, you made me jump.' Natalie had to act normally. Had to get through the day.

'Something's wrong. I know you, Nat. Look, it's getting busy in here. Let's go out to the terrace; you probably need some air.'

Natalie let herself be led out to the terrace down the steps past a bronze statue of a naked man astride a horse. A very naked man.

'*L'angelo della città* – the Angel of the City. I'd heard this was here, but I didn't imagine he'd look *quite* so pleased to see us!' Cate laughed.

They took the last few steps onto the canal front terrace where Peggy Guggenheim had thrown her legendary parties. Turquoise and white poles marked the entrance where the eccentric gallery owner had once moored her private gondola.

'Peggy knew anyone and everyone in the art world. Imagine the conversations!' Cate said. 'And some of her parties were so extravagant, wild and decadent. It's said that she staged a re-enactment of the sinking of the *Titanic*, jumping naked into the Grand Canal with a whole orchestra following! Phil and I watched a programme about her once; well, I watched it, I think Phil was playing on his phone.'

Natalie stared down into the canal. She was almost tempted to follow Peggy's wild stunt – without the nudity – and jump in. If only the water wasn't so cold and dank. And knowing her luck, she'd be sure to be arrested or knocked unconscious by the ill-placed oar of a passing gondolier.

Cate pulled out her phone. 'No messages – phew! Even now, I'm half-expecting Phil to be delayed by some last-minute problem but it looks like he's taken off on time. I can't believe we'll soon be together in this amazing place. It's incredible… unique.' She waved a hand towards the canal. 'I'm sure Phil's going to be over the moon at being back here. That school trip changed his life. He was always interested in art but when Evan took him to see an oar-making workshop, he was so inspired, it made him even more determined to train as a craftsman. And of course, it was Evan's uncle Seb who first employed him.'

Natalie tried to block out Cate's voice; she studied the row of carved lions' heads positioned low on the museum's façade as though ready to lap the canal's green waters.

'Nat, you really don't look well. Let's go to the café, sit down, get you a cup of tea.'

'Okay.'

No pot of tea could solve her problems but she followed Cate back through the museum to the paved area on the other side of the sculpture garden where cheerful yellow and white chairs flanked small tables for two. Natalie ordered tea for them both. Cate leant back in her seat, her expression serene, her limbs as relaxed as a ragdoll's; it was impossible that she could know her husband's dirty little secret.

'There, that's better. Maybe put some sugar in it.' Cate pushed a small dish of colourful paper sachets towards her.

'No, thanks.' Natalie squished her teabag against the side of the metal pot, trying to coax some flavour into the not quite hot enough water. The throbbing in her head was increasing.

'I don't normally take sugar either but sugary tea works wonders when you're stressed. Phil's mother always says...'

'Just stop!' Natalie hadn't meant to say the words out loud.

'Stop what? Please tell me what's wrong. I want to help, whatever it is.'

'It's nothing.'

'You're grinding your teeth.'

'Am I?' She poured out her tea; she couldn't drink and teeth grind simultaneously. Nor respond to Cate's insistent questioning.

'What's wrong? I can't have a friend who won't talk to me. It's bad enough having a husband who bottles things up.'

'Please,' Natalie said quietly. 'Please. Don't. Keep. Talking. About. Phil.'

Cate's hand flew to her mouth. 'Oh, no. I didn't think. I can't imagine how hard it must be being single at nearly forty when everyone around you seems to be married with kids.'

'I'm perfectly happy being single, thank you very much. I'd rather be single than with the wrong man.'

'What's that supposed to mean?'

'Nothing.' Natalie turned her head towards the waitress clearing cups away from the adjoining table. 'It was just an observation... about people in general.'

'No, it wasn't. You meant something about me and Phil. Don't try and wiggle out of it; I know you too well.'

'It was nothing, honestly. Well, nothing to do with you.'

'Well, something's upset you. Oh, I know what it is. How stupid of me! I shouldn't have mentioned our school trip, not after knowing what happened to you.'

'Don't worry about it,' Natalie mumbled. She ripped open a packet of sugar and poured it into her tea, took a sip and pulled a face. She signalled for the bill. 'Let's go. You'll want a bit of time to relax and freshen up before Phil gets here. Lucia and I won't meet you until eight tonight when we'll film you together at the palazzo; we'll use that as part of the first episode, I expect.'

Tonight, meeting Phil: she didn't know how she was going to get through it. But she had to do it. For her career. And for Floella. But most of all, she wasn't going to give Phil the satisfaction of seeing her rattled. She was determined to give him the impression she hadn't given him a moment's thought since she'd scarpered that night.

She scraped back her chair. Cate didn't move.

'Sit down. We're not going anywhere. Not yet. There's something wrong, something to do with Phil. I know you only spoke to him for a few minutes on that school trip – don't tell me you fell for him too?'

'Of course not. Look, Cate, stop pushing it. I'm sorry I'm not my usual chirpy self but I'm not going to tell you why. I don't see why I should and I can't tell you anyway.'

'Whatever it is, I'll understand. I won't let it destroy our friendship. Nothing's going to change, I promise you.'

'Everything's already changed. And it's nothing to do with you. This is all about me.'

'Something went on between you and Phil.' Cate's voice trembled.

'Shut up! Don't make me say something I'll regret.'

Cate grabbed her by the arm. 'Whatever happened between you and Phil back then, it can't hurt me now but I have a right to know. I'm his wife. And you're my best friend. If you don't tell me, I'll be forever wondering what went on. Tell me, whatever it is.'

Natalie couldn't meet her eyes. 'Okay, but don't say I didn't warn you... Phil isn't the man you think he is. Phil was the boy who attacked me.'

Cate's mouth dropped open. She stared at Natalie. Nat was lying; she knew she was. But why? Cate was sure she'd done nothing to upset her since she'd arrived in Venice. The only possible explanation was that her old friend still harboured a bitter grievance from their school days. Wasn't it enough for her to know that her cruel revelations about Cate's mother had irreparably wrecked Cate's relationship with her dad and destroyed her happy childhood? Evidently not. Natalie's lust for revenge still wasn't satisfied. Now she wanted to break up Cate's happy marriage. How bitter and twisted was she? If Cate wasn't so angry, she could almost feel sorry for the pathetic creature.

Cate gave a bitter little laugh. 'What is it they say, Natalie? Revenge is a dish best served cold? You still haven't forgiven me for not believing you that night, have you? You didn't want to be friends again, did you? How stupid I was to think that you did.' Cate's voice dropped to a whisper. 'Now you want to have your revenge by telling these lies, trying to destroy my marriage. Because I know... I *know* that Phil would never ever do something like that.'

'You're wrong. It was Phil in that alleyway, even if you don't want to believe me. But I'm sorry, I shouldn't have said anything. I did want to be your friend again but finding out who Phil is has brought all the horror back. It was him. Ask him, see how he reacts, if you dare.'

'I wouldn't dream of accusing Phil of something I know he'd never do. And who do you think I'd believe – the father of my children or a jealous ex-friend who's harboured a grudge for twenty-five years? You're pathetic, Natalie; I feel sorry for you. You can stick your fake friendship and your stupid TV show. Don't bother turning up with the film crew later. Phil and I will stay at the palazzo tonight. We'll catch a flight home tomorrow.'

Natalie fell back into her seat as though she'd been knocked off her feet by a rogue wave. 'You can't just go. Everything's set up... You've signed a contract.'

'Sue me.' Cate strode away.

'Cate!' Natalie jumped up, catching her shoulder bag strap on the handle of her chair. The waitress appeared by her side the same instant, brandishing a card reader; they hadn't paid for the drinks. Natalie threw down a note; this was no time to wait for a receipt. Untangling herself, she hurried through the garden exit out over a little bridge and into a courtyard. Cate's blonde hair and floaty dress were nowhere to be seen.

A sign on the wall pointed to the vaporetto station but she knew Cate would have had more sense than to go that way knowing that Natalie would catch her up if the Number One did not come immediately. Ignoring the dingy passageway that led off the courtyard, Natalie wandered around the corner back onto the *fondamenta*.

She scanned both sides of the narrow canal. No one around but the straggly queue outside the gallery. Natalie buried her head in her hands. She'd lost the star of *Luxe Life Swap*'s new series. Cate had gone.

Natalie's heart raced; her palms were sweating. She half felt she might be sick right there in the canal. How could she possibly break the news to Floella? Flo had worked so hard to build her business against the odds; she'd made such sacrifices. Natalie should have kept her mouth shut, gritted her teeth and got through the filming. Her ordeal would only last a few days. Flo-Go Productions was Floella's life. Everything was riding on the success of *Luxe Life Swap*; Flo's team had pulled out all the stops. In one afternoon, Natalie had blown the whole thing sky-high.

28

Cate shrank back against the narrow passageway. Natalie hadn't seen her; she let out a breath. She watched her old friend disappear back in the direction of the *fondamenta* from where they'd entered the gallery. She waited another minute. Natalie did not return.

Cate knew she should head back to the palazzo and make a start on packing her bags but she wasn't yet ready for Nunzia's polite enquiries, and the thought of soaking in her ludicrously large bath before Phil arrived no longer promised to be the relaxing experience she'd envisaged. Instead, she followed the signs to the vaporetto stop, looking over her shoulder every few yards like a second-rate spy in a film noir – all she needed was an upturned collar and a cigarette. To her surprise, the signs led her down a narrow passageway from which she emerged onto a small bridge. Ahead of her rose the great dome of Santa Maria della Salute. On an impulse, she climbed the steps and slipped through the entrance door. The scent of the old church instantly calmed her, like the smell of books in the care home's library.

There must have been several dozen tourists inside, eyes raised to the altar, but they barely disturbed the peace of the vast interior. She wandered in and out of the side chapels, eyes straying over the paintings. She stood for a while in front of Titian's *Descent of the Holy Ghost*, marvelling at the rays of light emanating from the white dove, the apostles falling back in alarm. There wasn't enough time to linger over Tintoretto's *Wedding Feast at Cana*; she'd have to come back another day. Except she wouldn't. Tomorrow, she'd sweep up her bewildered husband and head back home without seeing half of the places she wanted to. Thanks to Natalie, she'd never return to Venice now, never share the fizz of a peach bellini at Harry's Bar with Phil, never lean back against the crimson leather seats of a gondola steered by a man in a stripy top singing 'O Sole Mio'.

An idea flicked across her consciousness. Quitting the TV show didn't mean she had to leave Venice. She and Phil could move into the Hotel Danieli or The Gritti Palace for a short break. It would cost a fortune but she deserved a treat after the emotional upheaval of the last few days and it would solve the problem of where to stay whilst the old vicarage was still occupied by the Italian count and his wife. She shelved the idea as quickly as it came. Thanks to Nat's allegations, even a stay in five-star luxury would be tainted. Nat wasn't telling the truth, yet a tiny kernel of doubt remained lodged in Cate's brain like the repetitive tune of an irritatingly catchy pop song. How many times had she switched on the television or opened a newspaper to see a wife or mother accompanying an abuser or murderer to court, convinced beyond a shadow of a doubt that he was a good, kind, loving guy, only for their heart to be broken into a thousand pieces when the truth came out?

Cate could trace Phil's tiny signals of discomfort – the fiddling with his belt loops, the nearly imperceptible foot jiggling, the flashes of impatience – back to the day the TV people sent the email revealing that Venice was to be their destination. And she didn't believe for one moment that a last-minute work crisis had prevented him from boarding their original flight. Something connected to this city had disturbed his peace of mind and however infinitesimally small the chances were that Phil was guilty of such a sordid act, Cate couldn't sit outside Caffè Florian gazing into his eyes whilst the orchestra played as if Nat's words had never been uttered.

Cate couldn't flee Venice and her old school friend, however much she wanted to jump on a plane. She needed to see Phil's reaction the moment he and Natalie came face to face.

* * *

Natalie watched the small queue shuffle its way into the Guggenheim Collection. Phil's plane would be touching down in not much more than an hour. She should be contacting Lucia, not wandering along a canal side in the back streets of Dorsoduro too cowardly to face the inevitable phone call with Floella that would follow. She had no one she could ask for advice, nowhere to turn. Her parents knew nothing about the world of television and she was reluctant to worry them. The motley collection of ex-colleagues and vague acquaintants who passed for friends wouldn't care enough. There was only one friend she'd ever truly confided in: Cate, the best friend she'd lost and won and lost again.

She carried on down the *fondamenta* in the direction of Eraldo's workshop. Her heart gave a little skip at the thought of him, dark head bent over his workbench, beavering away up there. She stopped outside Pietro's window. He'd changed the display again. A riot of gold, shocking-pink, royal-blue and white masks glittered enticingly. She'd probably never go inside and up the spiral staircase again. When she left Venice, she'd be leaving Eraldo for good. Tears pricked her eyes. She couldn't understand why she felt so emotional about a man she'd only met a handful of times.

* * *

Nunzia had pressed Cate's silk shirt dress. At least she'd look in control tonight even though her insides were churning as though a fairground's worth of bumper cars were hurtling round in there. Breathing slowly, trying to remember everything she'd read about the power of mindfulness, she began brushing her hair, focusing on the sensations of every stroke. Her colourist had done a wonderful job, but what did that matter now?

If Dad hadn't kept her and Mum apart for so long, things would have been so different. After Nat's revelations in the dormitory, Cate had confronted him the moment she'd walked through the front door. Dad had admitted everything. Her mother had gone travelling like he'd said but then she'd returned to Venice. For more than a decade, he had known exactly where she was. He hadn't told her where to find Mum; he'd deprived her of a mother's love, kept the two of them apart.

She'd cried and raged, spent her evenings shut in her room, headphones blocking out the sound of the telly blaring from the lounge. She'd shunned their Saturday-morning trips to Annie's café for a hot chocolate, buried her head in her schoolbooks and danced for joy the day she got a place at Durham University more than two hundred miles away.

She'd taken the train up north, not letting Dad drive her there, pressing her arms to her sides when he went to hug her goodbye. In Durham, she'd reinvented herself as Cate. She'd persuaded herself she wasn't lonely, batting away memories of Dad holding the back of her bicycle and cheering when she'd pedalled off all by herself, of him bringing her chicken Cup-a-Soup in bed when she'd felt unwell. Then one day in the college bar, she saw the boy she'd fallen for all those years before. The one Natalie had been talking to by the paintings of the Madonna in the Accademia gallery.

Phil hadn't remembered Cate at all but by halfway through her second year – and his last – he'd proposed. It was a quick registry-office wedding so no one needed to give her away. Until Dad had fallen ill, she'd only seen him two or three times a year. Phil, Oli and Max were all the family she needed. They were her world. But once again, Nat's words threatened to smash it to smithereens.

A ringtone blasted from her handbag. She threw down her hairbrush and grabbed her phone. Without looking, she knew it would be Phil telling her he'd got through security and was waiting to collect his bags.

'Hi, darling!' She could hear the shake in her voice.

'Mum?'

'Max? Is everything okay?' Max only sent messages and memes. Like most eleven-year-old boys, he seemed astonished that anyone used their all-singing, all-dancing smartphones for making actual calls.

'Yeah, 'course it is.'

Cate knew it wasn't. She'd have to tread slowly, keep Max on the phone until he worked up the courage to tell her what was bothering him.

'How's cricket?' Always a safe subject.

'Great.' His voice perked up. 'We beat Harrow by sixty-three runs yesterday.'

'How many did you score?'

'Thirty-four, but Piers and Omar were really good too.'

'That's wonderful, darling. What did Nigel – I mean Mr Benn – say?'

'He was pleased, he said he was ever so proud... but he wasn't there. He's taking some time off.'

'He's not ill, is he?' She couldn't imagine Hillingdon without Max's House Master, a tall, thin man in corduroy trousers, such a stereotype of the kind, absent-minded teacher, Cate was surprised he didn't have leather patches sewn onto the elbows of his jackets.

'Mr Benn's wife left him. They're getting divorced; she's been having an affair with the school gardener. They say Mr Benn collapsed. He's gone into a clinic.' Her son's words came out in a rush.

'No! I can't believe it!' Vera with her homemade scones and no-nonsense brogues was the last person Cate could imagine as a modern-day Lady Chatterley.

'It's true, Mum. It's not fair, is it? He's such a nice man.' Max's voice wobbled. 'We're all going to be extra well-behaved when he comes back.'

'I'm really sorry, sweetheart. It must seem strange not having Mr Benn around but the doctors will make him better. He'll be back soon, I'm sure.'

A pause.

'Are you worried?' Max seemed to love boarding school just as Oli did but she knew what a steadying, reassuring presence Mr Benn was.

'Mum... I messaged Dad yesterday. He said he was still in England, but you're in Venice. He said he got held up by work then the green protest and that's why he didn't go with you. But... everything is okay with you and Daddy, isn't it? I mean, I know people get divorced and...'

'Oh, darling! You mustn't worry about things like that. Daddy's on his way right now; he told you that, didn't he?'

'Yes... but...'

She pictured him chewing at his nails, the habit she'd given up trying to change.

'Sweetheart, listen to me. I know some people get divorced but that's not going to happen to us. When Daddy and I got married, we made a vow to stay with each other for ever and ever. Life doesn't always go exactly as we expect, sometimes we get a little bit annoyed or frustrated with each other, but whatever life throws at us, good or bad, Daddy and I are going to stick together. I promise you.'

'Promise?' Max's voice was small.

'Promise.'

'Okay... Mum, I've got to go; it's teatime and it's sausages today.'

'Ooh, lucky old you!'

'Yeah, I hope there's second helpings... Got to go. Love you, Mum.'

'Love you...' Cate said but Max had already gone. She pictured him flying down the wide, wooden staircase at Hillingdon, shirt untucked, socks falling down.

Outside the window, barges and gondolas moved unhurriedly down the canal. She realised she was still holding the phone. A text pinged through. Phil had cleared security.

29

'Natalie!'

She turned her head at the sound of Eraldo's voice. Of all the moments he could walk out of the shop, he had to choose this one. The dim, shady entrance dulled his dark eyes but his brows knitted in concern as he came towards her. Her hand went to her damp, dishevelled hair.

'Natalie, are you okay? You look terrible.'

'I bet you say that to all the girls.' She gave a haven't-got-a-care-in-the-world laugh.

'I'm sorry, I did not mean...' He twisted his hands together.

'It's okay, I know. I was just kidding.'

'Kidding, that is joking, yes? But I think perhaps this afternoon, you have nothing to laugh about. Why are you not with Cate? I thought you were to visit the Guggenheim collection together.'

'Yes, we went there together. Everything's just fine.'

'I do not think so... but if you do not wish to tell me, that is okay.'

'It's not that... I don't know...' Her voice cracked. 'I just don't know where to begin. Everything's gone wrong.'

'Ev-err-ree-thing?' The way he drew out the word and half-raised his eyebrows almost made her laugh. 'I have taken a break to have a coffee; why do you not join me? Tell me about this "everything". Let us go to a nice place I know. You do not mind walking?'

'I don't want to keep you from your work. Are you sure you want to go for a coffee? I know you've got a coffee maker upstairs.'

'Yes, and that coffee is okay, I suppose. But sometimes, I want to go out somewhere, have a few words with the barista, sit in a chair, and let someone else bring it to me. I like Da Michele. It's been run by the same family for more than seventy years. My papà and my *nonno* before him used to take me there. And you will see a little more of the real Venice as we walk.'

'I'd like that.'

They walked together in silence in the late-afternoon sun. Despite the unsolvable situation she'd created, she felt her cares temporarily subside as they cut through narrow streets past ancient churches and crossed vast *campi* where groups of young boys straight out of school played competing games of football, balls flying in every direction.

Eraldo stopped by a café's red canopy. The few small tables outside appeared to be occupied but he didn't seem deterred, holding open the door for her. The aroma of coffee and toasted bread filled the small, tiled interior.

'*Salve!*'

'*Salve*, Eraldo. *Un caffè?*' The tattooed barista was already twisting the basket into place.

'For you, Natalie?'

'The same, please.' She glanced through the window; no seats had been vacated, no one looked in a hurry to move.

The barista said something in Italian. Eraldo shook his head.

'What did he say?' Natalie asked.

'He says he can ask that old fellow to move; he and his dog have been hogging that outside corner table for nearly two hours. But I know him; he has no family, so he spends a lot of the day here talking to whoever comes by. We can sit inside instead.'

'I don't want to keep you too long,' Natalie said again. She squeezed into a small corner booth.

'Do not worry, I will let you know if I get bored.' His eyes twinkled. He put their coffees on the table and sat down opposite her. 'Now, tell me.'

'It's Cate's husband, Phil. He's somebody I knew a long time ago.'

'An old boyfriend?'

'Absolutely not!' she snapped so loudly, the barista turned around. 'Sorry... it's just... oh, I don't know. I don't know where to begin.'

Eraldo ran his hand through his hair. 'It is okay. You do not need to tell me. Perhaps we do not know each other so well.'

'Sometimes, it's easier to talk to a stranger.'

'A stranger?' His face clouded. 'I thought perhaps I was a little more than that.'

She fiddled with her teaspoon. 'You are... I just meant someone who can see with fresh eyes.'

His smile returned. 'I hope I can do that.'

Natalie looked into his eyes, warm and sincere. 'It was on our school trip...' she began.

It was easier to tell her story than she thought it would be,

Eraldo gently encouraging her each time she faltered. When she'd finally unburdened herself, he sat quietly for a moment or two before speaking.

'Perhaps it is for the best that Cate is going home. You will not need to see this man who caused you such hurt. It does not seem a good thing now, but perhaps in time, you will be glad.'

'But the show... Floella's always been so good to me.'

'Floella is a kind, good person; I think she will understand. She would not expect you to have to spend time with a man who did this to you.'

'I can't believe he's wrecked my life again. He's destroyed my one chance to present a prime-time show. Floella might forgive me but there won't be another opportunity like this. They'll have to set up the whole Venice sequence again; I expect they'll wait for Mandy to come back now.' Natalie's phone beeped. 'That's bound to be Lucia, confirming this evening's arrangements. I don't know how I'm going to tell her all her work's been for nothing.'

'Answer it; ignoring it will not make things better.' His voice was gentle.

She reached into her bag. 'It's Cate!'

'What does she say?'

She hardly dared read it. But whatever Cate had written couldn't make things any worse.

> Phil is at the airport. Will do filming tonight as planned. See you and Lucia later.

She passed the phone across the table.

'So that solves one problem,' he said. 'But now you must choose. Leave the show or meet Phil, knowing what you know.'

'I'll just have to be professional.' She bit her bottom lip.

Eraldo's hand reached across the table; it closed over hers.

'You are very brave, Natalie. I wish I could do something to help.'

'You already have. Just listening has helped. I've never spoken to anyone about what happened that night, except Cate, and look how that turned out.'

'You did not tell your mum and dad?'

Natalie sighed. 'I couldn't. They were both so excited about the trip. Neither of them had been abroad themselves. It was such a big deal for them... How could I tell them it had all gone wrong?'

Eraldo squeezed the hand he was still holding. 'I wish I could be there when you meet this Phil but I fear it would look very strange.'

Natalie sipped the coffee she'd so far ignored. 'I wish you could too but this is something I need to do alone.'

'I wish you luck. And afterwards, you will join me for dinner, I hope. You have eaten risotto in Venice already?'

'Yes, of course.'

'Let me take you to La Gallina Verde. Whatever risotto you have eaten, I guarantee tonight's will be even better.' He smacked his lips.

'Thank you, *grazie*! It will be something to look forward to.' But she knew that when she came face to face with Phil, the thought of devouring a fragrant heap of glistening grains of rice would be the last thing on her mind.

* * *

Cate sprayed on a little more perfume. Chanel No. 5 had been her go-to for decades. It wasn't the most original choice but even as a twenty-something, it had made her feel grown-up, sophisticated, ready to take on the world. But it would need more than a spritz of scent for her to feel confident that she could cope with whatever the evening threw at her.

She'd know from the expression on Phil's face if he was guilty. And if he was then nothing would ever be the same again; all her cherished memories would be tainted. She wouldn't ask him for a divorce, for Oli and Max's sake, but she'd insist on separate bedrooms. They'd live parallel lives in their once happy home, drifting on in a marriage of convenience until both boys were old enough to head to university.

She stared into the mirror. *Please let there be some other reason for Phil's odd behaviour.* Perhaps meddling Lucy had hit the nail on the head with her suggestion that he was playing away. She almost wished Lucy was right. An ill-advised affair between Phil and their neighbour Kiran would be a hundred times less distressing than finding out the father of her children was responsible for the attack on Nat.

She opened a blue, velvet box lying on the dressing table and took out her diamond pendant, a gift Phil had chosen for her last birthday. It took several attempts to do up the catch; it usually fastened so easily.

She checked her watch for what felt like the hundredth time. Below the floorboards, she heard the scraping of a chair. The film crew were getting into place to capture the moment when she and Phil were reunited. Judging by the enthusiasm with which Lucia had greeted her an hour before, Natalie had dropped no hint of the slightest disruption to the smooth running of *Luxe Life*'s schedule. Cate would put on her widest smile, give the audience what they wanted to see: two wealthy, privileged people, living their best lives and still so in love.

Outside, the canal was bathed in golden light; the sun was starting to set. A private water taxi was approaching the palazzo. She knew even before it turned towards the waterfront entrance that Phil and some of the camera crew were aboard. Taking a deep breath, she opened the bedroom door, began descending the wide steps to the *piano nobile*. She opened the door to the Red Room. Greeting Lucia, and Natalie – who avoided her eyes – she perched on the edge of a crimson couch.

Voices in the hallway. The hefty wooden door swung open. Phil, smart in an ivory linen suit, strolled in. She rushed towards him.

'Cate, I've missed you so much.' He wrapped his arms around her. She buried her face in his neck, the same old familiar scent.

'I've missed you too.' She turned to the camera, all smiles. 'Darling, can you believe it? I told you the new presenter was someone I'd been to school with but Natalie was actually on that school trip to Venice where we first met.'

'Small world! Pleased to meet you, Natalie.' Phil held out his hand.

Natalie shook it. 'Small world, indeed.'

Cate looked into the eyes of the man she loved, dreading what she might find there.

30

The director stood by the chaise longue. 'Three, two, one.'

Cate and Phil clinked glasses on cue. Tiny bubbles rose to the surface of their drinks, sparkling in the soft light from the antique wall sconces.

The Prosecco bottle stood on a low, glass-topped coffee table with lion's paws for feet, its label turned towards the camera. The exclusive vineyard, located just a few kilometres north of where they were sitting, had paid handsomely for the subtle product placement.

'To our new Venetian adventure,' Cate said. Her face was painstakingly made up, her pink dress chosen to contrast prettily with the room's red hues, a diamond necklace nestled in her gently tanned cleavage. She was no longer the grim-faced, angry individual who'd stormed off that afternoon.

Phil gazed adoringly at his wife. 'Our new adventure and all our other adventures to come.'

Cate smiled. None but the most discerning viewer would spot the slight stiffness around her jaw.

'Well done! That is the end of our filming for tonight,' Lucia said. 'We have an early start tomorrow morning. The most prestigious glass factory on Murano will be giving you a private demonstration of glass blowing.'

'How early?' Phil put the back of his hand to his mouth, stifling a yawn.

Lucia opened the folder she clutched to her chest like a newborn baby. 'A private water taxi will collect you at six thirty. That is why I have arranged for the count's personal cook to create a meal for the two of you here tonight. It will be less tiring for you than going out. I know it is not a long flight from London, Phil, but travel can be exhausting.'

'Giovanni used to work at the Hotel Cipriani,' Natalie added. 'He's a marvellous chef.'

'I am so happy to be sharing a meal with my wife, I wouldn't care less if it was beans on toast.' Phil turned to Cate. 'You don't know how I've missed you.'

'Me too.' Cate looked rather bashful, as though she wasn't used to her husband being so effusive.

'Well, it's been lovely to meet you again, Phil. I'll leave you to enjoy your meal, which I promise you is not beans on toast.' Natalie picked up her bag. The crew were packing up, careful to lift their equipment to save scratching the glossy floor.

Phil stood up. 'It's been lovely to meet you too. Or should I say, meet you again. I'm sorry I don't remember speaking to you in the art gallery but I do remember trying to escape my raucous classmates! It must be fate, you and Cate meeting again like this. It's going to make our stay even better.' He stepped forward and planted a kiss on both Natalie's cheeks.

Natalie stood frozen, arms pressed to her side. 'Goodnight. I'll see you tomorrow.'

'I'll look forward to it.' His smile reached his eyes, warm and friendly. Natalie couldn't detect a trace of guilt.

'Goodnight, Natalie.' Cate's cheek brushed hers lightly, both women kissing the air.

'You go ahead, Natalie; do not wait for me,' Lucia said.

Natalie didn't need to be told twice. Stepping out into the dark street, getting away from Phil and Cate, was like casting off a heavy, itchy sweater on a warm, spring day.

A familiar figure was walking towards her. Eraldo! Without thinking, she broke into a run.

'Eraldo! I thought you were meeting me at the osteria.'

'I could not sit there, waiting. I was worried about you. What was it like meeting that man, Phil?' He kissed her twice, his faint stubble rough against her cheek. How good he smelt. She wished she could fling her arms around him, lose herself in a comforting embrace.

'It was hard, really hard. But it was really strange too. If I didn't know what he'd done, I would have said he's the nicest guy I could hope to meet.'

'Perhaps that is why Cate finds your story so hard to believe... Shall we go to La Gallina Verde, if you have not lost your appetite?'

'For risotto? Never!'

They set off through the back streets, her arms swinging loosely by her side, free of the tension she'd been holding inside for hours.

'Careful!' He steered her around a dropped ice-cream, a pink slick spreading across the paving.

'Thanks! I didn't spot that.'

'I expect you are still thinking about this Phil.' He took her hand in his. 'It is not far to walk now.'

'Good,' she said automatically, though she'd be happy to tackle the entire length of the Grand Canal in a pair of high heels if he kept hold of her hand.

A metal sign in the shape of a hen told her the osteria was ahead of them. The narrow *calle*, lit only by the lights from the row of eating places, wasn't wide enough for outside tables, but the view through the osteria's small window looked cosy and inviting.

'You are happy to eat here?' He indicated a menu propped open amongst a selection of old musical instruments displayed in the window. 'The owner's grandfather was a musician before he opened this place after losing an arm in the war.'

'How awful.'

'The orchestra's loss was the city's gain. He could create far better dishes with one hand than most of his rivals could with two. His son had a talent for both music and cooking and luckily, he chose to continue with this place and his grandson has followed him.'

'It looks perfect.'

Eraldo pushed open the door. A tall woman in a short-sleeved, black dress covering a prominent baby bump ushered them to a table, leaving them with a couple of menus whilst she went to fetch a bottle of water.

'She is married to the original owner's grandson,' Eraldo explained. 'Perhaps the child she is carrying will continue the family tradition.'

The woman smiled, obviously catching his meaning. She placed a blue, glass bottle on the wooden table.

'Some wine, Natalie?'

'You choose.' She'd been half-tempted to clear out the hotel mini bar before meeting Phil, but the fear of saying something to Cate that would destroy their tentative truce had prevented her from sampling even a small Peroni.

Eraldo ordered their wine without fuss.

'I recommend the seafood risotto to start: the house speciality,' the waitress said.

'That sounds good; I'll have that,' Natalie said.

'For both of us.'

'And today's special.' The waitress nodded towards the blackboard. 'It is a fish from the lagoon: very good,' she added for Natalie's benefit.

'Perfect, I'll have that too.' Natalie felt her shoulders relax. It was good to sit back and chill whilst someone else made the decisions.

'The same. A side of polenta too, to share.'

'How was your day?' she asked, content to let Eraldo talk until the waitress returned carrying their wine chilling in a bucket. The woman uncorked the bottle with a flourish and poured a little for Eraldo to taste.

'*Perfetto, grazie!*' He turned to Natalie. 'This will go beautifully with the risotto. They use saffron in that dish. Venice has a long tradition of using exotic spices; it was one of the trades that made the republic rich.'

'You're very proud of your city, aren't you? Why did you choose to go and study in London?'

'I was young.' He gave a wry smile. 'Venice seemed small, insignificant compared to London. I imagined it to be the most exciting city in the world.'

'And was it?'

'For a while! Especially when I met Floella and her friends. We were one big gang, working hard all week but at weekends – what parties we had! Sometimes, we would all pile into someone's little car and head for the coast. Brighton – it was not, how you say, an exotic, white-sands beach but it was fun.'

'You didn't want to stay?'

'I missed Venice but when I came back for Christmas one

year, I found that many of my friends had moved away to other towns. The population here is declining, forced out by the number of tourists renting properties that would otherwise be people's homes. The rents for shops are rising, pushing out the Venetian artisans as foreign investors move in. They say one day, there will be no Venetians; the city will be one big theme park: an Italian Disneyland.'

'That would be terrible.'

'I did not want to be one of the people who left, abandoning my city to such a fate. I knew then that when I had finished my course, I had to return here. And I do not regret that. How could I, with food like this.' He laughed.

She scooped up a forkful of the risotto which had just arrived, bringing the scent of the sea to their small table. 'This is so good.'

'The secret is cooking the rice just so. Creamy yet the centre of each grain of rice is still firm to the bite.'

'You look so serious!'

'Food for Italians is a serious business, especially here. Venice is a marvellous place. I do hope your bad experience in the past has not spoiled it for you. In future, when you think of this city, perhaps you might think not of creepy *sottopassaggi* but of historic eating places and food like this.'

'I will. I like it here a lot.' Her eyes strayed to the cello nestled in an alcove, a trio of violin bows mounted on the wall. An old-fashioned dessert trolley rattled over the tiled floor as the waitress headed for a table on the far side of the room.

'It seems to suit you; you look so much more relaxed.'

'It is such a relief to come and meet you. I almost forgot about tomorrow. I'm with Cate and Phil all day long, filming on the lagoon islands. First, we go to Murano for the glass blowing, then onto Burano and the island of San Giorgio Maggiore.'

Eraldo frowned. 'I do not think this is right. Call Floella. Explain. She would not want you to do this. It is not good for you here.' He tapped his forehead.

Natalie pulled the head from the langoustine decorating the edge of her dish, and carefully broke off its pink shell. She dipped her hands in the lemon-scented finger bowl and wiped them on her linen napkin.

'I can't quit,' she said. No matter how much Eraldo's suggestion made sense, she wouldn't, couldn't leave Floella in the lurch. Through years of short-term relationships that fizzled out before they had a chance of getting serious and fleeting friendships with people who never really got close, Flo was a constant presence in her life.

He took the wine bottle from the cooler, topped up both of their glasses. 'You are loyal, I understand. I just hope this man does not say anything that will cause you more distress.'

'Phil didn't even remember we'd spoken at the Accademia gallery as schoolchildren; at least that's what he said.'

'He looked perfectly normal? No change of expression, no twitch, no blinking?'

'No, nothing.'

'There is a name for people who experience no guilt, who have no empathy for their victims.'

'Psychopaths... but I can't imagine Cate could be married for years to someone who shows no feelings, and the way he acts around her, the way he talks about their two sons, it just doesn't fit.'

Eraldo scooped up the last few grains of his rice. He paused, the fork halfway to his lips. 'Maybe you are wrong.'

'What do you mean?'

He chewed on the mouthful then cleared his throat. 'It seems to me... if this husband of Cate is not a psychopath or a first-class actor then perhaps he was not the person who attacked you.'

She swallowed a large mouthful of wine. The risotto, so light just moments ago, sat in the pit of her stomach like a pile of builders' rubble dumped in the Grand Canal.

'I was only fourteen; Phil ruined my life.' Her voice cracked; tears pricked her eyes. 'Phil groped me in that alley. If I had not got away from him, I don't know what else he might have done. First Cate, now you. Why doesn't anybody believe me?'

31

Eraldo leant across the table. 'I do believe you, Natalie, I promise you. I believe that a man – a boy – assaulted you. But how can you be so sure this was the husband of your friend? You told me he was wearing the costume of the Plague doctor: a mask over his face, a cape up to here...' He raised one hand to his chin. 'A black hat, like so.' He put the other hand to his forehead.

'I knew it was him, the boy I'd spoken to in the gallery. He was the same height; he knew my name. He called my Natalie.'

'But his voice, you said it was strange, you did not recognise it.'

'It *was* strange, distorted, a fake creepy voice. Okay, I admit that voice could have been anyone's but he was wearing those fancy trainers. They had bright-yellow laces; that's why I noticed them straight away.'

Eraldo scratched his forehead. 'Those trainers were expensive, aspirational, I guess. To you, these were something you had only seen on pop stars or footballers, in fashion magazines, something kids at your school could only dream of, but this school Phil attended…'

'Hillingdon.'

'Yes, Hillingdon: an exclusive boarding school that costs a fortune. Those pupils were sons of lawyers, tech millionaires, even people related to your royal family. Is it not possible that one of those rich pupils had an identical pair? Another boy who overheard one of your friends calling you by your name.'

Natalie let out a sigh; it was as if all the fight had gone out of her. 'Maybe you're right; any one of the boys from that school could have seen me leave the masked ball, slipped away and followed me. I was convinced it was the boy I'd spoken to at the gallery; that's why I couldn't get over it: that it was someone who'd seemed so nice. What with that, and Cathy – I mean, Cate – not believing me, it stopped me from trusting anyone for all these years. I've always feared I was a bad judge of character, that friends and boyfriends would let me down. I've carried that with me my whole life.'

Eraldo leant across the table, picked up her hand and squeezed it. 'But you think highly of Floella, one of the best people I know. And you are here with me tonight. I am not a bad person, I hope.'

She couldn't help laughing. 'Maybe I've developed better judgement with age.'

'I do not think that is it. You thought the boy in the Plague-doctor costume was someone you knew but when he suggested you walk down that *sottopassaggio*, you were scared; you told me you went with him for fear of looking silly… You were a good judge of character; your gut instinct was right.'

She let go of Eraldo's hand so the waitress could put down their plates of fish.

'You're right. My gut was telling me to run… All these years,

I've had a problem trusting other people but maybe what I needed to do was trust myself.'

Eraldo cut into his fish. 'I know how hard that is. For years, I blamed my ex-wife for our break-up but if I look back with a clear head, I can see there were signs from the start that we would not be happy together, things I chose to ignore... and also things that I should have said or done differently.'

'Regrets are so hard to deal with. I wish I hadn't said anything to Cate. She was the best friend I ever had. We had the chance to start over and maybe I've wrecked our friendship over nothing.'

'It certainly was not nothing. You can explain to her, give her time... Come, eat your fish; it is so fresh.' He picked up the wine bottle, distributing what was left between the two of them.

She ate a forkful of fish, simply grilled, the flesh cooked just so. Her appetite had returned. Neither spoke as they ate but each time she glanced up, his eyes met hers.

'I am glad to see you eat like this. You were looking so pale. Would you like dessert or just coffee?'

'Coffee, then could we walk for a while, if you are not in a rush? It is such a beautiful evening.'

'Of course.' He nodded to the waitress.

The espresso was dark and rich as melted chocolate, giving her brain a little kick that woke it from the pleasant fuzz induced by the wine.

Eraldo paid the bill. They stepped outside. The *calle* was quiet, their only companions a couple emerging from the restaurant next door. Eraldo took her hand in his. They crossed a small *campo* boarded by a narrow canal. He stopped by the bottom of a flight of stone steps at the base of a small, brick bridge. He stood and looked at her. Her pulse was racing; she felt as though she was holding her breath.

'Shall we cross over?' he said.

Did he just mean the bridge or was he thinking of some other line?

She forced herself to be brave. 'That depends on whether I follow my gut instinct.'

He slipped his arms around her. 'What is your gut telling you?'

'Not to talk any more.'

He lifted a hand to her face, his fingers traced her cheek, his thumb finding the line of her jaw. 'Is that all?'

'And to trust what I'm feeling.' She tilted her head towards his.

His lips brushed hers. 'And what are you feeling?' he whispered.

'Good.'

He kissed her properly this time. She wrapped her arms around him, eyes closed, lost in the moment.

Eventually, they pulled apart.

His eyes glowed in the semi darkness. 'Still feeling good?'

'Better.' She laughed.

'Good. Because my gut is telling me to do that again.'

* * *

Cate and Phil sat at either end of the magnificent antique table as though they were paranoid dictators meeting to discuss an arms trade, not a long-married couple reunited after several days apart. Cate would have rearranged the seating if Nunzia hadn't gone to so much effort: white plates rested on golden chargers, wine was poured in finely etched glasses, urns trailed foliage onto a lavishly embroidered linen runner. It felt as though she and Phil had stepped into an oil painting at the Accademia. Phil seemed relaxed and happy but it was hard to read his face; the Murano glass chandelier cast peculiar patterns across his features.

'Tiramisù.' Nunzia put down dessert in pretty glass bowls.

'*Grazie*! Would it be possible to take our coffee in the library?' Phil said.

'That would be nice,' Cate agreed.

'Of course.'

Cate ate her tiramisù as quickly as was decent, keen to leave the resplendent dining room for the cosier library. Nunzia ushered them down the long corridor and held open the heavy door. Cate sat on a high leather armchair, glad she was wearing heels so her feet could just touch the floor.

'You look like you're sitting on a throne.' Phil laughed. He didn't sit down, wandering around the room whilst they waited for the coffee to appear, running a hand over the wooden carvings, screwing up his eyes to see the details on a tapestry, peering at a table lamp.

Nunzia put down a tray, dimmed a lamp and glided from the room.

At last, Phil sat down on a matching chair. 'Just the two of us. I thought it would never happen! Oh, Cate, I'm so glad not to be spending another night on my own. I was hopeless without you, I felt like old Ted with his face pressed up against the window when there's no one at home.'

Cate frowned. It was so out of character for Phil to gush like this. Was he feeling guilty for something he'd done when they were apart? No, Lucy had to be wrong. Phil wouldn't play away. But something was making him more emotional than usual.

'Ted must be missing us,' she said. 'I'm glad the TV

company has been sending us some updates. He looks happy enough, but who knows what's going through his doggy head.'

'Ted will be fine. Now get off that huge chair and come and squeeze up with me; there's room for two on this.'

She clambered down, kicked off her heels and squeezed on next to Phil, between the arm of the chair and his familiar body. She snuggled into him, resting her head in the crook of his neck, inhaling his cologne, the smell of his skin. They were in a fancy palazzo hundreds of miles from the old vicarage, but now it felt like home.

'Tell me everything,' he said. 'All about your trip to the Guggenheim Collection, and you didn't tell me much about Burano; did you get to the Lace Museum? I'm so glad about you meeting Natalie again; it must have been so much fun doing those things together.'

'Yes, it was.' Cate was glad he couldn't see her face. She so much wanted to tell him about her fruitless trip to find Mum but she knew he'd urge her to try again and she just couldn't face it. 'The Guggenheim collection was amazing,' she said instead.

'Not my thing but I'm glad you liked it. Did you see the Kandinsky?'

'You remembered! He's one of my favourites.'

He twirled a strand of her hair around his finger. 'Of course I remember.'

She twisted around in the chair, slipped her arm around the back of his shoulders, looked into his grey-blue eyes. Could she risk telling him about what Nat had said? They could laugh together at the absurdity of it all. But how could he carry on filming with a smile on his face knowing what he was accused of? He might even demand they go back home and she couldn't let him sacrifice the publicity opportunity for the business he'd poured his heart and soul into because of Nat's groundless accusations. But there was something she could ask him, something that might set her mind at rest.

She planted a kiss on his lips. 'I missed you. It got me thinking... about Kiran.'

'Kiran? Our neighbour?' He repeated her name without a moment's hesitation. 'Why her?'

'I was thinking she must get lonely when her husband goes away on those business trips of his. Maybe we shouldn't just have dinner with the two of them; maybe sometimes, we should invite her over.'

'That's kind of you. Why not? Even better, why don't you and her go out for a coffee or lunch or something? She could probably do with a friend and... maybe, tell me if I'm speaking out of turn, but I know you see Lucy and some of the others from time to time but I've got the feeling that if they weren't wives of my friends, you probably wouldn't see them at all.'

'So, you're happy for me to spend more time with Kiran.'

'Of course, why wouldn't I be?' He pecked her on the nose.

'No reason.' She laughed with relief.

'What's funny?'

'Nothing, nothing at all... I love you, Phil.'

'I love you too, you daft old sausage. I don't know about you but I'm getting cramp squashed up in this chair. Shall we go and stretch out somewhere more comfortable?'

'Are you thinking of that huge great bed of ours? Did you see the painted cherubs and grapes on the headboard? They're incredible.'

'It's not the cherubs I'm thinking about.' He gave her a cheeky grin.

Cate slipped down from the chair. 'Come on then, what are we waiting for?'

* * *

Phil rinsed his toothbrush and put it back in the silver-plated tumbler. The edge of the bed where Cate lay was just visible in the corner of the bathroom mirror above the pair of his and hers basins. His wife's long, smooth legs poked out between the two edges of a sumptuous, velvety robe identical to the one he was now wearing. Cate was humming to herself, a habit he never pointed out in case it made her self-conscious.

He ran a hand over his jaw; he'd shaved that morning and being pale, he didn't get much of a five o'clock shadow.

'Phil, are you okay?' Cate called.

'Sure, everything's fine, I won't be long.' It was half-true. He didn't feel as bad as he had feared. Why had he thought that coming to Venice would make things harder? It wasn't the city that was to blame; it was his own cowardice. And he carried the guilt and the shame wherever he went. No change of location could make him feel worse. Or better.

He splashed some water on his face. Sometimes, he hated the sight of himself in the mirror. This marble bathroom, the basket of expensive unguents he could massage into his body or rub on his face, even his beautiful Cate waiting for him on the bed, who looked like a goddess and whose skin smelt like sugar and roses, had all come at a terrible price. Cate didn't deserve someone like him, his touch on her skin like toxic pesticide drifting across a meadow.

'Phil?'

'Coming!'

He padded over to the bed, his feet cosseted in the complimentary monogrammed slippers the TV company had provided. He perched on the edge.

'You look tired, darling,' Cate said.

'I think the travelling has just caught up with me. And it's a really early start tomorrow for this glass-blowing trip.' He gave a yawn he hoped sounded realistic. 'I don't think I can stay awake another moment.'

'Don't worry. There's always another time.' She pressed her soft lips against his. 'Goodnight, Phil.'

He shrugged off the dressing gown and crawled under the covers. Cate switched off the bedside light and snuggled back against her pillow. She closed her eyes.

Her breathing became heavier as she drifted off to sleep. He lay staring at the ceiling.

32

Natalie adjusted the hard hat they'd all been issued with even though they were safely positioned far from the glass furnace. Three men moved in silence; the tip of an iron rod glowed white hot. Another man was forging a red and orange vase, his face a picture of concentration behind his safety goggles. It was hard to imagine how the globule of molten glass could be turned into a precious *objet d'art* by nothing more than the glass blower's skill with hands and mouth, yet that was precisely what was happening right in front of her.

Cate's blonde hair and mint-green blouse glowed in the ethereal light. Natalie fought the urge to cough, desperate not to break the artisans' concentration. Phil's hands were thrust into his pockets, his forehead beading with perspiration in the heat, causing the make-up girl to be on full alert with her fluffy powder brush. Lucia had abandoned her trusty folder in the corner, watching with arms folded. The camera crew moved around, quiet as cats. There was no need for Natalie to speak; Cate's and Phil's rapt faces expressed more than any words, and the necessary explanations would be added in Natalie's voice-over once Floella had chosen her edit.

One of the glass shapes began to take on the form of a cheetah, or perhaps a leopard – she had no idea how to tell the difference.

'*Incredibile!*' Lucia gasped, immediately clapping her hand to her mouth.

'Don't worry, we'll edit that out,' Natalie said.

The glass blower carefully set the creature down to cool, signalling for them to stay back. He removed his goggles.

'That was superb, an experience I will never forget,' Phil said.

The make-up girl dashed forward. After a quick dusting of powder, Phil repeated his comment for the camera. His words sounded as natural as though he were saying them for the first time. Was he a good actor, a natural liar? Natalie studied his face. No, he wasn't acting, just trying to do his best. Despite her initial conviction, she was now almost entirely sure that Phil wasn't the one who'd followed her that night.

He caught her looking. 'Was I okay? Do you want me to say that again?'

'No, second time was perfect.'

The director nodded in agreement, signalling at the cameraman to stop the filming.

'Thank you again for this,' Phil said.

'It's a pleasure, Phil,' Natalie said.

Cate glanced at her sharply.

Natalie smiled, flashing Cate what she hoped was a 'speak later' look. Cate turned away, feigning an interest in the glass leopard.

'I was hoping to speak to someone about creating a chandelier for Cate's dressing room. We were talking about that over breakfast, weren't we, darling?' Phil draped an arm around his wife's shoulder.

'Phil's so thoughtful. It will be a gift for my fortieth birthday so the details will have to be a surprise but he has such a good eye, I know I can leave him to commission something exquisite.'

'We will talk to the showroom manager; he deals with all such enquiries.' Lucia glanced in her folder. 'We could see him in his office now if you would like to follow me.'

'Yes, thank you, Lucia.' Phil shook the nearest glass blower's hand. '*Grazie*.'

The man nodded, turning back to the furnace without speaking but with a twitch of a smile.

Cate hung back slightly, allowing Lucia and Phil to walk side by side down the long factory corridor. Natalie let out a breath. At last, she could talk to Cate. Apologise, try to explain.

'You should audition for the Royal Shakespeare Company when we get back,' Cate said coolly. 'The way you were chatting to Phil earlier, you'd think you were best buddies.'

Natalie slowed her steps. 'I can say a few words on a TV show but I'm no actor… and I don't think Phil is.'

'What's that supposed to mean?' Cate's eyes swivelled in Phil's direction. He and Lucia had stopped to look at a vintage advertising poster high on the wall.

'Cate, look at me, please!'

Cate sighed melodramatically. She turned her head.

'I've been thinking… about Phil. I'm sorry for what I said yesterday. He's a nice guy, like you said. He seems kind, genuine. My gut tells me he wasn't the person who attacked me.'

Cate's eyes narrowed. She regarded Natalie, stony-faced.

'Perhaps you should have waited to meet him before you started throwing accusations around.'

'Please listen. The boy in that alleyway was the same height as Phil, he was wearing the same designer trainers. And he knew my name. I'd assumed it must be Phil.'

'That's a pretty big assumption, don't you think? Wouldn't exactly stand up in court, would it?' Cate's voice dripped with sarcasm.

'I didn't think any of the others knew my name. Phil was the only one of those boys that I spoke to on our trip. I was far too self-conscious to go up and talk to anyone at the masked ball before I sneaked away. But I shouldn't have jumped to conclusions. I really am so, so sorry I said those things about Phil. I'm going to find a way to make it up to you, honestly I am.'

'Good luck with that project! What are you going to do? Buy me a bellini?'

'Please, Cate.'

Cate was silent. Natalie could almost see the cogs of her brain turning. 'I suppose it must have been traumatic for you, thinking you were going to meet your attacker again. I can see how you'd think that it could have been Phil. Not knowing him the way I do, I might have thought the same.'

'Thank you,' Natalie murmured. Cate was being so gracious, she felt even worse.

'You know what we could do? We could ask Phil who it might have been. There were no more than twenty boys from their school on that trip. Maybe he'll remember who else wore the Plague-doctor costume that night, who else had the same trainers as him.'

'I'm not sure I want to know. What would I gain? There's nothing I can do now; it's all too late.'

Cate squared her shoulders. 'We could go to the police.'

Natalie waited until Phil and Lucia disappeared into the factory office before she replied. 'No, there's no point. What would the police think? Two schoolkids fumbling in an alleyway, my word against his. There's no evidence, no CCTV, no DNA. Coming here, it's made me realise it's time to move on.'

Cate threw up her hands. 'But it's wrong. That boy might have done the same to somebody else. He might still be doing it now.'

Natalie shook her head. She looked down at the floor. 'It's over. Please don't say anything, and I'd rather Phil didn't know.'

'Okay, I'll keep your secret, like you've kept mine about me trying to visit Mum.' Cate gently touched Natalie's arm. 'But if you ever change your mind or want to talk, you know you can.'

'Same here. You can talk to me even if we're no longer friends. I know we can't start again, not after I said those things about Phil.'

Cate fixed her brown eyes on Natalie's. 'It's too early to talk about being friends again. But it meant so much when you came to Burano with me; that hasn't changed. You were there when I needed you. I won't forget that... We have been through a lot together, haven't we?'

'Yeah, we have,' Natalie said quietly.

Cate twisted a lock of her hair. 'You know, part of me wants to strangle you... and part of me wants to go back to how we were a few days ago. You were wrong to think Phil attacked you; I was wrong to think, even for a moment, he might be having an affair. But I know there's something up with him: something not quite right. I need someone I can really talk to. It's hard to be friends right now but maybe we can be... friendly acquaintances?'

Natalie smiled. 'Okay, that's fair enough: friendly acquaintances. It's more than I deserve.'

Cate laughed. 'It does sound a bit ridiculous, doesn't it?'
'A little.'

Cate smoothed down her hair. 'Acquaintances after all these years... Oh, dammit, Natalie, you are my friend, no matter what.'

'I don't know what to say.' Natalie's voice caught.

'Nothing. Just give me a hug.' Cate held out her arms.

'A quick one or I might cry,' she mumbled into Cate's hair.

The office door opened. They sprang apart.

'You didn't need to wait out here,' Phil said.

'I didn't want to stand in there with my hands clamped over my ears whilst you talked about my gift. Did you get everything sorted?'

'Yes.' A grin spread over Phil's face.

'You will love it,' Lucia added. 'And now, you might like to visit the showroom to buy some smaller items to take home: a little souvenir, a present, perhaps.'

'Something for the boys – they're both mad about animals,' Cate said.

'A monkey or a bear,' Phil suggested.

'I expect there is a whole menagerie to choose from. Are you happy to have the cameras rolling whilst you look?' Lucia said.

'Of course. I'm getting used to being a star,' Phil joked. 'So, Cate, Natalie, any thoughts what sort of animal we should look for?'

'How about a nice green turtle?' Natalie suggested.

Cate started laughing. 'Anything but a turtle! Do you remember Shy Kelly's face?'

Natalie let out a snort: laughter mixed with relief.

Phil looked from one to the other. 'Who's Shy Kelly? What's so funny?'

'It's nothing, darling.' Cate gave her husband a peck on the cheek. 'It's just a joke between old friends.'

'Let's go and find those gifts,' Natalie said.

'And afterwards,' Cate said quietly, 'I want to know all about your date with Eraldo.'

'We went to La Gallina Verde; it was a really nice evening. The seafood risotto was out of this world.'

'Are you sure the risotto was the best bit?' Cate smirked.

Natalie's face heated at the memory of their kiss. 'Shut up!' She laughed.

33

'Most people come to Murano just for the glass factories; I am glad I have been able to show you something more,' Lucia said.

'The mosaics in the church were some of the best I've seen – such artistry!' Phil said. He took his wife's hand to help her into the water taxi.

'Next stop, Burano.' Cate's voice was bright but the corner of her eyelid flickered.

'We won't need to spend much time there,' Natalie said quickly. 'We'll have a coffee break then just take some footage of you strolling past the rainbow-coloured houses. Unless of course there's something particular you want to do.' She caught Cate's eye.

'Thanks,' Cate mouthed.

Natalie gave a no-problem shrug. If she were Cate, she'd have been desperate to return to her mother's house to make another attempt to see her but it was Cate's decision; she had to respect that.

'That's all fine by me,' Phil said, plonking himself down on the boat's cushioned seating. 'You girls have been before and

I'm not desperate to see the museum. Lace making isn't really my thing, not like that glass blowing. Thanks for arranging for those blue lions to be sent straight to the palazzo, Lucia. I think the boys will love them.'

Lucia consulted her ever-present folder. 'Burano is so photogenic, we will definitely need some footage but you are right, Natalie, a quick stop is best. We have a strict time slot for filming at the *campanile* on San Giorgio Maggiore; we cannot be late. But we still have time for coffee in Burano when we arrive.' She looked at the director, who responded with a nod of his head.

Lucia turned to the driver of their water taxi. 'Burano, *per favore.*'

He turned the steering wheel; the boat sped straight towards the island, bypassing the detour Natalie and Cate had made to Mazzorbo. They disembarked on Burano's bustling waterfront. Lucia led the way, the director and camera crew following along, arguing good-naturedly – according to Lucia – about their chosen camera angles for the post-coffee filming and which row of the colourful houses would best demonstrate the beauty of the island.

The spot Lucia had chosen for their coffee wasn't on the canal side where Natalie and Cate had lunched but on a wider *fondamenta* where the houses were even more colourful: hyacinth blue, bright orange, canary yellow, a pink that would send Barbie into ecstasies.

Lucia ushered them towards some outside seating where she had arranged for a substantial area to be reserved for the crew and all their paraphernalia. 'Coffee and a *bussolà*, everyone?'

'What are they?' Cate asked, popping her handbag on a spare chair.

Lucia put on a mock-shocked expression. 'What are they? They are the most famous biscuits in all of Venice. The original and best are from this island. All ingredients natural, nothing artificial. You must try one. And I recommend a *caffè shakerato*, espresso coffee shaken with ice cubes – perfect on a hot day like this.'

'I'm not arguing with that!' Phil smiled. He'd been looking more relaxed as the day went on but every now and then, Natalie noticed him gazing into space as though his mind was far away.

Lucia organised the drinks and biscuits. Natalie leant back in her chair. The day was going better than she dared hope. The glass blowing was going to make great television and the sun-saturated colours of Burano were a guaranteed crowd-pleaser. Beyond the edge of their shady umbrella, the sky was an unbroken, paintbox blue. Even the biscuits were as good as Lucia promised – crunchy with a hint of vanilla – though the ice-cold coffee was a little sweet for her taste.

She would have loved to stay put all day but the crew were already standing up, arguing over who would carry which bits of kit. She was glad she had nothing bulkier than a shoulder bag to lug around. The day was only going to get hotter.

Cate and Phil finished their drinks and, after a quick appraisal by the make-up girl, were soon gamely walking back and forth along the *fondamenta*. Cate's bright smile never faltered but Natalie sensed her friend's relief when Lucia called time and they all made their way back to the water taxi, leaving Burano and Cate's estranged mother's house far behind.

The waterfront at San Giorgio Maggiore was practically deserted. Phil gave his arm to Natalie to help her out of the water taxi.

'Compared to the other islands, few people come here and

even fewer film here,' Lucia said. 'But Floella and I wanted the viewers to see you exploring a part of the lagoon that's outside the normal tourist bubble.'

'Our viewers like to believe they are discerning people,' Natalie added. '*Luxe Life Swap* provides an upmarket type of armchair travel, not a tick list of the same old top ten must-see sights. Back in England, the count and his wife will visit London but we won't just show the viewers red buses and Big Ben. The Venetians will walk up Parliament Hill for a view over the city, see the flamingos in St James's Park, explore the backstreet boutiques of Mayfair, take in a private tour of the Queen's Gallery at Buckingham Palace.'

'I've never walked up Parliament Hill myself; perhaps the countess has never been up the tower here,' Cate said.

'Quite possibly,' Lucia said. 'But she will have missed out. The views from the top are sensational. Fortunately, there is a lift we can access from the back of the church.'

'I was wondering how we'd get the crew up there.' Natalie tilted her head back to take in the soaring bell tower.

The female camera operator said something in Italian and laughed.

'She says if they had to climb up, we would have a mutiny!' Lucia said.

'I'm very glad we don't have to.' Natalie threw a glance at Cate's spindly heels.

* * *

'This is amazing!' Cate flung out her arms.

'It's truly magical.' From the top of the tower, Natalie had a perfect view across the water to the Doge's Palace, the soaring *campanile* in St Mark's Square, the terracotta rooftops and church towers, the lagoon beyond. She could already envisage the viewers' oohs and aahs.

Lucia organised more shots. Although to Natalie's eyes, everything was going swimmingly, the young woman's brow was creased.

'Is everything okay, Lucia?' Natalie asked.

'Yes... but here, I cannot help feeling sad. This view reminds me of how vulnerable Venice – my city – is. All built on this lagoon. Layers of mud on sand, sand on clay, all held up by stakes of oak or pine. This bell tower where we stand was built in the nineteenth century, but the original was built more than five hundred years ago. I pray it will survive another five hundred years but some say Venice will not be here in a hundred.' She pressed her lips together.

'Why do you say that?' Cate asked. 'Is it climate change?'

'In part, but it is human greed that is destroying the Venice I love. I know this show we are making will try to show the real Venice, the ancient buildings, the typical foods, the old crafts, but all this is under threat from fake experiences and cheap copies of everything. Our handmade masks, our food, even our coffee sold by people who do not care about anything but making money. They do not care about the ships pulling on the pilings on which this whole city is built or losing the people and places that make it special. And you are right about climate change. The rising water level, the high tide – *acqua alta* – that makes such amusing photographs for visitors posing in their tall, rubber boots destroys the very places they come to see.'

'That is so sad. We could add some additional information to the webpages that our viewers visit,' Natalie said. 'We could draw their attention to the importance of supporting the people and places that keep the real Venice alive. I know that is not much.'

'But it is something,' Lucia said. She checked her folder. 'And now we must not be late for our appointment at the Giorgio Cini Foundation; we have special permission to film in the maze.'

'I hope we don't get too lost; I wouldn't want to miss lunch,' Phil joked.

'Fortunately, the hedging they planted is not so tall; you can see over it so we will not have that problem,' Lucia said seriously. 'Do not worry, you and Cate will have a very nice light lunch; it is all arranged.'

'Are you joining us, Natalie?' Phil said.

'No, Lucia and I will eat with the crew once they've taken some footage of you enjoying your food.'

'Tonight, we go to George Clooney's favourite restaurant,' Phil said. 'And you must eat with us, Natalie; I insist.'

'Nat might have a date with someone else.' Cate smiled.

Phil laughed. 'Cate tells me you have become rather friendly with a handsome watch restorer. But if he has not yet arranged to see you tonight, I hope you will tell him you are busy. Absence makes the heart grow fonder. I'm living proof of that.' He turned to Cate with a boyish grin.

'I would be delighted to join you,' Natalie said. She longed to see Eraldo again but perhaps Phil was right. A short absence might make the heart grow fonder. But soon she'd be back in England for good. And whatever they had between them would come to an end.

34

Natalie paused outside the mask maker's doorway. The last few days had passed in a blur of activity. All the filming for *Luxe Life Swap* had gone to plan. Cate and Phil had done everything the director had asked of them: strolling around St Mark's Square, taking a private tour of the Doge's Palace, holding hands on a gondola ride along the narrowest and most picturesque canals. The footage of the couple they'd taken in the maze and at the top of the spiral staircase at the Palazzo Contarini del Bovolo was sure to prove particularly popular. But half of Natalie's mind had been on Eraldo; they'd snatched together what time they could but when they were apart, she couldn't help wondering if he was missing her as much as she was missing him. She could hardly bear the way the days were rushing past. The thought of saying goodbye to Venice, never to return, seemed inconceivable. The place she'd associated with fear and loathing was becoming more and more dear to her with every day that passed.

She pushed open the door to Pietro's shop. The bell

jangled. Pietro looked up. He stood his paintbrush in the empty jam jar on his desk.

'Natalie! *Buonasera*! I call Eraldo for you?'

'*Buonasera*, Pietro. No, do not tell him I am here yet. I would like to look around.'

'At my masks?' He raised his eyebrows. 'You are usually not so happy to see them. Perhaps they are now familiar to you or is it that now when you visit my shop, you associate it with happy things?' He glanced meaningfully towards the spiral staircase.

Her cheeks warmed. 'Perhaps.' Whatever the reason, today was the first time she had stood amongst the masks without feeling a prickle of unease. 'I feel so rude always rushing through your shop and I would like to buy a gift for my friend Floella.'

'*Allora*, something bright, happy, sparkly.'

'You must know her.'

'When Eraldo speaks of her, I imagine a bold, brave lady who will wear a carnival mask like she wears a pair of jeans.'

'That's Flo.' Natalie smiled.

'What colour is her favourite?'

'Purple, definitely purple.' She picked up a carnival mask decorated with feathers. 'This is made from papier mâché?'

'Of course, by hand – by me!' He touched his chest. 'You like this? I will wrap it for you; you go upstairs. I warn you, you need to shout loudly for Eraldo's attention; he is working on the watch for your friend Cate.'

'Maybe I shouldn't interrupt him if he's busy.'

'No, no, go up. I think you will be a most welcome visitor.'

She climbed the staircase with a spring in her step. Eraldo was bent over his workbench, headphones in his ears. He looked so intense, she didn't know if she should stay and wait for him to look up or leave him to his work.

'Natalie!' His smile answered her question. He put down his magnifying glass, put on his tortoiseshell glasses and came around from behind the workbench. 'Come here!'

'Hi! I hope I am not interrupting… I mean, I am interrupting but…'

'*Basta*! Enough! Stop talking and kiss me,' he murmured, pulling her into his arms. Warmth flooded her from top to toe. She didn't need to ask if he'd missed her.

'I'm so pleased to see you,' she said.

'I was not sure if you had any spare time today. Come sit, shall I make coffee?'

'No, just a glass of water, please. I wish I could stay longer but we are filming later.'

He swept an auction catalogue aside. She sank onto the low couch.

'The filming, it is going well?' He walked over to the sink and ran the tap.

'Very well. Cate has been so professional; they both have.'

He handed her a glass of water and sat down beside her. 'But you have more to do today?'

'I'll need to liaise with Lucia and then go back to my hotel to get changed. We're filming at Caffè Florian later but we are waiting until dusk.'

'You will have the most beautiful light. Venice at night, it is so special. But your film crew, they are so busy, are they not demanding overtime?'

'They have a day off tomorrow; we all do.'

'Ahh.' He ran his hand over his stubble. 'I suppose you will find some fun things to do with your old school friend.'

'She may suggest we do something but I will say no. Cate... perhaps I should not say this... but Cate is worried about Phil. He has been distant lately. He is not the sort of man who talks about his feelings but maybe some time alone together will help them.'

'And you?'

'I'm not sure what I will do but I would like to go back to Burano.'

'It is a beautiful place but have you not visited twice already?'

'Yes, but last time, I was there for just an hour with the film crew and it was all work. And with Cate, well... that was a strange day.'

'Strange, how?' He leant back against the couch, folding his hands together.

She took a sip of water. 'It was something to do with Cate, something personal. It meant we didn't get to go to the Lace Museum, and that is somewhere I want to see. My gran and Mum both sewed and crocheted. Gran made beautiful, embroidered tablecloths and pillow slips. I can't sew to save my life but I've always admired that sort of work.'

'Burano lace is the best in the world. You know Leonardo da Vinci commissioned the women of the island to make the altar cloth for the cathedral in Milan? Some still create the handmade lace even though it takes months, sometimes years, to finish a piece. That type of devotion to a craft, that desire to keep the old ways alive is something I can understand. They say the museum is very interesting. I've always meant to visit.' He gave a half-shrug.

'I would love you to go with me. I don't suppose you could spare the time tomorrow?'

His forehead wrinkled. 'I have not taken off a single day for

I do not know how long. I find it hard when I begin a new project like the watch I am creating for Cate.'

'I see, I should have realised. Sorry, I shouldn't have asked.' She took a long draught of water.

'But I am glad that you did ask. I know I should take a whole week off, take a proper holiday. Tomorrow, I *shall* take a break.' He smiled. 'We will spend the whole day together but now I must work.'

Natalie glanced at her watch and jumped to her feet. 'Oh! So must I. I have to run.'

'Tomorrow, nine at the vaporetto stop?'

'Tomorrow!' She scuttled down the stairs.

Pietro waved a package. 'Natalie! Floella's gift! Pay me next time. You are always in a rush!' He shook his head, chuckling.

* * *

It was tempting to stand under the rain-head shower for longer but Natalie had no time to spare. It was her own stupid fault she was running late; she'd walked the wrong way from the mask maker's shop and had doubled back on herself, her head full of thoughts of her outing with Eraldo the next day. She tutted at herself. She needed to concentrate, not daydream like a teenager. She still hadn't decided what to wear for the evening's filming. The clothes she'd worn earlier were perfectly clean, but the viewers of *Luxe Life Swap* were used to Mandy Miller's ever-changing wardrobe.

She grabbed a floral sundress from the wardrobe. Too skimpy even for the evening. Her pink top was nice but mysterious creases seemed to have appeared whilst it was hanging up. The green skirt wouldn't do; she knew Cate was wearing her green maxi dress from Simona Rinaldi tonight. Today's dress would just have to do. She would chuck on a bright-orange scarf, big hoop earrings and change her handbag. Swiftly, she emptied her shoulder bag out on the white bedspread, sorting through the inordinate amount of debris it had mysteriously accumulated over the last few days.

She quickly selected the essentials: lipstick, mirror, purse and tucked them into her clutch bag. She'd keep the leaflets from various landmarks, but the expired vaporetto ticket, the sachet of sugar – why on earth had she picked that up? – and receipts for coffees she'd never bother to claim and other tat that was now scattered over the bed could be safely chucked away. Her hand hesitated over a scrap of brown paper, the piece of torn envelope that Cate had discarded. There was no reason for Natalie to hang onto Cate's mother's address but she could not bring herself to throw it away. She opened her purse and slipped it behind her stash of euros.

35

Eraldo put down his coffee cup. 'What a perfect morning! I had forgotten how beautiful Burano is. I have not been here for many years.'

'I probably know it better than you now,' Natalie joked. The stretch of eating places along the canal was now almost as familiar to her as the walk from her small hotel to the vaporetto stop but the vivid colours of the shops and houses still took her breath away.

'You chose a good place for coffee.'

They were back at the café she and Cate had visited, the espresso as rich as Natalie's mum's Sunday lunch gravy, the sun warming her face, the sky a chocolate-box blue. And the company... well, there was no one she'd rather be with than Eraldo.

She studied him surreptitiously as he turned to look over the canal. Sunglasses had taken the place of his tortoiseshell frames, his usual jeans swapped for cargo shorts. She was rather glad he wasn't wearing something more figure-hugging;

his muscular, brown arms and perfectly formed legs were more than enough to get her heart racing.

'What are you thinking?' Eraldo asked.

'Just wondering what made me decide to paint my flat in shades of beige.'

'Beige? No! I think that is not you. But perhaps back in England, these bright colours might seem odd. Even here, I do not understand. How can blue and orange look so good together?'

Natalie laughed. 'It's a mystery but I like it here. It's wonderful to come back again and not be in a rush. No Lucia in charge, checking her clipboard, no Cate deciding where to go.'

'Just the two of us.'

'Yes, just us.' She sipped the last of her coffee, glad she too was wearing dark glasses. She was already self-conscious enough about her growing feelings for him without having them written all over her face.

'*Allora*, so where shall we go now? The Lace Museum or shall we walk around?'

'Let's just stroll about for a bit first.'

Everyone else seemed to share the same idea. The canal side was busy and the little bridges were nearly buckling under the weight of the crush of phone-wielding day trippers.

'If you cannot beat them, join them. That is what you say?' Eraldo took out his phone. 'We could take a selfie and send it to Floella. She said she would like one. Here, lean that way... Yes, this is good... What do you think?'

She took the phone. 'It's nice. I managed not to blink.'

'I will send it to you and to Flo.'

Her phone pinged. 'I've got it.' She already knew she'd be sneaking peeks at it tomorrow whilst she was out with Cate and Phil. But she couldn't imagine why the ever-busy Floella would want a photograph of her and Eraldo together.

They squeezed their way off the bridge, resuming their walk along the path. A young woman in five-inch heels and a dress that just covered her underwear was marching towards them giving a running commentary in French, phone held aloft. Behind her, a flustered young man was clutching what looked like an armful of outfit changes.

Eraldo pulled Natalie to one side. 'Watch out!'

'Thanks, I almost ended up in the canal!' Natalie joked. 'This island is too photogenic; those influencers are a menace.'

'Let us go under this archway. It will be quieter. I remember we can walk to the main piazza that way.'

The small brick *sottopassaggio* led them into a square of houses, deserted except for a serious-looking child riding his mini scooter. Washing hung across balconies, the sound of someone practising the piano drifting from a ground-floor room.

'This is nice, so peaceful,' Eraldo said.

The square led through into another. Natalie recognised it at once. A striped curtain was pulled across the door of the orange house where Cate's mother lived. The flowerpots around the doorstep had been freshly watered, dark patches in the soil. The marmalade cat was back lolling in the sun. Natalie realised Eraldo was talking. She hadn't taken in a word.

'Sorry, I was miles away.'

'Looking at the plants? Whoever lives there takes a lot of care of them.'

'Mmm,' Natalie murmured. How she longed to knock on the door of the orange house, run up the stairs and tell Cate's mum what a kind, loving person Cate was. She'd beg her not to throw away this one chance to spend time with her own daughter. No matter what had happened in the past, couldn't she spare Cate just one hour? Wasn't she curious to see the woman who'd taken the place of the little baby she'd left behind?

Natalie went to turn away but a movement from the balcony stopped her. The swing seat was now occupied. A woman sat bent over, her black hair caught up in a floral scarf. She was stitching something: a hem of a skirt, perhaps. Natalie craned her neck. The woman wore a red top paired with jeans, a younger look than the simple A-line smocks favoured by some of the island's elderly. It was hard to tell but she could be in her late fifties: the same age as Cate's mum.

'Natalie?' Eraldo was looking at her curiously.

'Oh, sorry. Where shall we go now?'

'Piazza Baldassarre Galuppi. We will get a good view of the *campanile*. I am sure you noticed it before; it leans like the tower in Pisa.'

'I did see it from a distance, with Cate.' Natalie needed to focus on sightseeing with Eraldo, not fretting over her old school friend's problems. But she couldn't help glancing over her shoulder as they walked away.

'We can visit the church and the shops, if you like and after that, a nice lunch; the food on this island is legendary,' Eraldo said. 'And maybe then you will tell me what is really so interesting about that orange house.'

* * *

An elderly waiter cleared away their lunch plates, his sleeves rolled up, revealing a chunky, stainless-steel watch.

Natalie gasped. 'Do you know how long we've been sitting here?'

Eraldo checked his own vintage timepiece. 'Nearly two

hours. That is the sign of a good lunch... and good company. And I am paying today, no arguments.'

'Okay, thank you but next time, it's on me.'

'Even after two hours of talking with me, you will still want to do this again?' His lips twitched.

'I hope I did not bore you telling you about Cate. I can't believe she will be going back to England without trying to see her mum again. But I know you're right: I can't interfere. It's up to Cate to try again.'

'All you can do is listen if she does want to talk, and be a good friend. Let us go; some people are waiting.' He inclined his head towards a woman who was glaring in their direction.

Natalie caught the waiter's eye. Eraldo took out his wallet.

The woman's sour expression transformed. She elbowed her partner in the ribs as if to say, *See? I told you we would find a seat.*

'Now, the Lace Museum. We cannot allow you to miss it again,' Eraldo said.

Natalie picked up her handbag. 'To the museum, third time lucky!' She hoped it would be interesting enough to take her mind off the woman in the red blouse sitting stitching on her balcony.

* * *

Phil kept his eyes on the young woman pressing the tiny squares of gold-leafed glass into place. He'd adored the Titians and Tintorettos they'd seen that morning but it was a particular privilege to watch a twenty-first-century Venetian artist at work using techniques honed over centuries.

'Such skill,' Cate murmured.

Phil nodded. He wished he could concentrate on the

woman's skilful fingers but his thoughts kept straying to that other workshop more than twenty years before.

He stared into the glittering mosaic until he was almost dizzy trying to block out his memories, but it was no use. He'd never forget the wonder of silently watching the oar maker as he worked, the look of pure concentration on the man's face, oblivious to Phil and Evan standing there. Phil could still smell the scent of fresh wood that filled the air, remembered the early-morning sun lighting the dust motes. He'd wished so many times he could go back and stop time, stay in that blissful moment, oblivious of what was to come. But no amount of wishful thinking could undo what he'd done.

36

'Two tickets for the museum, please,' Natalie said.

Eraldo pointed to a poster behind the counter. 'Look, we are in luck; there is a live demonstration of Burano lacemaking today.'

The cashier handed over their two tickets. 'Yes, you *are* in luck. Few people practise the craft today and most of them are too elderly to sit here for hours showing visitors the old ways but Signora Gherardini has kindly come today. She started learning at just six years old and attended the lacemaking school when it was here. Now she is eighty-six and she still creates the most intricate work just for pleasure.'

'How lovely.' A memory of Natalie's grandmother embroidering pillow slips in her high-backed chair came out of nowhere. Sunday afternoons, the same every week: her mum clattering in the kitchen, waiting for Dad to come home from his shift; Grandad dozing in front of the racing, jolting awake with the roar of the crowd as the horses turned into the straight. She'd been so lucky without even realising. She couldn't imagine Cate's life: a mother who'd absconded, an awkward truce with a fast-fading father.

'You will find Signora Gherardini sitting upstairs where many of our rarest pieces of lace are displayed. You are just in time; she is leaving soon,' the cashier continued.

They found the old lady sitting on a rush-seated chair just like those in the black-and-white photographs displayed in the stairwell. A rectangle of white cotton was spread over a fabric bolster cushion resting on her lap. A glass of water and a wicker basket of sewing equipment rested on a nearby table. Her grey head was bent over her work, knobbly veined hands knotting fine white threads together with the ease of someone blessed with much younger fingers. There was something almost holy in the old lady's silent devotion to her craft. Natalie stood quiet and still as though she were listening to a priest reciting the catechism.

Signora Gherardini coughed. She laid down her lace and reached for the glass of water. With a flash of her beady, dark eyes and a smile, she acknowledged her small audience as though she had only just noticed them standing there. She coughed again and with an apologetic gesture, began gathering up her things.

'That was so absorbing. I'm so glad we didn't miss watching her, even though we only got to see a few minutes,' Natalie said. 'It will make it much more interesting to look around now I've seen someone actually make the lace.'

'Years and years of practice and still it takes months to make just a small tray cloth or some such item,' Eraldo said.

'Look at this, isn't it beautiful.' Natalie's eye had already been caught by a mannequin modelling an antique bridal dress decorated with the most delicate, hand-stitched work. She wandered over to a wooden cabinet watched over by a young woman in her late twenties sporting a lace-trimmed blouse, a vibrant mango-coloured skirt and a name badge spelling out *Belinda* in capital letters.

'These pull out,' Belinda said, fanning out the cabinet's shallow, glass-topped drawers. 'There are samples of lace in each drawer. This for example is a wonderful example of eighteenth-century *Punto in aria di Burano*. I leave you to look but ask me any questions that you like.'

Natalie gazed in wonder. 'I cannot imagine how much work went into these. Such skill!'

Eraldo looked over her shoulder, his now familiar warm, amber scent distracting her momentarily from the exhibits. 'Machines have done so much for humankind but handcrafted work like this can never be beaten. It is a tragedy that one day there may be no one alive who can create something like this – and they call this progress!'

'My grandmother was a friend of Signora Gherardini,' Belinda said, smiling at the memory. 'She too attended the lacemaking school from an early age. Such tales she would tell me about it! Sadly, she is no longer alive. How I wish she had written down her memories or recorded them, but one doesn't think...'

'Did she teach you or your mother the craft?' Eraldo asked.

'She died when I was too small to pick up a needle and my mamma... well, Nonna wanted Mamma to follow in her footsteps and learn to make lace. But Mamma had a mind of her own: a rebel, I suppose. She thought lacemaking, sewing and homemaking were all ways of tying women down. She was determined to leave this small, backward island – that is how she saw it – and have adventures all over the world. I am not like her; I was born on Burano and I love it and these old crafts, though sadly I have no talent like this.'

'But your mother came back to Burano, if you were born here,' Eraldo pointed out.

'Yes, after her adventures. Perhaps they were not as exciting as she hoped. She lived in England for a year or two; I guess that is where you are from?' Natalie nodded. 'She fell in love there with an English boy, Terry.'

Natalie's breath caught. Was Cate's dad called Terry? She couldn't quite remember; it might have been Jerry. But this had to be more than a coincidence. She glanced at Eraldo.

'Mamma and Terry's relationship did not last. She went off travelling again for a while but after two years, she settled back here. Nonna had mellowed, she didn't try to mould Mamma any more; she was just so glad she had come back home. Mamma told me she picked up a needle out of boredom one day and immediately, everything made sense; she loved sewing, the very thing she had tried to escape! She never had the skill to make lace for a living so she worked in a boutique out there on the piazza... Oh, excuse me a moment...'

Belinda turned to an older lady, answering her question in Italian. Natalie couldn't understand what they were saying but she heard the name Lina loud and clear. That was Cate's mother's name; this time, she was sure. She clutched the edge of the display unit, her heart racing.

'Sorry about that,' Belinda continued. 'The lady was asking when my mother, Lina, was coming in; Mamma volunteers here once a week.'

'I...' Natalie hesitated. Eraldo's hand squeezed hers, whether in encouragement or warning, she wasn't sure. But she couldn't stay quiet. 'Could I ask you a question? I will understand if you cannot answer.'

Belinda smiled. 'Of course. I do not know the story of every piece of lace but I will try to answer you.'

'It is not the lace...' Natalie opened her bag. She took out the scrap of brown envelope, now more creased than ever. 'Your mamma, Lina, she lives here on Burano? Is this her address?'

Belinda stared at her as though Natalie was the first human she'd ever encountered. She took the paper from Natalie's hand. 'It is Mamma's writing, I am sure of that. And our address, although the number looks wrong... You would think this was a three and a one, not a five and a seven. But that is typical; even I cannot always read her handwriting. But where did you get this? Why do you have it? Have you come from England to look for Mamma?'

'I... well...' Natalie did not know how to answer her.

Belinda's eyes filled with tears.

'It is you, isn't it? I would never have guessed... We look nothing alike. You are Catherine, aren't you? The older sister I have never met.' She grasped Natalie's wrists. 'Oh, Cathy! Cathy! My mamma's little baby girl!'

37

A delivery barge piled high with crates of fruit was heading for a landing spot. The day was already warm, *La Serenissima* basking under a blue sky. But Natalie suspected it was nerves rather than heat that were responsible for the dampness spreading under her arms, the trickle of sweat down her chest. She hurried along the *fondamenta*, dodging a dachshund on an extendable lead.

Her meeting place came into view. Cate, already perched on a white, metal chair, raised her hand. Natalie let out a breath; she slowed her pace a little.

'Hi, Cate!' She walked up to the table.

'Hi, I got you a cappuccino and a pistachio croissant; it's so early, I guessed you hadn't had breakfast.'

'Thanks, you're right.' Natalie sat down, her back to the canal. 'Where's Phil? What did you tell him?'

'Not much. He's quite happy for me to disappear for an hour. He's discovered the palazzo's home gym. He's working on his quads and his abs or something – don't ask me what!' Cate laughed.

'You're not a gym bunny nowadays?' Natalie gingerly lifted her dangerously full cappuccino to her lips.

Cate stretched her well-toned arms over her head. 'No, just Pilates... but you haven't met me to talk about workouts, have you? What is it? Your message sounded a bit cloak and dagger. It's something to do with Mum, isn't it?'

'How...?'

'You went to Burano with Eraldo yesterday; what else could it be? Don't tell me you went back to the house?'

'No, of course not. You can't imagine how tempting it was, but it wouldn't have made any difference.'

'Why, what have you found out? For goodness' sake, Nat, spit it out.'

Natalie brushed some sugar off the aluminium tabletop, reached into her bag and smoothed out the scrap of brown paper.

'You kept it? Why?'

'Just in case... but look: that's not a one at the end of that number, it's a seven, and that's a five, not a three.'

'Maybe, but it still looks like a one and a three to me. Is that all?' Cate sighed. She picked up her coffee. 'Wait a moment... you're smiling. You know something, don't you?'

'I didn't meet your mum but I found out she's still living on Burano, the same little square we went to but a different number house. And... you have a sister, a half-sister who works at the Lace Museum. I met her when—'

'A sister! You met my sister?' Cate interrupted. She stared at Nat, lips slightly parted as though waiting for more words to come, her expression unreadable.

Natalie took a bite of her croissant, tasteless in her dry mouth. She felt so vulnerable under Cate's searching gaze. Was Cate angry with her? Had she handled this delicate matter all wrong, ruined their friendship again for the final undoable time? She wished Eraldo was with them; she longed to reach out and squeeze his comforting hand.

'Oh, Nat,' Cate croaked at last. She gave a big sniff. 'That's wonderful. What's my sister's name? Does she want to meet me? Please say she does... And my mum, does she know? Does she want to see me?'

Natalie swallowed the lump of pastry. 'Your sister's twenty-eight, she's called Belinda. She's so excited about meeting you. Your mum, she doesn't know you're here yet. She's away visiting friends. Belinda wants to tell her face to face when she gets back home this morning.'

Cate leant across the table. 'And if she wants to see me...'

'We'll clear a time tomorrow. I'll talk to Lucia and we'll work it out.'

'I don't know how I'll get through the filming today. I'm so excited and nervous.'

'Well, you'll have to start by getting changed; your sleeve's dragging in that saucer of coffee.'

'Ugh.' Cate examined her arm. 'I'll put a dress on, but not my favourite one. I'll save that for tomorrow. Do you really think she'll want to see me? Am I finally going to meet my mum?'

'Of course you are. I'm certain she'll want to see you.' Natalie crossed her fingers under the table. She would have crossed her toes if she'd been that dextrous. 'I'm so glad you've got this chance. Get that breakfast down you then you can get back to the palazzo and tell Phil all about it.'

Cate's face clouded. 'No, I can't do that yet. You'll need to find an excuse to separate us. Take Phil off to see some amazing old artworks or something.'

'But why?'

'This Belinda you met, she might think her mum wants to meet me. But what if deep down, she doesn't? Or what if she does meet me and I'm not what she expects? What if she rejects me again?'

'Oh, Cate, she won't.'

'She left me. Left me when I was a little baby and she never came back. Dad kept us apart but maybe she thinks it was *me* who didn't want to see her. Please, I don't want Phil to know, not until I'm sure I've really got Mum back in my life.'

'Okay, if you're sure that's what you want. We'll find some sort of furniture workshop or something like that to take him to. He'll be so interested in watching old Venetian artisans at work, he won't give a moment's thought to where you are.'

'Thanks, I really appreciate that. I'd better get back and change before Lucia arrives to collect us. I don't know how I'm going to get through this cookery class she's arranged. I'm so jumpy, I'll probably cut off my thumb whilst I'm chopping an onion.'

'Please don't! I don't want any more disasters!'

Cate's face changed. 'There's something I need to warn you about.'

Natalie put down the last piece of croissant she'd just picked up. 'What?'

'It's Phil. He's being a bit weird about this whole cookery-lesson thing.'

'It's only making a risotto. And if he's a little bit rubbish, it will just endear him to the viewers.'

'I know, but he gets in a bit of a flap when he has to do something that's outside his comfort zone. He's used to running his company, being successful... I suppose he's not very good at not being good at things.'

'Thanks for warning me. I'm sure he'll be fine once he's in the kitchen. Now get that coffee down you and we can go.'

'Okay.' Cate downed her remaining cappuccino in one. 'I'll see you later then. And thanks again about Mum. I really can't believe it.'

'I'll meet you at the restaurant.' Natalie gave Cate a kiss on the cheek before setting off in the opposite direction.

Her phone buzzed. A message from Lucia: everything was in place; nothing was left to chance. Today was going to be a good day. Cate worried too much. There was no way a successful businessman like Phil was going to have a meltdown over a simple bit of cooking.

38

Phil refastened the ties on his *Ristorante Nico* apron.

'*Tutto bene*? All good?' Nico Facetti, the owner and head chef, beamed at them.

'All good.' Phil hoped he sounded convincing, confident even. *Come on, Phil, you can chop some vegetables.*

Nico twisted an onion. 'We do not cut that way, we cut this way. And we keep the handle of the knife like this – and then it is simple.' The blade sliced up and down so rapidly, Phil was amazed the guy had any fingers left. A pyramid of evenly chopped cubes materialised on the wooden board. Across the stainless-steel counter, Cate's face was a picture of concentration.

'Shall I try now?' Cate said, picking up a short-handled knife.

'*Certo!*'

Cate wasn't half as fast as Nico but she chopped neatly and she'd remembered all the celebrity chef's hints and tricks to complete the job without her eyes pricking with tears.

'And now you, *signore*.'

Phil took a knife from the bewildering array of kitchen implements.

'Ah, no. That is the knife for the cutting of the fish.'

'Of course.' Phil hadn't even started cutting the onion and he was already messing up. He created intricate marquetry with the finest of chisels so why did the prospect of using paring knives and wooden spoons, spatulas and graters feel as cumbersome and unnatural as swimming in a ski suit? The steam from the other end of the kitchen where black-uniformed staff were beavering away, and the heat and bright lights from the camera crew were making him sweat. He looked around. The make-up girl with her ever-ready powder puff had disappeared.

What a chump he must look, dithering over such a simple task. They probably wouldn't even use this bit of film; no one tuned into *Luxe Life Swap* to see a red-faced, middle-aged man prepping veg. He took a deep breath and began chopping.

'*Bravo*, Phil! You see, it is easy when you have the correct technique.' Nico spoke in the same tone of voice Cate had used when they'd been struggling to house train Ted. 'And now we check on our beautiful fish stock.'

Phil nodded. When he'd agreed to take part in Mandy Miller's iconic show, he hadn't signed up for this. He couldn't cook, wouldn't cook – unless you counted making things on toast. But at least there was no chance of setting a pan ablaze with the oily Nico getting right up into his personal space. He'd almost forgotten the humiliation he'd felt in that school cookery lesson. There had been so many humiliations before he was blessed with Evan's protection.

The rugby pitch was flooded, afternoon sports lessons cancelled and the headmaster had decided he wasn't going to leave a whole year group to their own devices. To the horror of their motherly school cook, the kitchens were commandeered. They'd never had a cookery lesson before but everyone else seemed to take to it except for Phil.

Phil didn't know how he'd managed to set that pan on fire. He could still hear his classmates' giggles turning to panic as the cook fought to put out the flames, the ear-splitting ring of the fire alarm. Everyone had been forced to stand outside in the cold and the rain, moaning and bitching that it was all his fault. They were still making snide remarks on the rugby pitch the next week and he'd got in such a state that he'd somehow sent the ball down to his own try line instead of kicking it into touch.

He didn't care about being good at cooking or sports for their own sakes. He cared about being picked on, bullied, isolated. Failure told people you were weak. Weakness made you a target. All these years later, he could still feel Mr King's hand on his thigh, his minty breath in his face. That oh-so-soft voice whispering in his ear, 'Who do you think they'd believe, Philip? You or me?'

'Phil!'

Cate's voice snapped him back to his task.

'How much stock did you say?' They must be adding the stock now, mustn't they? Even he could recognise a ladle.

'No stock yet. First, we must add the white wine.' Nico sloshed some into Phil's pan, clearly deeming him incapable of doing it himself. 'Aah, the smell – mmm, *delizioso!*'

'Delicious,' Cate agreed, beaming at the smarmy chef.

'And now the stock, little by little. Let the rice absorb one ladleful of liquid before you add the next.'

Little by little. Phil could concentrate on this one simple thing. Mindfulness, wasn't that what they called it? Now that Nico was supervising proceedings on the other side of the kitchen, not hovering over Phil's shoulder, he could relax. If only he could get Mr King's voice out of his head.

* * *

Cate inhaled the warm, stomach-rumbling aroma of shellfish stock and white wine. It was such a privilege to be taught by a chef who'd entranced thousands of Parisians with his Michelin-star fusion food before feeling the pull of his native Venice. And she was grateful their jam-packed day was keeping her occupied until tomorrow's potentially life-changing encounter. There was something almost mesmeric about languidly stirring in each ladle of fragrant liquid.

She'd looked at the text from Belinda – her sister! – a hundred times: the one telling her that yes, her mother, Lina, wanted to see her. Tomorrow, she'd slip away to Burano whilst Natalie and Lucia took Phil to a *squero*. He was so excited to visit a boatyard where he could see the gondolas being worked on, he'd barely questioned why Cate wouldn't be there.

She glanced across the counter at him, his face so endearingly serious, you'd think they'd been entrusted with cooking a six-course banquet, not rustling up a risotto no one but themselves would eat. Cate wasn't worried about how hers would turn out. She was a decent home cook; she'd never have the talent of a starry chef, but it was the taking part that mattered. The only failure was the failure to try something new – that was what she'd always instilled in their two boys.

It was an attitude that flummoxed Phil. He'd stood on the sidelines at every infant school sports day, not understanding how she didn't care that she'd trailed in last in the mothers' race (though she'd started jogging round the park after that) or how she and Max were still smiling after failing to finish the wheelbarrow race, lying in a tangled heap on the playing field laughing and laughing until their sides ached.

There were worse foibles for a husband to have. Phil was only ever hard on himself, never on the boys. She smiled fondly at him, hoping the simple task of stirring risotto would provide him with the confidence boost to tackle the tiramisù they'd be making after lunch. But Phil didn't seem to be stirring his. Should she lean across the counter and interfere or let him find his feet?

'Ah, Cate!' Nico waltzed up. He plunged a fork into her pan and held a few grains of rice aloft. He blew gently on the morsel before raising it to his lips. '*Perfetto*! Now remove from the heat and we stir in a knob of butter.

'And how are you doing?' He clapped a hand on Phil's shoulder, making him jump. 'But what is this! You have not been stirring? It is stuck! Stuck to your pan!' He held up a forkful of Phil's creation, examining the rice, congealed, crispy and brown, as though it were something unpleasant stuck to the sole of his shoe.

Phil didn't reply, staring into the pan as though he had no idea how it had appeared in front of him.

'Try adding some more stock. It's probably just burnt on the bottom. Most of it will probably be fine,' Cate cut in, ignoring the expression writ large on Nico's face.

'It's ruined.' Phil banged his hand against his forehead so violently, she flinched.

'It's only a risotto,' Natalie interrupted, obviously trying to channel Mandy Miller's relentless good cheer. 'Don't worry, we won't show this on the programme. Could you stop the filming please, Lucia? Why don't we all take a little break? I'm sure you'll have more luck with the tiramisù after lunch.'

'I'm not doing this any more,' Phil said.

'But Phil...' Cate gave Natalie a helpless glance.

'You don't understand.' His voice was bleak. 'I can't fail. I can't.'

He started to wrench at the ties on his apron, struggling with the double bow.

Cate reached out a hand. 'Here, let me. You're knotting it tighter.'

'I can manage!' Phil snapped.

Ignoring his outburst, Cate gently pushed his hands away. 'There you go!'

Phil stood silently, balling up the stock-splattered apron in his hands. He seemed to have shrunk several inches. Now she really was getting worried.

'Phil!' She needed to get him out of the kitchen, out into the fresh air.

Phil raised his head. Cate's breath caught. She could hardly believe what she was seeing. Her husband was doing something she'd never seen before – not even on the days Oli and Max were born.

Phil was crying.

* * *

Despite wearing an apron, Cate had managed to splash fish stock on her dress. She pushed aside the pang of irritation. Even though she and Phil were sitting in a rather smart wine bar around the corner from *Ristorante Nico*, her appearance didn't matter. Nothing, not even tomorrow's trip to Burano nor the nagging realisation that she'd failed to make the usual call to the nursing home to check on her dad, was as important as discovering what had made Phil fall apart. But Phil wasn't making it easy.

'You need to tell me what's bothering you. It can't just be messing up in the kitchen. I couldn't care less about the risotto and we can pay for the pan if it's wrecked.'

Phil gulped another mouthful of red wine.

'Talk to me, Phil.'

He twisted his hands together. 'I do love you, Cate. You know that, don't you?'

She waited for the 'but', the wine churning in her empty stomach. Was the relationship that had sustained her for two decades about to collapse? Had his seemingly casual attitude to their neighbour Kiran been a clever bluff?

She looked into her husband's dead eyes. 'Are you leaving me, Phil?'

He shot forward in his seat. 'Leaving you? How can you think such a thing?' Her words seemed to knock a spark of life back into him.

'You're not having an affair?'

'Cate, Cate!' He shook his head. 'Of course not. You're more likely to leave me.'

'Why? I'd never do that. You're a great husband, a wonderful father. And a good man.'

'A good man? You wouldn't say that if you really knew me.'

'It's not just me who thinks that. Your children love you, your parents, your old friends like Evan and Lucy.'

'Evan.' He spat out the name. 'Sometimes, I wish I'd never met him.'

He reached for the bottle of Valpolicella. She placed her hand over the top of his glass.

'Phil. Talk to me. Whatever it is, you have to tell me or I'll be imagining something worse. It's Venice, isn't it? You haven't been yourself since the TV company told us where we were being sent. Is it something to do with Evan? Something that happened on your school trip? But you're still such good friends...'

'I don't blame Evan for what happened. It was all my fault. But it was all because I was scared. Scared of... *him*.'

'Of who?'

Phil bit his lip. Tears pricked his eyes again.

Cate waited.

'Mr King.' Phil dropped his head.

'One of the teachers? You've never mentioned him.'

'King was only there for a year. They didn't tell us why he left. I wondered later if they – the school – had found out about him and got him to leave quietly without a fuss. They used to do that, you know, schools like mine: move a teacher on with a good reference rather than cause a scandal.'

He reached for the bottle again. This time, she kept her hands folded in her lap.

'King was straight out of teacher training, young, handsome, charismatic. He taught PE; he was a brilliant cricketer. He wasn't very tall and with his baby face, he could almost pass for one of us. Most of the boys looked up to him, as though he were a cool older school chum. But all that charm was a front. I thought I was the only one he picked on but there were probably others like me: a scholarship boy, without a deep circle of friends, a boy who knew he didn't really belong, who was desperate to be accepted, to fit in. He could smell weakness; the more I failed, the more he'd goad me. I would never have signed up for the school trip if I'd known he'd be there. He joined at the last moment after the art teacher broke his hip falling off a ladder pinning the third form's watercolours to the classroom wall.

'He used to sneer at me, make me feel small; at school, he'd bash into me in the corridor accidentally on purpose, knock my books out of my hand. And in the changing rooms, if I wasn't quick enough, he'd corner me...'

Cate's hand flew to her mouth. 'He touched you?'

'He only ever touched me through my clothes, but I was terrified. I was so relieved to find we slept in dormitories in Venice like we did at Hillingdon. I knew he wouldn't dare creep in there in case someone like Evan was awake. Looking back, I don't think he was even interested in me that way. It must have been a power trip, letting me know what he could do to me. He preferred prettier boys with sharp cheekbones and pouty, petal-pink lips, so they said. Girls, too. The police found all sorts on his computer at the next school where he taught.'

Cate lowered her voice, conscious of three elderly ladies sitting nearby. 'Did he go to prison? Has he come out?'

Phil stared at a point beyond Cate's head. 'He can't go anywhere. Not any more. They say he ripped up his sheet and twisted it into a rope. And the weird thing is that when I heard he was dead, all I could think about was my trainers, that now I'd never get them back.'

'Your trainers? I don't understand.'

Phil rubbed his forehead. 'Grandad died a few months before we went to Venice. He left me a few hundred pounds out of his meagre savings. Dad got the rest; he insisted on using most of his share to pay for the school trip. I should have saved the money or bought something sensible but I longed for these trendy trainers with bright-yellow laces I'd seen one of the sixth formers wear.' Phil took another great swig of wine. 'I stupidly thought the other boys would see me differently, that people would want to be friends with me. My best friend Raj told me to save the money for uni, for books and stuff and not waste it on trying to impress people. Raj grew up on the same estate as me, he won a scholarship the same year I did, but he never seemed to care if anyone looked down their nose at him, or maybe he just didn't show it.

'I got the trainers delivered to the school; they arrived just in time for the trip. I felt I was the bees' knees when I got them out of my suitcase. A couple of the boys were impressed like I'd hoped but others just took the mick. King was even worse. He sidled up and hissed in my ear that they looked stupid on scum like me.'

Phil paused. He fiddled with the stem of his wine glass. 'The afternoon before the masked ball, one of the boys was showing us some magic tricks and King got out a pack of cards. He challenged us to a game of poker and told us all to put some money in. It was against the rules but the other teacher wasn't around and he knew no one would dare report him. Everyone was excited to play except Raj; he just sat and read a book and wouldn't join in. The boys were slapping down tens and twenties like it was Monopoly money. I lost all my term's pocket money. King said I'd have to sell dishcloths and dusters door to door round the council estate and everybody laughed.'

Phil picked up his glass, looking momentarily surprised to see it was almost empty, and put it down again. 'King poked my trainers with his toe and said I could put them in, joked they weren't worth much now someone like me had worn them. I felt sick at the thought of losing them, but everyone started chanting, "trainers, trainers, trainers", louder and louder. I saw Raj shaking his head but I didn't want to stick out like him so I put them into the pot. King won that hand, scooped up all the money and held up my trainers like he'd won the FA Cup. He wore them to the ball that night even though they looked stupid with his Plague-doctor costume. He did it just to taunt me. I was so glad when he disappeared halfway through the evening.'

Cate felt the tension she didn't realise she'd still been carrying lift away like a dandelion puff blowing through the air. Now everything made sense. The predatory Mr King had to be Nat's attacker. Her hand itched to reach into her bag for her phone, to give Nat closure, whatever that was worth. But right now, it was Phil who needed her.

She reached across the table to hold his hand. 'Why haven't you said anything to me before? Why have you kept it all to yourself?'

'Because whatever King did wasn't an excuse for what I did next. I knew being friends with Evan and his mates would protect me. I would have done anything to join their gang. And I hate myself for it.'

Cate frowned. 'I don't understand. You and Evan are best friends.'

'Not the way Raj and I were.' He finished his glass of wine in one gulp. 'If I tell you the truth, you'll despise me, the way I despise myself. And I just couldn't bear it.'

'Whatever you did back then, you were just a child. But I have to know.' Her other hand tightened around her wine glass. 'Phil, you have to tell me the truth or we can't go on. You have to tell me what else happened in Venice.'

39

VENICE, TWENTY-FIVE YEARS EARLIER

The room was stifling, the dormitory stuffy with the smell of eight boys. Phil wished he could switch on the light and absorb himself in his *Harry Potter* book but he couldn't risk disturbing the others.

He swung his legs out of bed, un-balled his abandoned socks, slipped his plastic room key into his pyjama pocket and groped his way across the room. He paused, hand on the doorknob, waiting, his breathing fast. One boy kicked at his bed covers in his sleep; no one woke. Six boys slept on; one other boy-shaped hump was missing. Evan wasn't there. Had he also gone wandering in the night?

The long, panelled corridor was quiet, lit dimly by wall sconces decorated with scrolls and leaves. Phil made his way towards the staircase at the end, his footfall softened by the patterned runner, as quiet as one of the hooded monks with candles who had walked there centuries before him when the building played host to holy men, not boisterous school groups.

He climbed the stairs. A wooden bench stood midway

along the upper corridor. He ran his hand along its sturdy back; even at this hour, he could not pass it without stopping to appreciate the fine carving. He'd never be as talented as the artisans who'd created St Mark's Basilica but one day, he'd learn to make something like this.

The arched doorway leading to the upper floor's outside balcony was half-hidden behind a sage-green curtain patterned with fleur-de-lys. Phil prayed the door had been left unlocked so he might spend the hours before breakfast watching the city of Venice as it woke up: the coming of the dawn, the changing colour of the sky, the delivery boats taking goods to businesses around the city, the rubbish barge with its red crane lifting sacks of refuse.

He pushed open the door. A sweet, pungent smell, heavy on the night air, hit him. For a moment, he was catapulted back into the stairwell of his London housing estate. A boy sat on the floor, pyjama bottoms rolled up, bare feet resting on the railings. The glowing tip of a hand-rolled spliff illuminated Evan's face. Phil's loud gasp came out before he thought to stifle it.

Evan swung around. 'Oi, Phil! Where are you going? Come here.'

Phil glanced over his shoulder.

'Don't worry, no one comes out here, at least not at three o'clock in the morning. And you haven't been here either. You've not seen anything.' There was an edge to Evan's voice.

'I'm not a snitch.'

'No, I don't suppose you are. Probably get you stabbed, where you come from. Sit down. Have a drag.' He held out the joint.

'No, I'm all right, thanks.' Phil leant against the railing. 'But why?'

'Why am I taking drugs, risking everything?' Evan's voice was sarcastic. He sighed. 'I dunno. Boredom? Stress?'

'You?'

'Yeah, me. Straight-A student, captain of the rugby team, bloody rich family. Sometimes…'

'What?'

Evan's face closed up. 'Nothing. Anyway, it's not heroin, it's only a bit of blow; it's no biggie. Some of my mother's friends snort coke on their girls' night out. She says she doesn't but I reckon she does. My father's pretty difficult to live with.'

'Yeah, it's no biggie.' It was for Phil. Drugs meant next-door's baby being taken into care and the guy who sat on a sheet of cardboard in the doorway of Poundland shouting incoherent profanities: everyday tales from the world he and Raj had left behind. Phil wasn't going to stay out here, risk being caught and going back to that.

'You sure you don't want some?'

'Nah.' Phil yawned theatrically. 'I'm off back to bed; think I could sleep after all.'

'Got an alarm clock?'

'Why?'

'Set it early, meet me downstairs at half six. My uncle Seb's arranged a private visit for me to a workshop where they make the gondoliers' oars. You like all that old craft stuff, don't you? I saw you studying those picture frames in the Accademia.'

'Me? Why?'

'You're my friend, aren't you?' Evan took one last puff, screwed the butt into the ground and flicked it away. 'If King picks on you again, I'll back you up.'

'I told you, I won't tell anyone,' Phil said. 'But be careful, Evan.'

But Evan hadn't been careful enough. The moment they

returned from the oar maker's workshop and slipped into the breakfast room, Phil knew something was up. Voices were hushed, faces pale. It didn't take long to piece the events together: the butt of a joint flicked an inch short of the edge of the balcony, the Latin teacher roused from his bed by a bout of heartburn, opening a window and smelling marijuana drifting down. Whispered voices told Phil the school was taking the matter extremely seriously. If a culprit did not confess, the others must not hesitate to report him anonymously. Someone knew who was breaking the school's zero-tolerance policy on drugs. The reputation, the very future of Hillingdon was at stake.

* * *

Phil stood at the dorm window. It was less than a week since they'd flown back from Venice; his pale arms still showed a hint of golden brown. Three floors below, Raj dragged his trunk across the courtyard. His father hauled it into the boot of his Corsa. The Burton suit he'd sported so proudly at last summer's prize-giving looked two sizes too big for him. Raj climbed into the passenger seat.

Evan sidled silently beside him. 'I really didn't think he'd be expelled; I thought they'd take him off the cricket team, make him spend Sunday afternoons helping the gardener weed the beds. Look at what happened to Jez.'

'Raj isn't Jez,' Phil said. Raj didn't have a father who'd paid for the new sports pavilion and who promised that his son would spend the holiday volunteering at a drug-prevention project.

'I didn't say it was Raj who did it, Phil, I swear.'

'I know.' Phil had seen one of Evan's best buddies sneaking

out of the headmaster's study, guilt written all over his face. 'I should have said something. Not to drop you in it, just to tell them it wasn't him.'

The passenger window rolled up and closed. The car stood idling on the gravel as though the two occupants couldn't quite believe they had to go.

Maybe it wasn't too late. Phil bolted for the door. 'I can't let him leave like this. Not when I know—'

Evan made a grab for him. 'Please don't say anything, Phil. If you tell them it wasn't Raj, they won't let it drop. They might even make us all take a drugs test. I'll never forget you standing by me, Phil. It means everything to me, you being such a good friend.'

Phil pushed past him, took the stairs two at a time.

Mr King was leaning against the newel post at the bottom. 'Where are you going in such a hurry, Philip?'

'Raj... he...'

'Best let him go. You wouldn't want to get Evan into trouble now, would you?'

'Evan? What do you mean?'

Mr King dropped his voice to a whisper. 'I don't walk around with my eyes shut, Philip. Pretty stupid of Evan, don't you think? But the school doesn't want to lose a boy like him. Bad publicity, no good for business. Best for someone like Raj to take the fall, wouldn't you say? One of your type, no one will miss him.'

'But...'

'Imagine how lonely and unpopular you'd be if Evan left. All the boys would blame you. There'd be no one to look out for you.' Mr King's hand strayed across Phil's backside.

Evan was coming down the stairs, his usual swagger gone. 'Oh, hello, sir.'

'Hi, Evan! I've put you on the team sheet for Saturday against Eton. Maybe you should start coaching Philip. He was just telling me what good friends you are.'

Evan slung an arm over Phil's shoulder. 'I'm starving, let's go to the tuck shop. Fancy some crisps?'

They walked out of the huge double doors and across the quad. The sky was a dull grey. Light rain was starting to fall. The green car had reached the far end of the long drive, two red spots fading into the distance.

40

Phil stared at the empty bottle of wine. 'So now you know I'm not the man you thought I was,' he said.

It certainly wasn't her husband's finest hour but Phil looked so wretched, Cate's heart went out to him.

'Oh Phil! Of course it wasn't right what you did, you should have spoken up and told the truth, but you have to forgive yourself. You were a child, just the age Oli is now, a scared young boy. If anyone's to blame for what happened to Raj, it's that sick, twisted teacher. And I'm sure it's not all as black and white as you believe it was. It sounds like Evan was a troubled young man who needed a real friend. And you *have* been a real friend to him. He would have dropped you long ago if it was just a matter of convenience.'

'We've got stuff in common now: business interests, dinner-party friends, our boys being at Hillingdon together. But don't you see? Underneath, it's all rotten. We're bound together by the selfish, cowardly thing that we did. I'll never have another friend like Raj; he's worth ten of Evan and a hundred of me. But I let Raj walk away. I never saw him again.'

'You didn't try to get in touch? Never phoned or messaged him?'

'I was too cowardly, too afraid of what he would say. I ruined his life, Cate. Coming back here brings more reminders every day. I can't forgive myself. Sometimes, I think you'd all be better off without me.'

'No! Don't ever say that. Oli and Max worship you. And how do you know for sure Raj's life was ruined when you haven't spoken since?'

Phil put his head in his hands. 'Sometimes, I look him up on Facebook,' he mumbled.

'But you don't do social media. You wouldn't even let me set up an Instagram account for the business; you said it was more exclusive that way.'

'I signed into Oli's account. It was easy enough to guess his password.'

'Phil! Honestly! Oli will think you're snooping because you don't trust him.'

'Oli doesn't post anything on there; he says only boomers use Facebook nowadays, whatever that means. I know how Raj is living, Cate. His posts and profile are there for anyone to see. He's such an open, honest guy, it wouldn't occur to him to make them private. He runs a coffee-shop franchise in a rundown shopping arcade; I've got a business that's patronised by the Prince of Wales. He takes his wife and three kids on caravan holidays; we've stayed in a suite at the Ritz. I've got everything he should have got.' He slapped his wrist. 'I've even got a Rolex. What a cliché!'

Cate fiddled with her wedding ring. Across the room, the man behind the bar was pouring glasses of champagne. She pulled out her phone and clicked on the Facebook icon she almost never used. 'I want to take a look at this Raj. What's his last name?'

'Why?' Phil sounded weary but he spelt it out for her. 'There's more than one user called that; he's the one with his family in his profile pic.'

Cate had no trouble finding him. 'What a nice smile he has! And his wife and kids look lovely.'

She studied the latest photograph Raj had posted. He and his family eating ice-cream sundaes at an outdoor café. She had the strangest feeling it was somewhere she knew. She used her fingers to expand the picture. The café where she and Natalie had drunk coffee earlier came into view. Cate checked the date. Raj had posted the photograph just that morning. She looked across at Phil, chewing the skin around his manicured nails.

'Now I understand why you've been so weird and jumpy. But don't you see? This is the perfect opportunity. I know it's not easy but don't you think it's time you apologised to Raj in person?'

Phil sighed. 'You're right, I know you are. Of course I should. I'll try and contact him when we get back home. He lives on the edge of London now; it's not that far away.'

'There's no point putting it off till then. Not when he's here.'

'What do you mean?' Phil looked blank.

'You didn't know?' She held out her phone. 'Read the caption.'

Celebrating our twentieth wedding anniversary with the kids, a once-in-a-lifetime dream trip to Venice.

'He's here? Oh, Cate, I can't.'

'You can. You've got to do it for yourself. And for him. I

already think better of you for having the courage to tell me all this. I know how hard it can be to bare your soul. Message him now; you can use my Facebook account. Tell him you're here and you'd like to meet. Keep it short and light.'

She forced herself to smile patiently as he typed and deleted, typed and deleted until finally settling on a two-line message.

'Do you think that's okay?' He slid his phone across the table. She pressed send.

'There, it's gone. And now it's my turn to confess. You're not the only one who's been keeping secrets.'

The colour drained from his already pale face.

'It's okay,' she said quickly. 'It's not an affair, nothing like that. It's about me. Tomorrow, whilst you're at the gondola workshop, I'm not going to be mooching around the shops like I told you I was. I'm going back to Burano. I'm going to meet my mother.'

'Your *mum*?' Phil gawped. 'But I thought... I assumed... she'd passed away.'

'I know I let you think that and I'm truly sorry. I haven't got time to explain properly now but I promise I'll tell you everything tonight when we're back at the palazzo. In the meantime, I've got to go.' She picked up her bag and squeezed out of the booth. 'One of us needs to go back to the restaurant to make that tiramisù before Lucia sends the film crew home. And with your cooking skills, it had better be me.'

For the first time in hours, Phil cracked a smile.

41

Cate had an hour to kill. She'd caught the waterbus far too early, terrified of messing up and being late but also yearning for time to sit by herself amongst the trees and flowers, safe in the knowledge that Nat was keeping a careful eye on Phil over at the *squero*.

She entered the little park on Mazzorbo, heading for the same bright-red bench she and Nat had sat on just days before. So much had happened since the two of them had strolled through here on their way to Burano. She cringed at the memory of visiting the house where she'd believed her mother lived, her foot in the door, the way she'd almost barged her way upstairs into a stranger's bedroom. Now she was going back to Burano by invitation, but still her emotions whirled like chunks of fruit in a blender. Phil's revelations, Natalie's relief that her attacker was no longer free to prey on others – yesterday was a day she'd never forget.

Of course, Cate hadn't shared Phil's own story; she'd only told Natalie about the prowling school pervert and his downfall. It was up to her husband to decide when – if ever – and with whom he wanted to share the episodes that had caused him such anguish. How thankful she was that she'd never shared Nat's suspicions that Phil had been her attacker. How Phil would have reacted was anyone's guess but the possibility that she might have irreparably damaged their marriage didn't bear thinking about.

Cate checked her phone. Again. Her new half-sister, Belinda, had promised to confirm the name of the café where her mum, Lina, would be waiting. Her own mother! But did Cate really want to hear her mum's excuses for staying away all these years? Wouldn't it be better to let the past lie? Dealing with her husband's anxiety about seeing Raj – who'd surprisingly messaged Phil straight back agreeing to meet – should be her priority, not chasing foolish dreams.

Cate sighed. She'd been wrong to come. She should go back to the waterbus, back to the man who loved and needed her, not sit here waiting for the woman who'd upped and left.

She picked up her bag. Her phone beeped. A message from an Italian number. It was Belinda.

> We are early, Mamma was too excited to wait.
> La Ciambella on Piazza Baldassarre Galuppi.

Her heart leapt. Despite her cool logic, Cate knew she couldn't just turn around and go. Not now. Maybe it was wrong to try and second-guess the reasons her mum had stayed away. She typed quickly, her message brief and to the point. She wasn't ready to share her emotions yet.

> I am early too. See you very soon.

She clicked *send* before she could change her mind. A message pinged through straight away but it wasn't a reply from Belinda. The message was from The Evergreens, asking her to contact them. Cate frowned. Dad had been fine when she'd checked last night. It couldn't be anything urgent; they would have called if it was. Anyhow, she couldn't stop and deal with it now; she'd be on the phone forever with chatty Sally on reception. Dad had kept her and Mum apart before. He wasn't going to do it again.

She stowed her phone in her bag and set off in the direction of the little bridge that led to Burano.

* * *

Cate had no memory of being with her mum, but she knew, even before Lina rose from her seat, that this slim, dark-haired woman was her mother, her own flesh and blood. Cate pushed her sunglasses up into her hair, wanting nothing, not even a layer of tinted glass, to come between them in this precious moment.

'Cathy, oh, Cathy!' Her mum clung to her, rocking her slightly from side to side as if she was still the baby she'd once soothed in her arms. Cate allowed herself to be held, feeling her toned arms and strong shoulders collapse against Lina's angular body like a half-baked soufflé.

Eventually, Lina let go. She lifted Cate's hair away from her face. 'You are so beautiful – and blonde now too.'

'A good hairdresser.'

'Every woman's secret weapon,' the young woman standing alongside Lina said. 'I am so pleased to meet you, Cathy. I have always wondered about you. *Che bello*! How beautiful it is that we meet.' She swiped tears from her eyes.

'My daughter, Belinda,' Lina added. The two younger

women embraced. 'Please sit down. Let us have some coffee together.'

Cate sat. Belinda ordered the coffee, smiling broadly as if to reassure the waiter who was looking a little alarmed by the sight of three weeping women.

For a while, none of them spoke. Cate gazed at Lina, searching for traces of her own features in her mother's face.

'I am sorry, I cannot help crying like this.' Lina sniffed. 'I have dreamt of this day for many years. Every year on your birthday, I have made a wish that you would come and find me.'

You could have come and found *me*, Cate wanted to say, but this wasn't the time for recriminations. She fiddled with the handle on the espresso cup the waiter had quietly set before her.

'I am so pleased to meet you,' Belinda said again.

Cate squirmed on her metal chair, not knowing where to begin.

Lina flicked her hand towards her untouched coffee cup. 'I do not know what we are doing here, amongst all these tourists! We must welcome you to our home.'

'You are right, you must come to the house.' Belinda peeled a note from her purse and wedged it under the sugar bowl.

'Thank you, that's very kind.' Cate said, getting up. She was glad to escape the curious looks from the family at the adjoining table. She pushed down her sunglasses and let her new half-sister link arms as they walked the short distance to the little square where her mother lived.

The marmalade cat she'd seen by the orange house was lying on the doorstep. Belinda scooped it up under one arm as her mother unlocked their front door.

'Tigre is our cat, though he likes to spend more time on our neighbours' doorsteps. I think other people feed him, although they say they do not. Please, come in. We will sit out on our balcony.'

Cate stepped into a narrow hallway, taking in its pale-pink walls, the samples of old, handmade lace framed and mounted on the wall.

'I will make the coffee,' Lina said, disappearing through a door at the end.

Cate waited in the hallway with Belinda. A folding umbrella and some unopened post lay on a half-moon table, watched over by several family photographs. An image of a girl in a bunny-eared hat feeding a baby lamb made her catch her breath.

'This is me... when we went to Wales. I must have been three or four.'

'Your papà sent Mamma a photograph every year. Most of them are in an album in our living room. I loved to look at them when I was a little girl, hoping you looked a bit like me. Come, let us go and sit outside.'

Cate followed her half-sister up the stairs and out onto the balcony, sinking into a green cushioned swing chair under a shady awning. She hardly dared to believe what she'd heard and seen. Her mum had kept and treasured Cate's photos; she'd yearned to see her daughter again. And her half-sister had known about Cate all along and dreamt of meeting her. How could Dad have let her go on that school trip to Venice, not telling her that the mother who loved her was living here?

'I still cannot believe you are really here!' Lina put down a tray laden with a metal coffee pot, cups, tea plates and an oval tin of Amaretti biscuits decorated with a whirly pattern of gold and pink. She perched on the edge of her chair, struggling to open the lid with her beautifully manicured hands.

'Let me. Your nails are too long.' Belinda prised open the lid, releasing a sweet, sugary scent. 'Please, take one.'

'Thank you.' Cate took one of the paper-wrapped biscuits. Lina poured out the coffee, holding the pot steady with both hands. Belinda threw back her drink in a couple of gulps and then stood up.

'Mamma, I think I will leave you two alone. Cathy and I have so much to catch up on... but you have so much you must want to say to each other.' Her sugar-almond-scented hair brushed against Cate's cheek as she bent to kiss her.

'Thank you, that's kind of you,' Cate said.

Lina stirred her coffee, even though she'd already added a sachet of sugar and stirred it just moments before. Cate undid the white wrapper on her biscuit even though she wasn't sure she could eat a thing.

'I saw the photograph in the hallway of me feeding the lambs.'

'Every year, Terry – your dad – sent one to me. This is the only one I have on display. It would make me sad to have too many pictures of you around the house.'

'Why did you leave?' Cate blurted it out. 'When I had my own children, I understood how strong a mother's love was. I couldn't imagine any circumstances where I would abandon my boys. It was Dad, wasn't it? Was he mean to you? Is that why you had to go?'

Lina fiddled with a stray strand of hair, taking a moment to compose herself. She licked her lips, swallowed and continued.

'No. I cannot blame Terry. He was always a good man, just a boy back then. I was so young when I fell pregnant: just a teenager. I was too scared to have a baby, too scared to have an abortion, too scared to go back home and disappoint my parents again. Terry surprised me; after the initial shock, he was thrilled to become a dad. I told myself everything would be all right. I even began to get excited and by the time I was five or six months gone, I knew I was willing to put my dreams of doing more travelling aside. I started to dream instead of a happy little family.

'I should have felt elated when the nurse handed you to me in the hospital but I just felt numb. She told me it was the exhaustion of the birth and I shouldn't worry. When I took you home, I struggled to breastfeed. I could not sleep. I would wake in the night to check on you, worrying about every little thing that could go wrong.'

Lina paused. She leant forward, resting her hands on the wrought-iron table, but that didn't stop them from shaking.

'I became convinced I was a bad mother, that one day, I would harm you. I began to imagine hurting you. I had visions of standing over your cot, holding a pillow and smothering you.'

Cate gasped, hardly able to take in what she was hearing.

'One day, I imagined feeding you from a bottle, putting bleach or some other poison in the milk. I could not tell anyone the truth; I believed they would take you away from me. But I knew you could not have a mother like me; you were not safe when I was around. You do not know how close I came to harming you.

'I could not tell Terry why I had to leave,' Lina continued, her voice so soft, Cate had to lean forward to catch her words. 'I did not want him to think I was a monster. It was easier for me to let him think I was selfish and uncaring, that I did not want to be tied down. Part of me hoped that once I'd left England, I could lose myself in travel, new places, new people, that somehow I could move on, but of course it does not work like that. It was many years later, when I was listening to a radio show, that I discovered I was not the only mother who had felt that way. I realised I must have been suffering from post-natal depression. I had not been mad or bad. I had been ill. It was such a relief to find a reason but so sad that I had not known to get help. When I was pregnant with Belinda, I spoke to the doctors so they could help me if it happened again.'

'Oh, Lina... Mum. It's terrible to think you suffered that way. I know how hard bringing up a baby can be. I was twenty-four when I had Oli and I still felt like a child parenting a child even then. And after him, we had Max and he didn't sleep. I still remember the struggles of being up half the night. I can't imagine dealing with that as a teenager and suffering from post-natal depression on top of it all.'

'I thought of telling Terry the truth once I realised what had been wrong with me. But it was too late and I knew he would blame himself for not being aware of how badly I was coping. I could see from the photographs he sent every year that you were happy, settled and you could not have had a better dad.'

'Dad kept me from you.'

Lina shook her head. 'No, that is not true.'

'I came to Venice, on a school trip, when I was fourteen. He never told me you were here. We could have met. You would have wanted to see me, wouldn't you?'

Lina turned her face away. 'Terry wanted to tell you, he wanted me to meet you, but I refused.'

'You didn't want to see me?' Cate's voice cracked.

'I wanted to see you, to hold you, with all my heart.' Lina's voice shook; she dabbed her eyes. 'But I told myself I did not deserve you. I could not come back into your life and turn everything upside down. I remembered my own teenage years: how difficult they were. But when Terry sent me a copy of the school's itinerary for your trip, I kept looking at it, imagining each day what you were doing, what you would think of the places you saw. I waited and waited for days until I could no longer stay away.

'The day you went to the Galleria Accademia, I waited in the Campo della Carità by the postcard seller's stand all morning. And then I saw a straggle of girls walking over the bridge. One girl was singing loudly, pretending to be Madonna. I hoped so much that it was your school. I went nearer, standing right by the foot of the bridge. It was not hard to pick you out. Oh, you cannot imagine the emotions I felt. I cannot even describe them. Love, pride, fear all rolled into one. How I wanted to rush up to you but you looked so happy, so carefree, I just stood and watched, telling myself it was better that way. I forced myself to walk away. For the rest of the day, I could think of nothing but you wandering around the gallery, imagining you exploring each room, wondering which painting would be your favourite.

'On your next birthday, your dad did not send a photograph. He never sent me any more. It was as though by not seeing you, I had made my choice – and I was too proud to contact him again. I met my husband, Belinda's papà, a few years later. He urged me to get back in touch with Terry. He told me I would regret it if I didn't. I said that you could choose to find me when you were older. I could not bear to try. I could not face the thought that you might reject me. I believed deep down, it was what I deserved. And in any case, you were always here.' She rested her palm against her heart.

Cate gulped. 'Why didn't Dad tell me? He let me believe it was his decision to keep us apart.' How could he have silently accepted the injustice of her sulks and strops, the way she'd grown away from him?

'Your dad loved you – loves you, Cathy. He was determined

to protect you in every way. He did not want to destroy whatever idealised picture you had of me. He loved you so much, he would rather take the blame himself. He could not bear you to experience the hurt and pain of knowing your own mother had chosen to stay away.'

Cate grasped her mother's hand. 'Oh, Mum! You had your reasons.'

'No reason is good enough, I see that now. I do not expect you to forgive me. I will understand if you go away and never want to see me again.'

'Of course I forgive you. And I'm going to see you again, and again. Venice isn't that far from England. I can visit you. You can visit me. We'll make up for lost time. And you'll meet my husband, Phil, and both my sons. You're a grandmother. A young, glamorous *nonna*! How about that!'

'Oh, Cathy!' Lina gasped, her eyes brimming with tears. 'Grandchildren, how wonderful! Do you have pictures?'

'Of course, not terribly good ones. I'll show them to you. But first, there's a phone call I have to make.'

Lina rose from her seat. 'Stay here for your call. I will start making lunch; I hope you would like to stay.'

'Thank you, I'd love to. I'll come and help in a moment.' Their first time in the kitchen together, mother and daughter. She could hardly wait.

Cate took out her phone and pressed the number for the nursing home. Sally on reception answered right away.

'Cate, I am glad you've got back to me, love. It's your dad. I'm afraid he's had a fall.'

Fear gripped her. 'Is he okay? Has he hurt himself? Has he broken anything? I'll fly right back.' The last filming session with Natalie, Phil's meeting with Raj, even her lunch with Mum: none of that mattered. Not if Dad was hurt.

'He's fine, Cate, love, I promise you. There's no need for you to rush back.'

'But when did this happen? Why didn't you phone me straight away?' Her heart was banging in her chest.

'I thought it was better to send a message so you could phone when it was convenient, you being on holiday like you are.'

'Anything could have happened. He could have hit his head. He could have...' She couldn't bear to say the words out loud. Dad had to be okay. He couldn't die. Not now, not before she'd tried to make things right.

'Cate, Cate, my love,' Sally soothed. 'If anything really bad had happened, I would have phoned you right away and kept on phoning until you answered. Your dad tripped over dear old Dot's stick. He caused quite the commotion, he did, but he landed face down on that big corduroy beanbag that Glenys's son insisted on donating to the residents' lounge. Hideous thing it is, we hide it away most of the time and only drag it out when we know he's coming to visit. It was more of a shock for dear Dot than your dad, love, but I did think you ought to know. Dot's been fretting ever since, but your dad, bless him, doesn't seem to remember anything about it at all. Now, no more worrying. I've got a note you're flying back the day after tomorrow, so you enjoy yourself. Venice, isn't it?'

'Yes, it's Venice. And thank you, Sally, it's such a relief that Dad's okay.'

Cate didn't deserve this second chance but she'd grab it. She'd take a cab straight to The Evergreens the moment she stepped off the plane.

42

The waiter put down two glasses of cold white wine.

'*Grazie!*' Natalie said. She closed her eyes for a second, turning her face to the sun. The last two days had been non-stop, running around with Lucia and the camera crew. *Luxe Life Swap* had filmed everywhere from the double-height ballroom of the Ca' Rezzonico to the secret nooks and crannies of the old ghetto. They'd completed the very last of their scheduled shots that morning, just in time for Cate and Phil to go and meet Phil's old school friend, Raj. It was hard to believe that the next time Natalie saw the pair of them, she'd be interviewing them for the final debriefing sequences at their restored vicarage.

Lucia snapped shut her folder. 'We have done everything! I cannot believe it! When Phil arrived here two days late, I did not know how we would manage. I was – how do you say – tearing my hair out!'

'Well...' Natalie decided to confess. 'Cate and I actually had an argument a few hours before he arrived and she threatened to go back to England.'

Lucia slapped her hand to her forehead. 'Now you tell me!

This, it scares me! I am so happy all our filming is done. I hope so much that Floella likes the results.'

'I'm sure she will. To the success of *Luxe Life Swap*!' Natalie clinked her glass against Lucia's.

'*Salute*! This is so nice and cold! And these small crostini – *deliziosi*! Try the one with olive paste, Natalie.'

She crunched into a salty oval of toasted bread. 'I am going to miss these *cicchetti* when I'm back in London.'

'I think that is not all that you are going to miss. What about this man whose name you can't help mentioning when we speak?'

'Eraldo...' It seemed inconceivable that the day after tomorrow, she'd be flying home. Leaving Venice, leaving him.

'Yes, the watch restorer. You have become very fond of him, I think.'

'I hardly know him.' It was what she was going to have to keep telling herself.

'But he is someone special.'

Natalie sighed. 'You're right. To meet someone like him was the last thing I expected.'

Lucia smiled. 'This is how you find love. Me, two years ago, I tripped over the long lead of a small dog. The owner was busy looking at his phone. The lead, it extended like this...' She flung her arms wide. 'I hurt my ankle; I was so cross. But I look into the eyes of the man who walked the dog and all this anger, it goes "poof" and that is how I met my boyfriend.'

'And he is still your boyfriend?'

'Yes... and I hope soon...' She fiddled with her unadorned ring finger. 'But we are not talking about me. What will you do, Natalie? You cannot let this man go.'

'I don't know what to do. I'm meeting Eraldo at his workshop later. He's taking me to his mother's home in Cannaregio to have dinner with his family tonight. It feels significant: something that you do when your relationship is becoming more serious. It should be the beginning of something, not the end.'

Lucia ran her finger around the rim of her wine glass. 'It does not have to be the end. Can he not go to England? Did you not mention he studied there and speaks the language? Surely with his talent he could work anywhere.'

'I couldn't ask him to. Eraldo is Venetian from head to toe. He's not just devoted to his work but to keeping the artisan tradition in Venice alive. Being in this city is what inspires him, what makes him tick – if that isn't a terrible pun.'

Lucia laughed. 'Ah, tick like a watch! Yes, I believe you are right. Venice is unique. Everywhere there are reminders of the talented artists and craftspeople who built this incredible city on mud. Venice must not lose the creative people; it must not become a theme park catering for tourists who do not realise they are driving out the very people and things that make it special. If things carry on like this, we will be eating hamburgers, not *baccalà mantecato*.'

'Eraldo has a cousin who is training to become a gondolier; he will be there tonight too.'

'That will be interesting. I am sure that you will have a nice evening. I am just sorry that it will make you both happy and sad.'

'At least we have a whole day together tomorrow.' Natalie tried to sound upbeat. 'Floella sent me a message a couple of days ago asking if it was okay if she booked me onto a later flight back.'

Lucia frowned. 'Was she worried that we would not finish on time?'

'I'm sure it wasn't that.'

Floella hadn't given a reason and Natalie didn't need one. There was no one she had to contact back in London, no close friend or lover coming to the airport to scoop her up in their arms. Not even a dog, like Ted, waiting behind her front door, scratching his paws on the mat.

43

'What if they aren't coming?' Phil said.

Cate laid down the café's menu. 'He'll come. That's him walking towards us now, isn't it? Looks like they've brought all three kids.'

Raj raised a hand and waved. The smallest of his three children, a little boy, ran towards them, Raj's wife in hot pursuit, her long plait flying.

Phil stood up.

'Phil! I can't believe it; you haven't changed a bit!'

'Nor you.' Phil couldn't help smiling at their blatant untruths. Raj was stockier, Phil's hairline receding at an alarming rate.

'This is my wife, Neelam.'

Dark smudges beneath Neelam's eyes told of the exhaustion of mothering three lively youngsters but her green eyes were bright and clear. And her smile was genuine. Perhaps Raj never spoke about his days at Hillingdon. Perhaps he'd never mentioned Phil at all.

'Pleased to meet you.' Neelam held out her hand. Phil shook it, a hard ridge of gem-laden rings digging into his flesh.

'This is Cate,' Phil said. How glad he was to have her by his side.

'Hello, I'm Rishi.' Raj's elder boy, smart in a pressed blue shirt, flashed a cheeky grin. All three children looked remarkably clean and tidy, shoehorned into their best holiday clothes.

Cate turned to Neelam. 'What lovely children.'

'It is a pity we cannot meet yours but I suppose they haven't broken up just yet. We shouldn't really have taken ours out of school but it's a special occasion and at this age, they can catch up easily enough. Raj is very strict about homework.'

Cate smiled. 'This café's a lovely choice; how did you find it?' she asked.

'Just by accident. We came here yesterday. The children haven't stopped talking about their *bussolà* since. They'd eat those biscuits at every meal if they got the chance.' Neelam laughed.

Phil studied the menu for something to do. It was okay for Cate, talking to Neelam so easily the way women did.

'What's everyone drinking?' Raj asked, immediately drowned out by a chorus of demands for fizzy drinks.

'Lemonade for me and Phil, please,' Cate said.

Neelam took charge of the ordering. Raj lounged back in his seat; his T-shirt and bright-orange shorts looked cool and casual. Phil's favourite linen jacket felt stuffy and formal but he needed somewhere to stow his wallet, map and phone, an issue Raj seemed to have solved by shoving his belongings into a mini Pokémon rucksack purloined from one of his kids.

The conversation was light, frivolous: the weather, the prettiest streets in Venice, the best place for gelato. Cate flashed him a 'see, nothing bad's going to happen' look but she didn't know what torture this was. He hadn't realised himself until today how he needed to feel Raj's anger, the anger he deserved. He wanted to feel the sickening pain of a punch in the gut, longed for the metallic taste of blood in his mouth as Raj knocked out a couple of teeth. Phil needed some sort of closure. He couldn't sit here making meaningless chit-chat as though Raj was some guy he'd met once on a golf course.

'So how did you come to look me up after all this time?' Raj said at last. Phil felt the words *you didn't bother before* left unsaid.

'Coming to Venice. Brings back memories of school, I suppose.' He felt his face burning.

'I'd never been abroad before we went on that school trip. I don't think you had either.'

'France once, camping. It rained a lot.' Phil gulped his drink.

'Played any rugby lately? I'll never forget that day you went to kick that ball into touch and it went flying down to your own try line. Fathead Horace couldn't believe his luck.'

Phil forced a laugh.

Raj turned his head. His middle child, the girl, was pulling on his arm. 'Daddy, are we going to tell them our secret?'

'Shh!' Neelam said.

'We're going to do something exciting but we can't tell.' The eldest boy nudged his sister. The littlest one said nothing, noisily sucking up the last of his cola.

'Raj thought we should do something fun together if you have the time,' Neelam said.

'We're free all afternoon.' Cate spoke before Phil had the chance to send her a 'please no' signal.

'Let's go, Daddy, let's go!' The girl started banging a spoon on the table.

'Stop that noise, Malini.' Raj put a firm hand on her arm. 'Okay, folks, time to go. I'll pay for this.'

Phil was about to protest but he caught Cate's warning look. Raj had his pride; he must remember that.

Cate bent down to the level of the littlest kid. 'Where are we going?' she whispered.

'Secret.' He giggled, stuffing his fist in his mouth.

'How exciting.' Cate played along.

Raj led them in the direction of the Grand Canal, talking about football all the way. Phil was relieved to discover they still supported the same team. Missed penalties, bad managers and dodgy refs filled up the conversation as they walked along.

'We're going on a gondola!' Malini jumped up and down, forgetting her vow of secrecy.

'You've given it away!' Raj pretended to be cross. 'Yep, that's where we're going.' He pointed towards the gondola station just beyond the Rialto Bridge where a small queue had formed. Phil opened his mouth to suggest they head to the out-of-the-way spot where he and Cate had taken their gondola, gliding down the equivalent of Venice's back streets, an experience that felt so much more exclusive than the trip Raj and Neelam had planned. He felt Cate's fingers press lightly on his arm, reminding him that this afternoon, they'd be doing things Raj's way.

The small queue rapidly dwindled; a gondolier signalled he was ready for another set of passengers. His black gondola with gold trim was as sleek as any Ferrari. The craftmanship Phil had the privilege to observe at the *squero* was as fascinating as any building they would pass. He realised he wouldn't care if they were sailing down the Thames.

'Hold back, guys.' Raj grabbed hold of his littlest one by the neck of his T-shirt. 'Mummy and Cate will get on first, then you lot can sit on laps; that way, we'll fit everyone in.'

The gondolier, straight out of central casting in his black and white striped top, helped Cate and Neelam step aboard, steadying them as they wobbled, laughing, to the two prime forward-facing seats. Raj plopped the kids down one by one. He signalled for Phil to go next.

'No!' The gondolier put up his hand like a traffic policeman. 'Only five.'

'But the kids are going to sit on our laps,' Raj said.

'And they weigh next to nothing. Please, it's a special occasion,' Cate wheedled.

The gondolier wasn't the sort of man to be turned to mush by Cate's full-beam smile. 'Next gondola, gentlemen.'

'We can't go without you,' Neelam fretted. Cate put her hand on her arm, said something soothing.

'Of course you can,' Raj said. 'We'll meet you back here in half an hour.'

Phil watched the gondola glide away, Malini and the older boy now spread out over seats facing the two women, the younger boy balanced on Neelam's lap. Now it was just him and Raj, alone at last. He felt as vulnerable as a child whose blankie had been whisked away.

'Are you getting on?' A woman in a yellow hat gestured to the next craft.

'What do you think, Phil? You and me on a romantic gondola ride?' Raj waggled his eyebrows.

'Umm, if you like.'

Raj laughed, flashing a couple of metal fillings. 'Let's get a beer. There's a bar round the corner.'

Phil followed his ex-friend to a teeny hole-in-the-wall place. Perched on a wobbly stool as Raj ordered two bottles of

Moretti, he had the gnawing feeling that Raj had known full well they couldn't all pile on the one gondola.

'How's biz, Phil? I heard you took over Evan's uncle's old company. It's doing pretty well, from what I see.'

'Yeah, turnover's up. I wouldn't say we're recession-proof but there's a pretty steady customer base for high-end, bespoke products.'

'Cate mentioned your boys are at Hillingdon. I was kind of surprised about that.'

Phil's face burned but he resolved to tell the truth. If he wasn't going to be honest, he might as well get up and walk away right now.

'It's a different place these days. Things have changed a lot. Proper pastoral care and all that. Oli was really keen to go and of course Max wanted to follow him. Oli's best friend, Evan's son, was already there.' He paused, waiting for Raj to react.

'They've got the right type of friends then.'

'Our boys, they're not awkward outsiders like us. Oli and Max are made for Hillingdon. They're not just academic, they're sporty too. They get leading roles in the school plays, they'll stand up and debate. I couldn't let my experience stop me from giving them the best education they can get.'

'My kids are at the local schools; they don't seem to be doing so bad.' Raj shrugged. He took a couple of swigs of his beer.

Phil tensed, waiting for Raj's next move.

'So, you still see Evan then. How is he? I often thought about him, wondering if he was okay, whether he moved onto harder drugs: ketamine, cocaine or something worse. I pray my kids never try stuff like that.'

'You knew it was him all along?'

Raj's brown eyes seemed to look right into his soul.

'So did you, Phil. I woke up that night in Venice, saw both your beds were empty. I was worried that you might be so desperate for Evan's friendship, you'd start taking drugs with him. People like us don't detox in luxury spas; we end up sleeping on the streets.'

'So, you knew that I knew it was him. When I didn't go to the Head to clear your name, you must have hated me.'

Raj ran his finger down the side of his beer bottle. 'I'm a realist, Phil, you know that. I was sad, disappointed but I didn't hate you. The law of the jungle ruled in that place and you needed Evan's protection. I saw that perv, King, in the changing room putting his hand on your knee. I knew it wasn't just a friendly pat; there was something about the look on his face. I should have spoken up too, reported King. So, I guess now we can call it quits.'

'No. No way are we quits! They would never have taken your word against King's. He would have charmed his way out of it then made your life hell. But what I did – or didn't do – was pure cowardice. I ruined your life and I've never forgiven myself. You were cleverer than me, more hard-working, a better person. And I'm the one who's ended up with everything.'

'And I've got nothing? Is that what you think? Tell me, Phil, what is it that you've got that I haven't? Is it your wife? Is she prettier than mine? Nicer? Kinder?'

'Of course not! Neelam's lovely. I never meant to imply—'

'Is it your kids then? It took me and Neelam a long time to conceive, but are your children better than mine?'

'No! No!' Phil didn't know how he'd lost control of the conversation. He and Cate had gone up Vesuvius once. He felt as though he were back there now wobbling on the edge of a crater, everything hanging on one false step.

'If it's not my family, it must be my job. We're both businessmen but I'll admit your business is worth more than mine.'

'Well, umm, yes.' Phil was back on safer ground. His furniture company turned over millions. Raj couldn't argue with that.

'You've made more money than me, for sure. You can buy all this stuff.' Raj flicked a finger against Phil's watch. 'That's a Rolex Submariner, isn't it? Nice! Very useful if you need to dive down a few hundred feet. I paid twenty-five quid for my Casio and it still tells the time.'

'I always wanted a nice watch and it's an investment.'

'Not a status symbol, then?'

Phil didn't answer. He turned his attention to the beer he'd hardly touched.

Raj sighed. 'I'm glad you've done well, Phil. I really am. You learning those crafts with Evan's uncle and taking over the business meant something good came of it all. And I'll admit, being a franchisee of Costless Coffee doesn't make me much money but there's no need to look down your nose at me.'

'I'd never do that, honestly! There's nothing wrong with running a coffee shop. People want to drink coffee. I want to drink coffee! I just know you could have done more.'

'Done more?' Raj's voice was laden with vitriol. 'I'll have you know I'm proud of what I do. You make beautiful works of art for wealthy people who have more than enough already. How many of them really appreciate what they buy? How many really appreciate you? My branch of Costless is in a rundown arcade sandwiched between a vape shop and a place that cuts keys but *I* make a difference, and you know what makes *me* happy?' He jabbed a finger at Phil. 'It's the single mum who pours her heart out and tells me I'm better than therapy, the staff who sneak free cuppas to the dishevelled lady pushing her belongings around in a supermarket trolley when they think I'm not looking, the three lonely old men who now meet each other for some warmth and company. I go home every night knowing me and my shop make a difference.'

Raj leant right over the table, his now beery breath in Phil's face. 'So, don't you ever tell me my life's not as good as yours. And I'll tell you something else you're wrong about. I wasn't a victim; I chose to leave Hillingdon. I could have fought my corner, told them what I knew, but I didn't. I'm not like you, Phil. I was proud to get that scholarship but I never wanted to be one of them. I never wanted to be anyone but myself. Sure, I would have got better grades, more opportunities staying there, but during the Christmas holidays, I'd found something I wanted more: a beautiful, green-eyed girl.'

'Neelam?'

'Yes.' Raj's face softened. 'She was working in my uncle's shop. We met up a couple of times and I could tell she liked me too. I could have chatted to her online, seen her in the holidays, but I knew some other boy would date her if I was away for weeks on end at school. So, in a way I was relieved to leave. It was that and protecting Evan too.'

Phil gaped. 'You wanted to protect him? Why? You weren't even friends.'

'It was his dad. I knew what he was like.'

'Evan did tell me once that they had a difficult relationship. When he died suddenly a couple of years ago, Evan was a bit all over the place, like he wasn't sure how he should feel.'

'His dad was a violent bully.'

'What?' Phil spluttered on his beer.

'One Sports Day, my dad had left his glasses in the glove compartment; I volunteered to run back to the car. Evan was with his parents; they'd just arrived. His dad was ranting about the traffic. Then he started having a go at Evan about something. He was pretty aggressive; he had his arm twisted up behind his back. I ducked down behind our car. I didn't want Evan to know I'd seen. His dad marched him off towards the sports field. His mum stayed behind for a few minutes leaning against their Range Rover, making a call. It was a windy day; she had one hand on her phone, the other fussing with her hair. Her skirt blew up before she could stop it. That's when I saw the bruises all over her legs.

'I stayed crouched behind our car until she walked away. A couple of years later, I saw her picture in the paper. "Tragic death of MP's wife". It said she'd died falling from a hotel balcony in Portugal late at night on a trip to celebrate their wedding anniversary. A freak accident. But I always wondered.'

Phil gulped. 'You think he pushed her off?'

'I don't know and I never will but I can't help feeling I'm partly responsible if he did. Things might have been different if I'd spoken up and reported him to the police that day.'

'She would have been too scared to tell the truth; she would probably have said she fell down the stairs.'

'That's what I tell myself on the good days. Other times, I'm not so sure. So, you see, Phil, I was as weak as you. We both failed to speak up, failed to do what was right. But we can't turn back the clock.' Raj picked up his beer and downed the rest of it in one. 'Now, drink up. We need to go and meet our better halves.'

'Cate really is my better half.'

'That's something we've got in common, buddy.'

Phil followed Raj in a bit of a daze. The waterbuses and taxis and gondolas were still gliding down the Grand Canal, the tourists thronging at the station excited to take a ride. He'd finally met Raj and the world was still turning.

Cate and Neelam's gondola was approaching, the two women and three kids waving like crazy. The sky was completely blue: a day for new beginnings.

'I suppose it's too late for us to be friends,' Phil said.

'A long time's passed.'

Of course Raj wouldn't be his friend; he'd been lucky not to get a punch in the mouth.

The gondolier was helping Cate and Neelam onto the *fondamenta*. Cate looked golden, radiant, free for a short while from the worries about her dad. It had been selfish of him not to insist they fly straight home but he'd had to see Raj today.

'Our wives are getting on well,' Raj said quietly. 'My Neelam's lovely but she's always found it hard to make friends. I can't remember the last time I saw her click with someone so easily. It's lovely to see.'

'Hi, Phil.' Cate gave him a kiss. 'Ooh, you taste of beer!'

'Come here, you lot!' Raj put out his arms. Three over-excited kids flung themselves on him, all talking at once.

'It was lovely to meet you both,' Neelam said. 'Cate and I have been getting on so well; we must meet up again when we're all back home.'

'It's so nice to make a new friend.' Cate smiled. 'I hope we can all have dinner soon. I've promised the kids they can meet Ted.'

'Cate says if we're good, we can take Ted for a walk,' Malini said solemnly.

'And if he gets all muddy and smelly, we can put him in the bath!' The littlest child collapsed into a fit of giggles.

'Still play tennis, Phil?' Raj asked.

'We've... umm, got a court at home, actually.'

Raj looked him straight in the eye. 'I haven't played since school but I reckon I can still thrash you.'

* * *

Natalie pushed open the door of the mask maker's shop. The bell tinkled.

Pietro set down a jar of varnish. '*Buonasera*, Natalie. *Bella*! You look wonderful!' He turned his head towards the spiral staircase. 'Eraldo, it is Natalie!'

'*Grazie*, Pietro.' She climbed the stairs, heels clanging on the metal treads.

Eraldo laid down the watch strap he was examining. 'Natalie! I have not seen that dress before. It is so elegant; I like it very much.'

'I'm glad.' She'd been concerned the deep-blue, V-necked dress was a bit over the top for a family meal but Lucia had convinced her that it was just the thing.

'Relax, please sit. I will quickly tidy up. I am a little late; Floella rang me, asking all sorts of questions about what you and I have been doing. She was delighted I have asked you to meet my family tonight.'

'She must have been surprised when you first asked me out.'

Eraldo closed a drawer. 'No, I think not. Floella likes to plan things, even in personal matters. Without her intervention, I would never have dared. I would have assumed you had a husband or boyfriend in London.'

'What intervention?'

'Remember the first day we met? I guessed she asked you to bring me that package for a reason.'

'I wouldn't put it past her!' Natalie tutted.

How Floella must have chuckled to herself as she sent Natalie on her errand. How well suited the two of them would have seemed: Eraldo, a man who had sworn off permanent relationships after his wife's untimely departure and lived in a city he'd never leave. And Natalie, a woman who couldn't bring herself to trust anyone long enough to even contemplate getting serious. Floella had brought the pair of them together for a fun-filled fling. But she hadn't predicted how things would play out.

Presenting a top TV show – Natalie's childhood dream – hadn't changed the way she felt about her life. Meeting Cate and Eraldo had. They had shown her what she was missing: a true friend and someone to love. She and Cate would be best friends for life now, but what were the chances of finding another man like Eraldo? Floella thought she'd been doing Natalie a favour. But she'd set her up for heartbreak.

Eraldo finished tidying away his tools. 'I am sorry you had to wait for me. *Andiamo*! Let's go! I hope you are hungry. Mamma is cooking up a feast.'

44

Natalie toyed with her cappuccino. Tomorrow would be the last time she would have breakfast Italian-style: standing up in a bar, coffee by her elbow, holding her paper-tissue-wrapped pastry. Cate was already on a plane home with Phil, looking forward to spending time with Ted and her dad before her boys came home for the holidays. Then, in a couple of weeks, the family would be travelling to Italy so Cate could try and make up for some of the time she and her mum had lost and Lina could meet her grandchildren at last.

Eraldo rested his elbow on the counter, his palm against his cheek. Sun streamed through the window, lighting up his dark hair. How could she let him go?

'My family enjoyed meeting you,' Eraldo said.

'I'm glad. I liked them a lot. Your mother is very kind and an incredible cook – those sardines! And that polenta with shrimp! I ate far too much.'

'That is the reason she liked you.' The twitch of his lips told her he was only teasing.

'Your cousin was so interesting. I knew making a gondola

must be tricky but the work he described is so skilled – and I had no idea how much upkeep they need too.'

'There has been talk of the *squero* closing down. It would be a tragedy; all that talent and knowledge would be gone. But he confided in me last night that they may have some good news. They are discussing working with a prestigious English furniture maker to create some bespoke pieces incorporating many of the techniques they specialise in. It will be an extra source of income for them. At the moment, it is all like this...' He put a finger to his lips. 'But he did tell me it was a surprise suggestion from a businessman who spent a few hours at the workshop whilst his wife was visiting Burano, so I thought of your friends.'

'Phil and Cate! It must be them. I expect they will start travelling here regularly if Phil has business interests and Cate will want to get to know her mum.'

'And what about you?' It was the question they'd both been avoiding.

'I don't want to leave.'

'It is hard to visit Venice without falling in love with her.'

'Not just Venice.' She felt herself redden.

He cupped her face in his hands, his eyes scanning hers. 'I have been thinking about... us. I do not want you to go back to England and everything we have to fade away. I have been asking Pietro's advice and he found this...'

He took his phone from his trouser pocket and opened up a website.

'A studio to rent in Hatton Garden, London,' she read.

'The centre of the jewellery and watch trade. I could make contacts, set up shop. It is good business there.'

She bit her lip. How easy it would be to urge him to leave Italy. But she knew she couldn't.

'No,' Natalie said.

He laid his phone on the marble counter. 'You do not want me to come to England?'

'It's not that. You would do well in London, of course you would; you'd get customers from all over the world. We could be together and perhaps you could reconnect with old friends of yours that Floella still sees. But England isn't right for you; something would always be missing. Venice, this place, it's deep within your soul. And it would be wrong to wrench you away from it.'

'I know you are right. But I do not want this to end.'

'Neither do I.' She did not know what else she could say.

His phone's jolly ringtone broke the silence.

His forehead creased. 'It is Pietro. He never calls.'

'Answer it.' She needed a few moments to breathe, to take everything in.

'Excuse me.' He walked towards the door, phone clamped to his ear. Through the window, she watched him, waving his free hand as he spoke.

She swallowed the rest of her coffee, nodded her assent to the barista as his hand moved to clear her half-eaten pastry away.

Eraldo returned just moments later. 'We have to go to my workshop.'

'It's okay, you go.' Whatever problem had arisen, she'd only get in his way.

'No, we both have to go. Floella's there.'

Natalie would have been less surprised if Elvis had strolled through the door.

'Floella, in Venice? What on earth is she doing here?'

* * *

'*Buongiorno*, Natalie! This is a nice surprise. I was not expecting to see you or Eraldo today. But your friend from England, she appeared.' Pietro inclined his head to the foot of the stairs. 'She is upstairs; you cannot miss her,' he added, chuckling.

'We are here, Floella!' Eraldo called. Natalie followed him up the stairs.

Floella had her shoeless feet up on the coffee table, looking as though it were her own sitting room. She got up and walked towards them, the bat-wing sleeves of her extraordinary butterfly-print dress stretched wide.

'Eraldo, Natalie, so wonderful to see you!'

Natalie was pulled into a hug, almost bouncing straight back off the sort of shoulder pad last seen in the eighties.

Floella released her and gave a little twirl, holding the hem of her purple frock. 'I picked this up in a fabulous little place in Cannaregio specialising in seventies' and eighties' designer vintage. Shame it was far too small to film in or we could have sent Cate there.'

Natalie tried and failed to imagine Cate in orange flares or a ra-ra skirt.

'You're both looking fantastic yourselves,' Floella continued. 'Your shoes are nice, Natalie.'

'Floella!' Eraldo's voice was stern. 'Stop all this talking about clothes. What are you doing here? Why did you not tell us you were coming today?'

'Who said anything about today? I got here yesterday morning. But coffee first: I can't talk when I'm gasping.'

'I have never known anything to stop you talking,' Eraldo said. 'But I will make you a coffee. Sit down, both of you.'

Floella sat back down. She tucked her legs up behind her; Natalie perched on the couch. She knew her employer well enough not to bombard her with questions; she had to wait for Flo to spill the beans.

'So, how's it going?' Floella jerked her head in Eraldo's direction.

Natalie felt a surge of irritation. This wasn't a game. 'As good as can be expected when I'm flying home tomorrow night. You were right to think Eraldo and I would be good together. But now what?'

A huge smile split Floella's face. '"Now what" is exactly the reason I'm here. But first, you can tell me all the things you've been up to, with and without that new man of yours.'

45

Cate scrambled out of the taxi, leaving the driver a far too large tip. Her feet crunched on the gravel path leading to the doors of The Evergreens. An elderly lady in a wheelchair, a plaid shawl wrapped around her shoulders, was examining one of the rose bushes. The glorious blooms, old-fashioned and blousy, were as heavily scented as the Duty-Free shop where Cate had hastily purchased some of her dad's favourite shortbread.

She pushed the button that swung open the double doors, pulling her hair from her ponytail clip with the other hand. Dad had always loved her with long hair. To think, as a teenager, she'd once chopped it off to spite him.

Sally looked up from behind the reception desk.

'Oh, Cate! How are you, love? You didn't rush here straight from the airport, did you? Your dad's going to be just fine now, so I hope you haven't been fretting.'

'I know how well you look after him.' The home was the best of the best: clean, well-appointed rooms, a comfortable lounge like something out of a gentlemen's club and a tasty, ever-changing menu. But she knew her dad would trade it all in a heartbeat for a daughter who loved him like she should. Tears welled in her eyes.

'I should have flown home yesterday; Phil would have been fine without me for a day.'

Sally reached under the counter for a box of tissues, concern written all over her round face. 'Don't be so hard on yourself; there's those that bring their mums and dads in here and we never see them from one month to the next. You're in here at least twice a week by my reckoning. You're a good daughter.'

'I'm not... The things I've done... the things I've said...'

'Now, now.' Sally patted Cate's arm. 'I reckon you've done nothing really bad. We all have our regrets, things we wish we'd done, things we wish we hadn't said. Some never get the chance to put things right but your dear dad's here and he'll be happy to see you, I'm sure of that. Whatever you think you've done, we can't go back. Your dad, bless him, can't remember yesterday but sometimes, his mind wanders back to the past as if it was just last week. Only the other day, he was telling me about your holiday to Wales as if he'd just come back. Reckons he had a turn at milking a cow.' She chuckled.

'Perhaps he did. We stayed on a farm. I was looking at a photograph recently.'

'Well then, that's a nice memory now, isn't it? Fancy you both thinking about the same thing. Call it coincidence, call it telepathy, whatever you like. Now, do you want to go to the visitors waiting room for a little while before you see him? I can make you a nice cup of tea.'

'I'll be all right.' Cate sniffed. 'Thank you, Sally. And I almost forgot, I've brought this shortbread. I thought it would be best to leave it with you to make sure Dad doesn't eat it all in one go.'

'He does have a sweet tooth, dear man, bless his heart.' Sally took the box, putting it up on a shelf behind her. 'The lift's arrived. I heard it go "ping".'

Cate crossed the foyer and pressed the button. The lift doors slid back, providing her with an unwelcome view of her red-eyed reflection. Gracie Fields singing 'Wish Me Good Luck' came from the speaker. Slowly, the lift took her up two floors, stopping directly opposite her father's room.

She knocked and walked in. Dad was sitting up in bed.

'Hello, love.'

His voice was cheerful. He was having a good day; her heart lifted.

She sat on the visitor's chair right next to the bed. 'I'm so relieved to see you're okay.'

He gave her a quizzical look. 'Of course I'm okay. Why wouldn't I be?'

'You had a fall.'

'A fall? I've not been up any ladders.' He gave a wheezy chuckle.

'You were walking across the lounge. Didn't you fall over Dot's walking stick?'

'Dot? Who's Dot? Who's telling you all this nonsense? Look at me! I'm fit as a flea. I walked ten miles yesterday.'

'Did you? That's a long way.' She knew it would only agitate him if she corrected him. The doctors said it was kinder this way.

He scratched his head, peering at her. 'You've changed your hair, Lina. It's always been dark.'

'It's blonde now. Do you like it?' Cate said.

'I do. But you look tired today, love. All this getting up for the baby.'

'Baby Cathy?'

His face lit up, like a child holding a buttercup under his chin. 'She's a lovely little thing, isn't she, our Cathy? I was singing to her today.'

'What were you singing?' She remembered 'Nellie the Elephant', her dad waving his arm like a trunk, making her laugh.

'I sang that boop-a-doo tune from *The Jungle Book*. She gripped my thumb with her tiny fingers and gave me the biggest smile.'

Cate took her dad's hand in hers, turning her head so that he couldn't see her tears. 'That's because baby Cathy is happy when she's with her daddy. And because your little girl loves you. She loves you very, very much.'

46

Floella was obviously enjoying herself, quizzing Natalie about the palazzo, the filming session on the Rialto Bridge, the climb to the top of the tower on San Giorgio Maggiore, the galleries they'd visited and the places where they'd eaten. Natalie was on the verge of flinging her coffee across the room in frustration. When was Floella finally going to explain what had possessed her to show up in Venice?

Floella set down her cup and folded her hands in her lap. 'So, you like Venice. I so hoped you would – and that the two of you would get together. That truly gladdens my heart.'

'But now Natalie is leaving.' Eraldo's voice was flat. He too seemed to find Floella's upbeat tone rather out of place.

'She will be back soon, I hope.' Floella smiled.

'What *are* you doing here?' Eraldo asked.

'Business meetings all day yesterday. I caught the earliest flight out – exhausting! It was only the promise of the Danieli's sumptuous breakfast that got me out of bed this morning.'

'You're staying there?' The five-star hotel was a far cry from Natalie's simple three-star bed and breakfast.

'I had a couple of meetings in my suite: got to make a good impression.' Floella spread her scarlet nails. 'Well, aren't you curious?'

'Yes!' Natalie almost shouted.

'I've been in meetings for...' Floella paused dramatically. 'For finalising Flo-Go Productions' new show. And it's thanks to Eraldo that I first had the idea. Do you remember a conversation we had a long time ago when you told me how overtourism was killing Venice? People flitting in for the day, causing all the wear and tear to the delicate structures but spending just a few euros on a Chinese-made mask and an industrially produced gelato shipped in from elsewhere?'

Eraldo nodded. 'I remember.'

'You were too polite to say but you were probably thinking that shows like *Luxe Life Swap* added to the problem by encouraging more visitors.'

'It is not the number of people but what they do when they are here. We welcome those who spend money thoughtfully, supporting the museums, the real Venetian restaurants and the old crafts.'

'Exactly!' Floella thumped the table. Cups rattled. 'That is what Flo-Go and our new partners want to showcase. We are going to produce a series that takes a forensic look at Europe's most visited cities. I'm thinking Vienna, Paris, Rome. But first of all, Venice. We'll dive deep into the culture, the artisan traditions, following the lives of a handful of inhabitants over the space of a whole year.'

'Wow, that's a big project,' Natalie said. A year in Venice: could she somehow get involved?

'It's a huge undertaking which is why we're partnering with a Canadian company. This is the real deal! This is going to be even bigger than *Luxe Life Swap*! The Canadians have got a popular presenter lined up; we've got more funding than I could have dreamt of. Everything's coming together.'

'Doesn't Mandy Miller want to do it?'

'I shouldn't really tell you this.' Floella dropped her voice to a stage whisper. 'Mandy's not signed up for any more shows with Flo-Go. Rumour has it, she's lined up to present a new dance competition on Sky set to rival a certain prime-time, Saturday-night show. So, letting the Canadians have first dibs on the presenter has enabled me to insist I have one of my best people out in Venice full-time. We've still got things to thrash out, paperwork to sign but it's yours, Natalie, if you want it.'

'Oh yes!'

She glanced at Eraldo, fearful she'd been too hasty, until she saw the smile on his face.

'Did you arrange for me and Natalie to meet just because of this?' Eraldo shook his head in disbelief.

'It was all a happy coincidence,' Floella said breezily. 'I had no idea Mandy was going to get rushed into hospital but when that happened, it gave me the perfect opportunity to get things in motion for Natalie to come out to Italy. I knew you'd love Venice, Nat; who doesn't? But then I thought it would be nice if you had another reason to stay.'

'That is why you sent her out with the package of watch parts? I thought it was odd you did not just send them by post. There was nothing very valuable or irreplaceable.'

Natalie gasped. 'You told me they were rare one-off antiques!' she exclaimed.

'I thought they were – my mistake.' Floella grinned. 'I did take a risk putting you in front of the camera, though. There was a chance you might have loved it so much, you'd be off looking for another presenting role.'

'Mandy Miller could be looking for a co-presenter. I've always fancied myself in sequins.'

'You wouldn't!'

Natalie laughed. 'No, I don't want to do a dance show, and not just because I've got two left feet. I think I'm going to be very, very happy with the job you've lined up for me. Fingers crossed it all falls into place.'

'Do not worry, Natalie,' Eraldo said. 'Floella would not mention this plan if she had any doubts.'

'And I would not have been matchmaking two of my favourite people if I thought you had to go your separate ways.'

'But I did not want to meet anyone; I was happy in my workshop all day.'

'And I wasn't interested either.'

'It was intuition, what more can I say?' Floella laughed. 'Now, what are we going to do today? I've no more meetings and we can't just sit around here. So, I'm thinking, climbing the *campanile* in St Mark's Square, drinks at Harry's Bar and dinner at the Locanda Cipriani – all on me. But first, a gondola ride. Are you in?'

Eraldo took Natalie's hand and pulled her to her feet. 'Why not? I live here so I never do these tourist things.'

'Sounds good to me,' Natalie said.

'Come on! What are we waiting for?' Floella clattered down the stairs, waved goodbye to Pietro and flung open the door to the street. 'We'll do Venice in style! We'll feel like we're contestants on *Luxe Life Swap*!'

'Except there's nothing about my life that I want to swap,' Natalie said.

'Nor me,' Eraldo said.

He took her hand. Together, they walked towards the Grand Canal.

* * *

MORE FROM VICTORIA SPRINGFIELD

Another book from Victoria Springfield, *An Italian Island Secret*, is available to order now here:
www.mybook.to/ItalianSecretBackAd

ACKNOWLEDGEMENTS

Firstly, a thank you to all at Boldwood Books, particularly to my editor Francesca Best, Niamh Wallace and Wendy Neale for everything from the editing to the famous Boldwood biscuits!

Thank you as always to my agent Camilla Shestopal of Shesto Literary for all her hard work over the last few years.

I am indebted to my romance author friend, Giulia Skye, whose background in television production enabled me to quiz her about what might go on behind the scenes of a reality TV show like *Luxe Life Swap*. I added a fair amount of artistic licence, so any mistakes are my own.

I've long been intrigued by school friendships. It's always fascinating to come across a lost school pal (or sworn enemy) in real life or online and to see how much or how little they've changed from how we remember them. The ups and downs of these formative relationships can reverberate through our whole lives as they do for Cathy/Cate and Natalie – even if we haven't seen our fellow pupils for decades.

This book was partly inspired by our school trip to Leningrad (as it was then) and Moscow where my good friend 'Sham' and I managed to get stranded after a trip to the theatre and somehow made our way back to the hotel in the cold and the dark negotiating two buses, a tram and a trolleybus with only one word of Russian – *spasibo* (thank you) – between us. Talking to anyone about a school trip in the eighties (or earlier) tends to bring up similar hair-raising tales of never-to-be-forgotten adventures. I wonder if teachers are more cautious these days...

I've been to Venice several times though thankfully not on a school trip! For anyone thinking of visiting, I'd recommend *101 Fabulous Things to do in Venice* from the Glam Italia series by Corinna Cooke – the strong sustainability angle helped inspire Eraldo's character; *Magical Venice* from The Hedonist's Guides series for inspirational photographs; the quirky *Venice for Pleasure* by J.G. Links first published in 1966 for walks and historical snippets and *A Thousand days in Venice*, a captivating, romantic memoir by Marlena de Blasi.

Finally, thank you to all the readers, bloggers, Facebook friends and fellow writers for your support and friendship. I hope you've enjoyed another virtual visit to Italy.

You can find me on: X: @VictoriaSWrites

Facebook: https://www.facebook.com/VictoriaSpringfield Author

Instagram: @VictoriaSWrites

ABOUT THE AUTHOR

Victoria Springfield writes contemporary 'wish you were here' evocative women's fiction set in Italy. Her feel-good books follow unforgettable characters of all ages as they deal with love, loss, friendship and family secrets. Readers can feel the sunshine!

Sign up to Victoria's mailing list for news, competitions and updates on future books.

Follow Victoria on social media here:

- facebook.com/VictoriaSpringfieldAuthor
- x.com/victoriaswrites
- instagram.com/victoriaswrites
- bookbub.com/authors/victoria-springfield

ALSO BY VICTORIA SPRINGFIELD

An Italian Island Secret

One Summer in Italy

BECOME A MEMBER OF THE SHELF CARE CLUB

The home of Boldwood's book club reads.

Find uplifting reads, sunny escapes, cosy romances, family dramas and more!

Sign up to the newsletter
https://bit.ly/theshelfcareclub

Boldwood

Boldwood Books is an award-winning fiction publishing company seeking out the best stories from around the world.

Find out more at www.boldwoodbooks.com

Join our reader community for brilliant books, competitions and offers!

Follow us
@BoldwoodBooks
@TheBoldBookClub

Sign up to our weekly deals newsletter

https://bit.ly/BoldwoodBNewsletter

Printed in Great Britain
by Amazon